NAUTICAL

LUCY LENNOX

Cover Art: AngstyG

Cover Photo: Eric McKinney

Editing: One Love Editing

Proofreading: Lori Parks and Victoria Rothenberg

Beta Reading: Leslie Copeland, May Archer, Shay Haude, Sloane Kennedy, and Chad Williams.

SPECIAL THANKS

To Samantha Marscot for coming up with the perfect title for Cal's story. You're a special kind of cornball. I still can't thank you enough for having so much patience with me four years ago when ~~we~~ you were coming up with the cover design for *Borrowing Blue*. Here we are after over twenty-five covers together, and your creativity hasn't dimmed. It's not easy to make a hot mess of ideas look pretty, but you manage it every time.

Thank you ❤

AUTHOR NOTES

The Caribbean towns of St. Mitz and Turshall Cay are fictional. All other locations mentioned in and around the British Virgin Islands, including the dive sites, are real.

Part of this story takes place on a Sunseeker Ocean Club Ninety motor yacht. Feel free to Google it to see photos of the spaces described in the book or visit my Pinterest board for the link.

A handy list of Wilde family members can be found at the end of the book.

Enjoy!

KEEP IN TOUCH WITH LUCY!

Join Lucy's Lair
Get Lucy's New Release Alerts
Like Lucy on Facebook
Follow Lucy on BookBub
Follow Lucy on Amazon
Follow Lucy on Instagram
Follow Lucy on Pinterest

Other books by Lucy:
Made Marian Series
Forever Wilde Series
Aster Valley Series
Twist of Fate Series with Sloane Kennedy
After Oscar Series with Molly Maddox
Licking Thicket Series with May Archer
Virgin Flyer
Say You'll Be Nine

Visit Lucy's website at www.LucyLennox.com for a comprehensive list of titles, audio samples, freebies, suggested reading order, and more!

Twenty years from now, you will be more disappointed by the things you didn't do than those you did. So throw off the bowlines. Sail away from safe harbor. Catch the wind in your sails. Explore. Dream. Discover.

— H. Jackson Brown Jr., *P.S. I Love You*

1

CAL

My brother King had tried to warn me about this. Well, not *this* specifically. Even King wouldn't have anticipated me being shoved buck naked into a closet on a superyacht in the Caribbean.

"If you never listen to another word I ever say," he'd said, "at least remember this: never trust a rich older man trying to get into your pants. They're manipulators and users."

If only he could see me now.

I looked down at myself with a sigh. At least there was a tiny sliver of light coming in under the closet door to illuminate my surroundings. The master closet was full of clothes, but none of them looked like they'd fit the showy style of the man who'd brought me here. Prescott Resnick was a pompous ass who'd probably popped his Izod collars when he was growing up in the 1980s. When I'd first seen him at the club in St. Mitz, he'd been wearing a yellow linen shirt unbuttoned about six spaces too many. I couldn't blame him, really. The man had a nice body. If I had a body like that when I hit forty, I'd probably want to show it off too.

It had been the bartender's whispered words in my ear that had finally lured me past the warning bells clanging in my head about the man.

"Says he owns the *Worthington*, and I heard she's looking for a new chief mate."

Suddenly, the preppy linen-clad peacock had been the possible ticket to a new job and an extension of my time in the Caribbean. If I could find an excuse to stay here a little longer, I wouldn't have to return to Hobie and deal with facing my future now that all of my original plans had gone to shit.

We'd spent the rest of the night dancing, drinking, and eye-fucking. When he'd finally brought me back to the yacht, my heart had tripped in my chest. The *Worthington* was stunning. She was eighty-eight feet of pure perfection, custom-crafted by an English company called Sunseeker and probably worth at least fifteen million dollars. I'd already scoped her out after finishing up my last gig captaining a small catamaran for a family's vacation. With the busy season ending, I'd been released from my job at the charter company and had been planning on flying home to Texas.

But the opportunity to stay a little longer as chief mate of the largest private yacht in port? Too good to pass up.

I wasn't proud of myself for giving him a little more credit because of his yacht, but I also wasn't going to forgo a night of hot sex with a fit older man in thousand-thread-count sheets when the alternative was the St. Mitz youth hostel with shared rooms and bonus cockroaches.

And the sex had been plenty hot. The man sucked dick like a champ, and if he'd slipped into referring to himself in the third person a bit there at the end, well, so be it. It wasn't like I was marrying the guy. More like I needed him to consider hiring me or at least introduce me to his captain.

Before I'd had a chance to inquire about the position, however, we'd been awoken by happy chatter just outside the stateroom windows. Prescott had shot out of bed like a missile.

"Jesus fuck! It's worth. Fuck, fuck," he'd squawked.

"It's worth what?" I'd mumbled, unsure of where I was and who he was. I'd rubbed my eyes and looked around at the lushly appointed room. *Ah, the Worthington. I remember now.*

"Hide! Fuck. Get in the closet!"

I'd blinked at him. Had I woken up on the set of a 1970s sitcom?

"Cal, get in the fucking closet. I'll distract them and you'll sneak off once we're clear, okay? Now go."

He'd scrambled to put his clothes on while I remembered mine were still on the top deck by the hot tub. Crap.

"Why am I going into the closet? And who's on board without your permission?" He'd spent way too much time last night lamenting how hard it was to keep hangers-on away from his precious ship since it was such a standout in every marina it docked. It had gotten to the point I'd started to feel a little guilty about being one of the people he'd been complaining about, but then I'd quickly distracted him by stripping down and luring him into the hot tub on the top deck.

The voices had come closer, and this time they'd seemed like they were right outside the bedroom door.

Prescott had looked at me with panic in his eyes. "Ah... work, um, people. Clients! And they can't know I have a... a..."

The handle on the stateroom door had jiggled, causing Pres to shove me hard into the closet and slam the door closed after me.

"Cheap fuck?" I muttered, feeling like gutter trash. I heard the snick of the stateroom door, and then Prescott's voice was loud and commanding.

"Oh there you are. I was just making sure everything was in order before your arrival. I'm afraid the cleaning crew hasn't gotten to the master suite just yet, so you might want to have a talk with the captain, I'm afraid." His voice faded away until I heard the snick of the door again.

I let out a breath and reached for the handle to open the closet door. There was no handle. I pushed on the door. No movement whatsoever.

"Fuck."

I moved my hands all around the edges looking for any way to open the closet door from the inside.

"I will not make a joke about being stuck in the closet," I

murmured, guessing at the time. Maybe it was around five in the afternoon. We'd stayed at the club till at least 2:00 a.m. and then had come back and raided the fridge in the galley before starting the sexfest. By the time we'd finally fallen asleep, the sun had been rising. Still, I felt completely out of sorts considering I'd been keeping sailor's hours all summer.

My stomach let out a loud grumble. I hadn't eaten in twelve hours. Fine. At least I'd gotten up an hour ago to pee. I couldn't imagine Prescott appreciating my urine puddled in his fancy leather deck shoes.

As my eyes adjusted to the clothes around me, I began flicking through the hanging items to select something to put on. At least when Pres realized he'd locked me in here, I could confront him with my dignity intact.

The softest shirt I came to was a T-shirt that felt like it had been washed a million times. I couldn't read the logo on it in the dark, but I figured at least it was old enough not to be anything too special. I slipped it on, noticing the fresh scent of the laundry detergent mixed with the faint traces of a Tom Ford cologne I recognized from a tuxedo I borrowed once from my brother-in-law Augie. That was expensive shit, way too rich for my blood. But it was sexy. I wondered why I hadn't noticed it on him the night before. He'd smelled more like rotten limes and cheap tequila.

I slid into a pair of uber-soft cotton lounge pants since they were the only thing I could find with a drawstring. At least I was comfortable. I pulled a thick bathrobe down and used it as a pillow to make myself a little nest after several bouts of banging on the door had only resulted in loud pop music being cranked up somewhere on board.

Stupid asshole. My brother was right. Older rich guys weren't worth the trouble. I closed my eyes and wondered how long it would be before Prescott returned to his stateroom. If only I hadn't left my phone in the shorts I'd tossed aside when I came on board, I could have at least been playing a game or catching up with my family.

Time passed like watching fresh paint peel on the side of a barn.

The temperature climbed in the little space until the Tom Ford scent was intimately comingled with the Cal Wilde scent. At some point the engines began rumbling, and I reassured myself that while Prescott Resnick may have been a pompous ass, he didn't seem like a felony kidnapper to me.

I was wrong.

"What the fuck?" I yelped when I felt the ship begin to move. The familiar sounds of the dock hands calling out and tossing ropes made it through the space under the closet door now that the music had been turned off. I banged on the door again and called out. "Hey! I'm stuck in here! Let me out!"

I racked my brain trying to remember the specs I'd read about the Sunseeker Ocean Club. If I wasn't mistaken, the master closets were right underneath the bridge where the captain would be currently sitting if we were underway. So why the fuck couldn't he hear me banging? Was the master suite soundproofed?

I thought back to the night before and couldn't help but hope it was, if only so the crew didn't lose respect for poor Prescott. He'd had a moment of begging and sobbing that hadn't reflected well on his ability to command a ship. There'd also been an unfortunate moment where he'd wanted to role-play pirate and mate, and let's just say the interlude had gone in a more... prisoner/warden direction.

"Fuck," I said again for the millionth time. "Fucking asshole."

The sex for sure hadn't been worth it, and now it was looking less and less likely I'd even want a job working for this jackass. How could he not have realized my fucking clothes were still on board?

Suddenly, the closet door opened and an arm shot in to grab something.

"Ah!" I squawked, jerking out of the way of the claw.

"What the hell?" the man shouted back. It wasn't Prescott. I could tell right away from the deeper voice and the dark arm hair this wasn't the prissy blond I'd spent the last few hours plotting to murder.

"Thank fuck," I said, shooting out of the closet and heaving in a big gulp of fresh air. It was blessedly cool in the dimly lit bedroom, and I was surprised to see the room was clean with all fresh linens on the bed as if I'd never been naked and coming all over the sheets. Had someone been in here cleaning while I was just on the other side of that damned closet door?

"Who are you?" the man demanded.

"Where's Prescott?"

He blinked at me. My eyes adjusted to the light enough to make out his features. He wasn't super tall, but he was certainly taller than my shrimpy self. He had wavy, dark hair sprinkled with a little salt at the temples, and his dark brows were furrowed as if confused about why a perfectly good closet would have spit out a semi-sweaty and cum-stained sailor.

"Who the hell are you?" he asked.

I mustered as much dignity as I could manage. "I'm a guest of the ship's owner."

He raised his brows in surprise. "Are you?"

"Yes. And I'm not sure he'd be happy with you sneaking around in his bedroom messing with his clothes."

The man crossed his arms in front of his broad chest, his mouth turning down in a frown. "Hm. I think he'd be fine with it actually." He squinted at my chest. "Wait. Are you wearing my shirt?"

Oh shit. Ohhhh shit. Was this guy married to Prescott? Had I just accidentally stowed away in someone's marriage... closet?

"Um..." I looked around desperately, wondering if I could make a run for it. Were we still close enough to the marina for me to make it on a midnight swim?

The man took a step closer, and I instinctively took one backward. He was giving me distinct predator vibes, and not the sexy kind. More like the pressing charges on a Caribbean island kind. "What's your name?"

"C-Cal..." I began. I was distracted by his piercing steel-blue eyes. I wondered if I'd find them this attractive when they glared at me across a jury box in court at my trespassing trial. "And yours?"

"Jonathan Worthington."

Worthington.

My eyes flicked over to the small brass plaque over the stateroom door. *The Worthington.*

"Oh," I said weakly, reaching out behind me for the closet door handle. I slid it open slowly, stepped back into the dark space, and slammed the door closed in front of me.

2

———————

WORTH

I stared at the closed door in shock.

What the hell had just happened? One minute I'd been reaching into the closet for a clean shirt to replace the one I'd spilled wine on at dinner, and the next minute I was dealing with a stowaway.

A gorgeous stowaway.

A gorgeous, *young* stowaway. The man had to be twenty years my junior.

His words finally reached my brain. He'd been asking for Prescott, my brother's fiancé, and if this was what it looked like, poor Lucas was going to be devastated.

I pulled the closet door back open. "Get out here and sit down. There." I pointed to the upholstered chair at the desk under one of the windows.

Cal winced and scrambled over to the chair, taking a seat so primly I almost wanted to say "Good boy."

"Explain yourself."

His clear blue eyes darted nervously around the room, and his dirty-blond hair stuck up everywhere like he'd stuck his finger in a light socket for way too long. He bit his full bottom lip with his top teeth while he considered how to lie to me. This was going to be good.

"I was doing some work for your... husband?"

"Mm. I'll bet you were," I murmured. "*Hard* work, was it?"

He blushed and looked down at his clasped hands in his lap. Were those my pajama pants?

"Ship work," he said, getting a second wind. He looked up and met my eyes. "I'm here for the chief mate job."

I barked out a laugh which caused him to jump and nearly tumble off the chair. "Are you? Well, I can tell you haven't learned how to dress for the job you want considering those are Ralph Lauren pajama pants."

He sniffed and looked out the window. "The chief mate of the *Worthington* has standards, and it is bedtime after all."

I bit back a laugh. "I guess it is. Where exactly are you sleeping considering the existing chief mate is still in the chief mate's rack?"

Cal flapped a hand. "I'm not picky. I'm happy to sleep on deck if you—"

I suddenly remembered something and snapped my fingers. "'Who Let the Dogs Out.'"

Cal blinked at me. "I'm... sorry? Is this a trick question? Is the answer Baha Men?"

"That was your phone, wasn't it?"

Cal stood up suddenly. "Shit. That's my ringtone for my grandfather. Where is it?"

"The captain has it on the bridge. We assumed it was left by someone on the cleaning crew. Along with... their clothing."

He looked worried. "I need to get it in case something's wrong at home." When he moved to stand up, I pressed him back down with a hand to the chest. I tried not noticing the warm feel of his muscles under my fingers.

"You're not going anywhere, and it only rang once about an hour ago. I'm sure everything is fine. Besides, you can't be much help from the middle of the Atlantic Ocean."

He looked both worried and resigned, and for some reason his expression made me want to reassure him, which was laughable, considering he was my stowaway.

"How far out are we?" he asked. "Can... can you take me back to St. Mitz? Please? I don't have any money, but..." He looked around my bedroom as if there were a treasure chest of gold bricks going begging. "I can... work it off? Or..."

I held up a hand. "I'm not sure I'm interested in the kind of work you do."

His eyes shot wide before they narrowed into a glare. "Sailing?"

"Is that what Prescott brought you on board a motor yacht for? *Sailing*?"

His cheeks flushed and he looked away again. "Well, that other bit was more of a... volunteer gig."

"Charity sounds about right," I said more peevishly than I'd intended. "Considering you couldn't pay me to touch that piece of shit."

The idea of this beautiful boy naked in bed with Prescott Resnick made my jaw tick. Lucas's fiancé was a snake, a man only out for himself. I'd tried so hard to unmask him as a gold digger, but Lucas wouldn't have it. He'd told me I was biased against everyone he dated, and I couldn't argue with that. It didn't mean Pres wasn't a manipulating asshole though.

Cal's brows furrowed. "That's not a nice thing to say about your husband. Even if he is a cheating bastard, Jon."

"I don't have a husband. And I go by Worth."

Something moved behind his eyes for a split second before he grinned. "Ah, then I didn't do anything wrong. Perfect."

I wanted to laugh. I wanted to release ridiculous giggles from my chest like bubbles coming up from the last scuba dive I'd taken. When was the last time I'd been so charmed by a stranger?

"I would say stowing away on another man's ship is considered wrong," I suggested.

"Is that a euphemism?" His grin was adorable and flirty, and I had to assume he was laying it on thick to keep himself out of trouble. "Because, if so, I'm here for it."

"Explain yourself," I demanded again, looming over him.

"Me?" he asked indignantly with a hand to his chest. "You're the one who kidnapped an innocent victim!"

I stared at him in disbelief. "Kidnapped?"

"Yes. I was just... um... inspecting the closet of this fine... vessel when you..." He sighed and slumped in the chair. "Fine, but can you sit down? You're making me feel like I'm in some kind of thirties mafia film, and I assure you I don't know where Bugsy went with the goods."

I sat down on the side of the bed. "Better?"

His shoulders came down from around his ears. "Marginally."

"Continue," I said with a sigh and a *Let's speed this up* motion with my hand.

"I was born in a small town in Texas called Hobie," he began, leaning back in his seat as if to get comfortable. It took me a minute to realize he was actually going to tell me his life story.

"Skip to the part where you boarded my ship."

"I wish that was a euphemism," he muttered. "You're no fun. You would have liked the story about the first time I rode on a pony." He sniffed and looked at his fingernails. "I can't imagine what your sex partners think. They're probably still removing their unmentionables when the door hits them on the way out."

My heart sped up a little at the sound of the word *sex* coming out of his mouth, but there was no way I was touching someone who'd slept with my brother's fiancé. "Focus, Calvin," I warned.

"It's Calgary actually."

"Sure it is. How did you meet Prescott?"

"We were dancing in a club when he asked me to come back to his yacht."

Why didn't that surprise me? "He told you this was his boat?"

"Technically, this is considered a ship. That's something most yacht owners tend to know. Are you sure you own it? The way you can tell is—"

"I know how to tell," I snapped. "I have a captain's license. Stop correcting me."

"Yes, he told me the *Worthington* was his. Then when we heard people on deck earlier, he freaked out and said it was probably his clients. I'm guessing that he lied. Please don't tell me he's the captain, because I swear I could really use the chief mate position and I don't think I can work for someone whose mouth was on my—"

"Stop," I growled. "I don't want any details. Do you understand?"

"No. I don't. You asked me to tell you what happened, and now you're saying you don't want to know. Which is it?"

We stared at each other.

I finally sighed and ran my fingers through my hair. He at least needed to know the sticky situation we now found ourselves in. "Prescott is engaged to marry my brother. And as far as Lucas knows, they are not in an open relationship."

Cal's face crumpled. "No. Oh shit. No. You have to know I didn't know that. I would have never ever even looked at that asshole, much less let him—"

I held up my hand again and ground my back teeth together. Cal snapped his lips shut and looked contrite.

I sighed. "It's not your fault. But we are now at sea on our way to Turshall Cay to pick up my sister's friends. From there, we're headed to the BVI for some island-hopping. I won't be able to return you to St. Mitz for a week."

His eyes went round, and he lost a little of his brash confidence. "Well, shit."

I couldn't help but laugh. "Right. So you see my dilemma."

Cal sat forward and rested his arms on his knees. "You have to tell your brother about this. He shouldn't marry that pompous dick."

"Lucas won't believe me."

"Then I'll tell him." He stood and put his hands on his hips. I was struck stupid with how sexy he looked wearing my old Pride T-shirt and pajamas. "Lead me to him. We'll fix this right now."

"No. That's not going to work. I might... have a history of trying to break him up with people." I hated admitting that out loud, but he needed to understand why it wasn't that simple.

"Why?"

"Well, once he dated a guy who'd been charged—but not convicted—of defrauding three previous paramours. I tried to warn Lucas that the guy was a serial swindler, but he didn't listen."

"What happened?"

I sighed. "The asshole found out I was sniffing around and took off. Lucas blamed me for ruining his relationship with my suspicions and the private investigator I'd hired." I mumbled the last part.

Cal's lips quirked up. "The what, now? The private investigator?"

"Then there was the time he dated a woman who kept asking him for a ring, only it had to be ten carats and it had to be a specific setting from Cartier, blah, blah. Clearly she was only into him for his money."

Cal winced. "That's a harsh thing to say about your brother."

His words stung, but he didn't realize that regardless of how incredible my brother was, sometimes people only saw the money he had. "I didn't mean it that way. I think he's wonderful. That's why I'm so protective. But Zara was about as deep as a buoy. Everyone but Lucas knew she was all about the flash. And my brother deserves more than that. He deserves more than someone who can't wait to get her name on his club memberships and asks on the third date if he wouldn't mind her making a few 'minor' changes to his town house with the most expensive interior decorator in town."

I leaned back on my hands on the soft bed. "I want him to find a companion who challenges him. Someone who values him and sees him for the smart, sweet man he is. Lucas doesn't even like a flashy lifestyle, and yet everyone he keeps dating is all about name-dropping and wearing the right clothes and..." I stopped when I realized Cal was eyeballing my own clothes.

"What?" I asked, looking down at my plain white shorts and button-down shirt.

He chuckled. "Asks the man who's probably wearing clothes worth more than my annual salary as a charter captain and standing on a yacht worth more than most people earn in two lifetimes. A yacht he named after himself no less."

I opened my mouth to tell him how wrong he was, to snap and

bite at someone who dared question me while trespassing on my fucking property, but I realized he was right. I was being a hypocrite. But that wasn't going to ever, ever stop me from being protective of my brother.

"I didn't name it," I muttered petulantly. "It was a gift. Sort of." I didn't mention the giver had used my own money to buy it.

Cal's jaw dropped open before he began a deep belly laugh. "Whose Christmas list do I need to get added to? Jesus. A gift?" His voice squeaked. "This?" He looked around at the two-year-old ship I still wasn't sure about keeping. The man who'd given it to me remained on my shit list, and as much as I loved this ship, I did not love the association to the man who'd named it.

"Irrelevant." I rubbed my jaw, the barest seed of an idea germinating. "Here's what we're going to do. I want you to seduce Prescott away from Lucas. Get him to dump Lucas and pick you instead."

"Um..." He scratched the back of his head like he was thinking about it before rolling his eyes and glaring at me. "How about no?"

I couldn't hold back my tongue. "That's not what you were saying last night."

Cal laughed, a clear sweet sound that filled my bedroom with a light it hadn't seen before. "That was when I thought he owned the biggest... *ship*... in town. Now I know he doesn't. Now I know his ship is tiny. Teeny tiny. Like a dinghy."

If he made me laugh any more, my sister was going to come to see what was the matter. "In exchange for your service, I will give you a fair shot at the chief mate position when Freya leaves next week. *If* you're qualified."

I could see the offer stopped him in his tracks.

"Fuck," he said. "That's a low blow. And of course I'm qualified. I'm qualified to captain this thing, but I'll accept chief mate if it'll keep me on the water."

His words stopped me in my tracks. If he had captain's credentials, maybe he wasn't as young as he looked. "How old are you?"

Cal lifted an eyebrow at me. "Are we sharing personal information now, Mr. Worthington?"

"Only yours."

"I'm twenty-three," he said defiantly, as if he knew full well I was going to judge him for it.

I squeezed my eyes closed and tried not to picture this baby boy naked. "Jesus," I said under my breath.

"I've been on the water since I was in diapers."

I sighed and shot him a look. "So, at least ten years, then, right?"

He crossed his arms in front of his chest. "Unlike your little captain's license that probably came free inside of a box of Cap'n Crunch cereal? I mean, what? Did you do a liveaboard course one week on vacation from your big corporate job?"

I bit back a laugh. "I'll have you know I earned an Inland Master in St. Thomas and am working on my Near Coastal."

Cal huffed, but there seemed to be at least a spark of approval in his eyes. "I hope you don't claim the hours spent lying in the sun sipping a daiquiri in your logbook."

I gave him an exaggerated frown. "Oh, those don't count?"

He opened up his mouth to argue with me when I held up a hand to stop him. "I'm sure you're working on a certificate upgrade of some kind and need logged days underway as well. I can give you that, and I'll pay you for your time."

Cal's eyes shot daggers at me. "Absolutely not. You're not paying me to fuck some asshole. This isn't *Pretty Woman*."

"You're not fucking anyone," I hissed. "Certainly not Prescott goddamned Resnick."

His full bottom lip quirked, and I had a sudden flash of what it would look like trailing kisses along my stomach down to my groin. I quickly filled my brain with other images. Business meetings, dirty urinals in public restrooms, skin cancer biopsies. I did not want to have sex with Prescott's boy toy.

"Then how do you expect me to seduce him away from Lucas?"

"We just need him to reveal his true colors. So... flirt with him, tease him, try to get him to make his attraction to you obvious. All we need is something to convince Lucas he's betting on the wrong horse."

He thought about it for a minute. "Fine. Then if you're not expecting actual sex, I'll take your money." Cal looked embarrassed for mentioning it. "I mean... just... whatever you were going to—"

"Yes, fine," I said quickly. "It's the least I can do to make up for the egregious kidnapping."

He lifted his chin. "Exactly. And don't for a minute think I'll let you forget it. I was trapped in that hellhole for *days*."

"You were in there four hours."

He grinned at me, and I realized with a jolt that this task was going to be the easiest thing in the world. One smile from this beautiful boy and Prescott Resnick wouldn't be able to hide his hard-on.

"Lead me to my stateroom, master," Cal said, standing up from the chair and stretching to his full height of well under six feet. I hadn't realized how small he was until I saw my pajama pants puddle on the floor at his feet. He was fucking adorable, but he also kind of looked like a child in his father's clothing.

I thought about where to put him. My sister and her husband, Jin, were in the other large stateroom at the bow, Pres and Lucas were in the smaller room down the hall from mine, and the final guest room had already been made up for my sister's friends who were joining us tomorrow. That left the crew quarters. Currently, the captain had a room to himself per his contract, and Freya and our chef, Julo, shared the other one.

I glanced at the long sofa against the wall in my bedroom.

"No," he said.

"You didn't even listen to my idea yet."

He lifted an eyebrow. "For shame, Mr. Worthington, sir. You're old enough to be my father."

The arrow hit its mark with a thunk. "I'm forty-two, not fifty!"

"Huh. You look older."

Cal was even cuter when he was trying to get under my skin.

"Hear me out," I began.

He put his hands on his hips and tapped his toe on the ground, which would have been ten times more impressive if the collar of his shirt hadn't gaped enough to show me a glimpse of smooth collarbone. "I'm listening."

"What if... I mean, think about it. How can I explain your presence here? What if I say you're my guest?"

"Your guest with benefits? Are we back to the *Pretty Woman* thing now?"

"No. No. They all know I would never sleep with someone like you." My heartfelt reassurance hit the room like a delayed depth charge.

"Oh. Right," he said weakly, plonking back down in the chair. "Of course. Sure. Silly me."

I lurched forward, trying to suck back in the words. Before I knew what I was doing, I'd knelt on the floor at his feet and put my hands on his knees. "No, Cal, that's not what I meant."

We both looked at my hands resting on his warm legs until I slowly removed them and lurched back to sit on the bed again. What the fuck? I didn't grovel and apologize to people for speaking my mind, and I sure as hell didn't give one whit about the feelings of this young man who was a complete stranger to me.

I wasn't the only one confused by my actions. Cal's eyes were wide and wondering. Fine. Maybe I cared a tiny bit about his feelings. I wasn't a monster.

"I, ah," I continued. "It's just that... I had a bad breakup and... never mind, not important. Anyway, it's not like I'm even..." I took a breath and tried to remind myself this guy didn't care about my love life and he was young enough to be my child. He wasn't, of course; he was an employee. Period. And if breaking up with Mason had taught me anything, it was never to get involved with an employee. Cal would sleep where I put him. He did not need to know any further information about me or my family.

"Suffice to say—"

Cal snapped his fingers. "Dive master!"

"What?"

"I saw the tanks on board last night. You dive, right?" He seemed to be coming up with this idea right in front of me.

"Well, yes."

"Tell them you hired me to be the dive master for the week, and because the boat is full, I agreed to sleep on deck. I'll just keep my... stuff... in here and use your bathroom."

"Is that skimpy outfit we found by the hot tub your 'stuff' because if so, I'm guessing your dive gear was accidentally left behind in St. Mitz."

He shot me a look of annoyance. "All of my stuff is in a storage locker back on the island. I stashed it there because the hostel is a cesspit full of freeloading assholes."

He was worse off than I thought if he was staying at a youth hostel. And so young. I cleared my throat. "We'll get you new stuff at Turshall Cay. They have a big dive shop and some clothing boutiques next to the marina. But I don't think dive master is going to work. If you're part of the crew, you won't have as much opportunity to be around Prescott. He needs to think you're—"

The door opened and my sister came barging in. "Worth, Lucas and I can't figure out—" She stopped and stared at where I sat facing Cal, both of us leaning toward each other with our elbows on our knees. "Who's this? What's going on?"

Cal stood up and strode confidently toward Natalia with his hand outstretched and his cheeky grin in full blast mode. "Hi. I'm Cal Wilde. You must be Worth's sister. He's told me so much about you."

I stared at him wondering how he'd even known my sister was on this boat. "Uh, Nat, Cal is..."

What the hell was I supposed to say? We hadn't had time to come up with our cover story yet.

Cal jumped in. "Worth's friend from sailing school. We were on the master course together. Hope you don't mind, he invited me to join you this week, and you know how hard this face is to say no to." He reached over and squeezed my face in his hands, making my lips turn fishy. I tried to keep my eyes from bugging out in surprise.

He was so charismatic, so charming, that I immediately dropped my shoulders. This was going to be a walk in the park. In addition to hopefully opening Lucas's eyes to the joke of a man he was engaged to, Cal would add some much-needed levity to the trip I'd been dreading. Maybe he'd even get the focus off me for a while so I could avoid the "you're a workaholic" lectures I was sure my siblings were planning.

Nat glanced over at him before grinning. "Not at all. The more, the merrier. I didn't know Worth had met anyone in St. Thomas. But that was five years ago. You couldn't have been more than..."

"I look a lot younger than I am," Cal said smoothly, moving over to make room for Nat. "Supposedly, it will come in handy one day, but for now, I'm used to being mistaken for a twelve-year-old." He winked at her, and I felt my heart rate kick up a notch.

"Why weren't you at dinner?" Nat asked. I could see the confusion on her face. I wasn't known for spontaneous decisions. This was also originally planned as a sibling bonding trip, and I'd given her hell for wanting to bring her own girlfriends with us.

I opened my mouth to stammer out some kind of excuse, but Cal beat me to it.

"I wasn't in great shape, I'm afraid. I asked if I could sneak away for a nap to sleep off a hangover." Then the charming fucker actually blushed. "I, ah, stayed out too late last night drinking with Martha and Bix Gerrywell. Those two have an Oyster 565. Most beautiful girl in the harbor at St. Mitz. Did you see it? Sixty-foot sailing yacht with twin rudders, flush decks, and the optional center board for shallow sailing. Gah! If your sweet brother here hadn't begged me to join you this week, I would have jumped at the chance to head to the Caymans with them. The *Marthine* is gorgeous under sail, especially with the purple spinnaker."

There had been no sixty-foot sailing yacht in the harbor when we'd left the docks, but my sister wouldn't know that.

I lifted an eyebrow at him and joined him in his charade just to see his reaction. "Well, you would have been bored to tears considering Martha and Bix spend their entire time on board playing solitaire and discussing agriculture futures."

Cal's nostrils widened as he bit back a smirk. "I love a good agriculture future, Worthie. You know that."

I coughed into my fist and turned to look out the window at the pitch-black water.

"Anyway," Cal continued. "I was just getting ready to hop in a quick shower before raiding the fridge. Would you like to join me for a glass of wine? Your brother said he'd break out the best chardonnay for me if I agreed to sleep on deck this week."

Nat shot me a look. "For god's sake. Inviting him here, then putting him on the deck? The king of the yacht can't deign to share his giant stateroom with an old friend? Shame on you, Worth. This bed is plenty big enough to share." She smiled at Cal. "You'll sleep in here with my brother or he can sleep on deck."

Cal's smile dropped. "No, I—"

"Of course he'll sleep in here," I said, trying not to think of how much money I'd paid for this ship, even if it had been a "gift." All that money and now I was bunking with a smooth-talking stranger.

Cal's head snapped to face me, and he looked horrified. "No. That's not... no. I'm very happy sleeping on deck. I'm a sailor, I..."

I held up a hand and turned back to Nat. "Cal and I have it under control. Don't worry. In the meantime, he's going to hop in the shower and meet us upstairs for something to eat." I flicked my head from Cal to the bathroom, and he hopped up to scurry in and close the door.

I led Nat out of the room and up the stairs to the galley while I tried desperately not to picture Cal's perfect young body naked in my shower. I was absolutely not falling for the tempting morsel. My one job on this trip was to try and reconnect with Lucas and Natalia while supposedly celebrating my brother's engagement. And if I could convince Lucas that he deserved better than a gold-digging user like Prescott Resnick, that would be a bonus. But if I fell under the spell of another man-child who no doubt had his own gold-digging tendencies, as evidenced by Cal's willingness to fuck a man like Prescott just for a chance to get on a yacht, then I would no longer have a leg to stand on.

Cal was a tool. Nothing more.

3

CAL

As soon as I stepped under the hot spray in the luxurious tiled shower, I let out a shaky breath. How did I get myself into these situations? Jonathan Worthington had looked every bit the yacht owner which only served to illustrate what an idiot I was for believing that Prescott prick was the one who actually owned something so refined and elegant. I normally had a preference for boats with sails, but ever since spotting the *Worthington* in the harbor the other day, I'd drooled over its clean lines and sparkling presence.

I huffed and shook my head. *Idiot.* I should have left the dance club and found my way to the hostel. Doc and Grandpa were probably wondering where I was since I'd never checked in after getting off my last job. We had a deal that I called every Sunday between gigs, and now it was Monday night.

I indulged in a luxurious body scrub and hair wash, using some kind of fancy-ass body wash in a brown and gold bottle. It smelled like cedar and lemon if those two things had been delicately blended in a boutique in Paris.

I raced through a quick drying off, found a new toothbrush in a cabinet for a quick freshening-up of my skunk mouth, and finally slipped back into Worth's soft clothes. As I pulled the T-shirt back on, I finally saw the printed design on the front.

It was a tiny fat gnome in a faded rainbow hat with the words *Teeny Bit Gay* underneath. I smiled and ran my hand over where it lay on my chest. Jonathan Worthington didn't look like a guy who'd wear this anywhere, much less wear it often enough for the print to have faded out from hundreds of washes. He seemed more likely to sleep in Brooks Brothers pajamas, crisply ironed and buttoned just so.

When I got up to the living area of the ship, I noticed everything in its place and probably as pristine as the day the ship had come out of dry dock. It was a gorgeous vessel with a combination of modern and comfortable furnishings. It didn't look as untouchable as I would have expected. Instead, there were colorful cushions on the dove-gray sofa, a soft quilt neatly folded in a basket in the corner, and a squat pottery jar in the center of the dining table filled with a messy mix of Caribbean wildflowers.

I ignored it all and headed for the narrow galley, spotting Worth, who stood at the counter slicing some kind of artisan bread on a cutting board. Even his movements looked elegant and refined as if the man himself was an extension of his sleek yacht and all of its high-end finishings.

"Better," Worth said, after giving me a quick up-down. It was a statement, not a question, and I tried not to apologize for whatever had offended him about my pre-shower self. The instinct to defend myself to this stranger set my teeth on edge, and I breezed past him to the fridge in search of something cold to drink. I refused to be cowed by men who thought they were more important than other people.

As soon as I reached for the handle of the fridge, the scent of something delicious finally breached my annoyance.

Worth had been right. I was starving.

I found a bottle of water in the fridge, but before I could rummage for something to snack on, I heard the ding of a microwave. Worth pulled out a dish of pasta that looked like something from a five-star restaurant. He placed two thick slabs of the bread on the side of the dish and slid it over to me.

"Forks are around here somewhere," he muttered, pulling open drawers until he found one.

"Oh, fuck me. This is incredible," I blurted after sneaking a bite right there at the counter. "I haven't eaten this good since—"

Worth cut me off with a head tilt at his sister. "Since the rock lobsters you dove for, right? Tell me again how that chef cooked them?"

He wasn't far off from the truth even though he was implying I'd been on some fancy yacht when I'd eaten them instead of the barefoot charter I'd captained for a family from Maine. Maybe he thought students of his beloved captain school had to be rich assholes like himself. Spoiler alert: they didn't. They could be young idiots who'd saved for years and sold their old truck for the chance to learn from the best.

"Grilled with simple lemon butter, but when you're eating it straight from the water..." I sighed. "There's nothing like it. I wish we could dive for some in the BVI this week, but they're protected right now. If you fish, we can probably do something similar with grouper."

I moved over to the table and sat down. Natalia was already lounging in a chair with a full glass of white wine. Her face lit up when I mentioned diving.

"I don't fish, but I love to dive. My friends are desperate to get certified this week."

"I can certify them," I said between bites. The pasta was incredible, and I tried not to moan again. "I mean, if you want."

Worth cleared his throat. If he hoped to remind me I was supposed to be a rich asshole on this trip, he was in for a surprise. I could pretend to be richer than I was, sure, but I wasn't about to be a jerk about it.

"Really?" Nat asked with a big smile. "Are you, like, a dive instructor or something?"

I nodded. "I have a current PADI instructor certification and an association with a dive shop back at St. Mitz. If I do their education and checkout dives, the shop will process their sea cards."

Nat's forehead crinkled. "But..." She looked from me to Worth and back again. "Is... is that what you do for a living? Teach diving in the Caribbean?"

She didn't sound judgmental, only confused. So I told her the truth.

"Not really. I spend as much of my life on boats or underwater as possible. I decided to get certified as an instructor when I realized how many people I sailed with would love to learn to dive if they could do it from the boat with a friend instead of being stuck in a dive shop back on the island."

It wasn't a lie, really. I just hadn't clarified that the people I sailed with were charter clients rather than my own rich socialite friends.

"That's fantastic," she said with a smile. "We're going to have so much fun! Are you single? I can't wait for you to meet my friends."

"Natalia!" Worth said.

She blinked over at him. "What? He's adorable. You know Mia will go nuts for him. And Jade too."

Worth's jaw tightened in judgement. "Cal isn't here for..." He trailed off as his brain most likely caught up with his offer for me to seduce Preston. "Just... stop harassing him, okay? He's not your entertainment for the week."

Nat rolled her eyes before winking at me. "My brother is a party pooper, but you probably already know that."

"Not true," I said, taking a sip of water. "I once saw him stay up all night pole dancing at an amateur—"

Worth's strong hand clamped over my mouth before I could finish. The warm scent of the Tom Ford cologne made its way into my nose, overpowering the seafood pasta in the very best way.

His stormy eyes met mine. "That's enough fun stories from the past, Calvin."

Our eyes stayed locked for a long beat before he pulled his hand away.

"It's Calgary," I muttered, digging into the pasta again. "How many times do I have to tell you that?"

Worth studied me for a minute before his eyes began to glitter. "Oh dear. You don't remember how everyone started calling you

Calvin after you wore those barely there swim briefs in Provincetown last summer? You remember, the red ones with the white Calvin Klein logo?"

My heart sped up. Did he think he could best me at a bluffing game? He had no idea who he was up against.

I met his eyes. "Those weren't even Calvin Klein. They were Studs from Australia. The company paid me to wear them in P-Town and Fire Island during Pride month. You should have seen the box of jocks and thongs they gave me as a thank-you present. Mm. So hot. But they run small, so... it was literally a pain in the ass to wear them. *Worth* it though."

I kept eating as if I hadn't just painted a picture for him that nearly made him choke on the sip of wine he'd taken.

Natalia sighed. "I love Fire Island. Worth has a house there, but he never uses it."

I glanced up at him. "Why don't you use it? My dream is spending the summer on Fire Island and the winter in the Caribbean."

Nat took another sip of wine. "He's a stodgy workaholic. It took us six months to pin him down on the dates for this trip. From the sound of things, you've seen more of him in the past few years than we have. Where are you from, Cal?"

"A tiny town in Texas called Hobie. My family owns a ranch there."

I noticed Worth's eyes widen in surprise. He must have thought I was a broke-ass sailboat bum who just magicked myself out of the surf in time to put the moves on his skanky future brother-in-law. I couldn't hold back a chuckle. "But don't ask me to rope a steer or anything. I'm the baby of the family, with the exception of my sister Sassy. By the time I came along, most of the cattle had been sold off. Now one of my brothers raises rare breed sheep on the land, and those guys are handled more with baby talk than ropes. It's a little bit embarrassing."

"What kind of rare breeds?" Nat asked.

I pictured the little fuzz-heads but drew a blank on the name of the breed for some reason. "Shit, I can't remember. I'll text Hudson and ask though. Maybe get him to send me some pictures."

Worth's eyes narrowed, and I realized he thought I was making all of this up the way I'd made everything else up. For some reason that disappointed me, as if I wanted him to know that there was more to me than a giant bag of lies.

"No, really," I said softly. "It's true."

"Mpfh." He stood up and took my plate to the sink. "Nat, you must be exhausted from the trip. You should get some sleep."

She ignored him. "My brother doesn't realize I'm twenty-seven years old and perfectly capable of deciding when I want to go to sleep. Tell me more about your family, Cal. How many siblings do you have?"

I bit my bottom lip while I considered how to respond. It was going to sound like a tall tale. "A lot." I shot a glance at Worth, who was pretending not to be listening as he washed my dish in the sink. "Um, there are ten of us."

Worth dropped his chin to his chest, and I tried my best to ignore him as I continued. "My mother is kind of a hippie. Or... she was. I'm not really sure what she's like anymore. My parents moved to Singapore years ago for my dad's job, so I was mostly raised by my grandfathers after that."

"The ranchers."

"Yep. Grandpa was a rancher. Doc was a doctor. *Is* a doctor, I guess. He ran the clinic in town until my brother West took it over."

Worth returned to the table to grab the bottle of wine before replacing the cork and putting it away in the fridge. When he finished, he gestured to me. "Come on, Cal. Freya has your phone on the bridge. You said you wanted to call home. You can use the ship's Wi-Fi."

I shot a wink at Nat and stood up. "Your brother is a bossy thing, isn't he? I guess I'll see you in the morning. It's nice to finally meet the woman Worth always speaks so highly of."

Nat seemed surprised by my words, and I wondered at the

siblings' relationship. It seemed friendly, considering the ribbing that Nat gave her brother, but what the hell did I know?

"See you in the morning," Nat said, hopping up and giving me a quick hug. "Glad you're here. We're going to have fun, even if we have to drag Worth with us screaming and kicking."

Once she'd descended the stairs back to her stateroom, Worth flared his nostrils at me. "Come," he said, as if I were a dog under his command.

"Beg your pardon?" I asked between tight teeth.

"I'm hardly going to sit here while you spin stories at my sister. I'm tired and ready to go to sleep."

I guess I couldn't blame him for thinking everything out of my mouth was a lie, but it still kind of stung a little. For some reason, I wanted him to think well of me, but then again, maybe it was human nature to want to be believed and liked.

He led me into the smaller room behind the galley that was clearly the ship's bridge. A heavily pregnant woman sat at the controls, monitoring several high-tech screens showing navigation and depth details as well as engine information. When the woman spotted me, her eyes widened.

"Freya, this is Cal. He's a... friend of mine joining us this week."

"Welcome, Cal."

I shot her my best smile and shook her hand. "Thanks. I'm excited to be here. You must be the chief mate I've heard so much about."

Her eyes flicked between Worth and me for a beat before she smiled. "That's me. Unfortunately this little sailor," she said, rubbing her stomach, "is landlocking me for a bit."

"Best wishes. My brother and his husband have an eighteen-month-old, and she's giving them a run for their money. They also have a three-and-a-half-year-old. It's chaos at home, but they wouldn't have it any other way. My grandfather says children keep you young even when they make you feel old."

Freya chuckled. "I'm good with one for now. We'll see down the road about adding to the chaos."

"Well, if you need any help while I'm here, please let me know. I've been on boats since I was tiny, and I'm good at moving heavy things and cleaning—two chores all ships need help with. Just say the word and I'm yours."

"Wow, be careful what you offer," she said with a wink. "Or Captain Vin will have you scrubbing the hull at sunrise."

"You're not cleaning the ship," Worth said, pinning me with his stare. "You're here as my guest this week, remember?"

"I can still help. I like to stay busy." I turned my smile on Freya. "Besides, my grandfathers would never forgive me if I let a pregnant lady do any hard work while it was in my power to do it for her."

Before Freya had a chance to stop blushing and respond, Worth grabbed something off a nearby counter before latching onto my elbow and pulling me out of the bridge with a stiff nod to his chief mate. "We'll let you get back to work. Have a good night."

When we stepped back into the galley, Worth slid the door to the bridge closed and shoved my clothes and phone into my arms. "She doesn't need any distractions," he said.

I looked out the window to confirm before I said, "We're going slower than the speed of a newborn kitten at rest, and there's no one around us for miles. What exactly do you think a quick conversation is going to do to cause—"

"Fine. Make your phone call or whatever you need to do, then come back down to my stateroom," he said. "We'll figure out the sleeping situation, and when we arrive at Turshall Cay, you can see about getting yourself some supplies for the week."

I froze. I could afford toiletries, a couple of cheap T-shirts, and a pair of swim trunks, but that was where my funds ended. My credit cards and passport were back at St. Mitz, safely stored in a locker at the charter company's office. I didn't make a habit of carrying anything valuable to a club or hostel, just enough to pay cash for drinks and a night's stay.

"Um, yeah. Sure," I said, before moving toward the fridge. "Thanks again for putting me up."

"Mpfh," he grunted before heading back down the stairs.

"Ooookay, then," I muttered to myself before finding a spot on the sofa in the living area. The sliding doors were partially open, letting in the familiar scent of the ocean in the night air. I took a deep breath and tried to steady myself.

It was much too late to call home, but I could at least shoot Doc and Grandpa a quick text telling them what was going on. Once I let go of the stress from the day's events, I brought up my texts.

Doc: *Didn't hear from you yesterday. Assume job ran late. All is well here. Love you.*

Doc: *Major is worried about you. Send us a text or he might initiate military-backed retrieval sequence.*

West: *Dude, answer your damned phone before Grandpa loses his shit.*

Nico: *What do you call that sailor knot that looks like a ball? I want to make one for Pippa.*

Grandpa: *I read an article today about a man who was lost at sea. Oh wait, that was my precious baby. My bad.*

Saint: *Why is Grandpa asking Otto and me about maritime rescue? Also, there's an old inn in St. Mitz that used to use old metal room keys in the shape of tropical fish. I want to give one to Augie. Find out if they'll sell you one and how much they want for it.*

Sassy: *Can I borrow your clarinet? Don't ask any questions.*

Doc: *At what point do I admit to you that I can do that Find My iPhone thing with your phone since you're still on our family plan?*

Grandpa: *Doc says you were safely on St. Mitz last night, but you're back out to sea today. What that says to me is you don't care anymore about two old men who may not live to see their grandson return from the deep.*

Doc: *Dammit, he hit send before I could get the phone out of his hand. Just let us know you're alive for Pete's sake.*

Sassy: *Wait. Did you play flute or clarinet? Either way, I need it.*

Charlie: *What's the American phrase for a nixer - like, doing work for cash to avoid taxes? Hudson says doing it under the table, but I think that's a sex thing and he's taking the piss.*

Sassy: *Otto says you played the drums. That can't be right.*

Hallie: *Send me the website for Bimbo Dan's again. My friend wants to book a sailing trip with you and I expect a kickback.*

Sassy: *Never mind. Stevie has a flute I can use. Even though he wasn't in band. Weird.*

By the time I finished reading all the missed texts, I was laughing so hard I was crying. Worth reappeared at the top of the stairs with a frown. "You're going to wake everyone on board."

"Oh, sorry," I said, sitting up from my slouch and sending a quick text to tell them I was okay. "Just catching up on messages from my crazy family. Like I said, I'm one of ten children. It's a little nuts."

Worth's eyes widened in surprise. "You weren't kidding about there being ten of you? Jesus. Was it a religious thing?"

"No. My mom is kind of a freak for natural methods, and unfortunately those don't work great for contraception."

Worth's nostrils flared and he pursed his lips together. "Yes, well. I'd like to sort out the sleeping situation so..." He took another look at me before clearing his throat and turning back to the stairs. "Come to bed, Cal."

The words sounded intimate in a way I'd never heard before—at least I'd never heard them aimed at *me*. It was oddly exciting, as if... as if we were lovers and he was calling me to bed because he wanted me there with him, to hold and love on. The idea of such a buttoned-up corporate type being vulnerable in that way almost made me laugh. A man like Jonathan Worthington was way more likely to tell his lovers to come the way a hunter would tell his dog to fetch.

Ever since Nat had found us talking in the stateroom, Worth had turned into exactly the type of man I'd picture owning a boat like this —controlled, stern, and a little bit cold. Which was odd because I could have sworn he'd been more open and talkative when he'd first found me in his stateroom. I wondered at the difference. Had it been a temporary slip, or had it been simply a figment of my imagination? Or maybe he was oddly friendly below decks and all business up top.

I snorted softly and stood up to join him in the stateroom to test it out. It didn't really matter though. I was here to do a job, and I needed a boss more than I needed a friend or lover. I would do just about anything to stay here in the Caribbean and continue living and working on the water and around boats, and if that meant putting up with the rich assholes my brother King had warned me about, then so be it.

4

WORTH

I couldn't get the sound of Cal's laughter out of my head. As soon as I heard him up there giggling, I had to see what was so funny. He was slouched down in my living room with only the company of his friends and family through his phone. He seemed like the very definition of the surfer or beach bum stereotype: relaxed and easy, friendly and warm. In other words, the complete opposite of me.

Which was as it should be. Except... except he seemed to be exactly the kind of guy my siblings wished I was. They'd begged me to come on this trip to reconnect since I hadn't taken any time off with them since before our father had died seven years ago, leaving me in charge of picking up the pieces after his disastrous decision to leave half of the family business to his fourth and final wife—Angela —the twins' mother, instead of leaving it to Lucas and Nat directly.

I'd spent the last seven years working my ass off and trying desperately to keep my head above water to make sure Lucas and Natalia never wanted for anything in their lifetime. It had taken all this time—and exhaustive legal negotiations—to finally wrench Angela's share of the business away from her and secure it for the twins.

Seeing how easy Cal was with Nat made me bristle, because of course it was easy for a kid bumming around in the Caribbean to relax and go with the flow. He didn't have thousands of people whose livelihoods depended on him.

"Come to bed," I said before returning back downstairs. My words reverberated in my head. It sounded like something you'd say to a beloved instead of a twenty-three-year-old stranger.

I closed my eyes and rubbed my hands over my face. What the hell had I gotten myself into? I didn't set out to lie to my sister, and it wasn't exactly the best way to start a trip whose sole purpose was bringing us closer together.

It's just a week.

A week of sharing a room with him. A week of listening to his easy laughter. A week of seeing those slender muscles move under his tanned skin.

I glanced up when I heard the bedroom door click.

"Sorry," he said, suddenly looking a whole lot less sure of himself. "I hope I didn't screw things up too much with your family. I mean... I don't even know if you..."

"It's fine," I said quickly. "And Nat is right. This is a king bed. You're tiny." I cleared my throat. "We'll be fine sharing."

I'd already considered switching with Nat's friends and having them share so Cal and I could have a room with two singles. But all of my things were in here, including my desk. The only way I could do the work I needed to get done this week was to sneak it in the privacy of my own stateroom.

"I don't mind sleeping on the sofa," Cal said, looking anywhere but at me. I didn't like the insecure Cal. I preferred the charismatic version who made up stories. "If you'd rather me do that."

"Don't be ridiculous. One big wave and you'll tumble right off. Get in bed." I tried not to notice his eyes widen and the pink flush steal across his neck.

He pulled back the blankets and climbed inside. "And I'm not that small," he muttered. "I can sail a hundred-foot trimaran by myself for fuck's sake."

I pressed the button to lower the window shades and tried to hide my smile as I got into bed next to him. "Tiny but strong," I teased. "Like Mighty Mouse."

He launched himself on top of me and pinned me to the mattress in seconds, with his hands holding my wrists up by the headboard and his knees squeezing my hips. I had no doubt my eyes bugged out of my head, and I might have made an embarrassing sound of surprise.

"Unhand me," I gritted out between my teeth. If Cal got any closer to me, I was going to lose all of my restraint and cross a line.

His fiery gaze met mine. "Don't underestimate small people. It makes you look like a jackass."

We were both breathing heavily, and I could see down the front of the open neck of the T-shirt he was wearing. The bumps of his chest and ab muscles were visible in the shadows, and I could even spot the shadowy hair of a happy trail. My heart rate ticked up. I wanted to lick all of it.

"When did I underestimate you, exactly?" I asked.

We locked eyes for a few heavy moments. The air in the room seemed thick with anticipation. "You're the one implying small is a bad thing, not me," I continued, because I couldn't keep from antagonizing him for some reason. Maybe it was a crazy, fucked-up defense mechanism to keep me from lurching up and taking his mouth in mine, a mistake that would surely bear impossible consequences.

Even twisted with frustration, his face was beautiful. His dirty-blond hair stuck up in different directions, and his top lip was fuller than the bottom one. I wanted to pull it between my teeth and suck on it.

I cleared my throat and pushed him off, rolling until I was the one pressing him into the mattress. His wrists felt slender and warm encircled in my larger hands, and as I'd flipped him, I'd felt his cock brush against my thigh. He wasn't the only one inappropriately turned on by our argument. "Don't get physical with me, *Calgary*. Or I will not hesitate to throw you overboard."

His face morphed from anger with a slight tinge of fear to a mischievous smirk. "Yes, Daddy."

If I hadn't been so distracted by the fact I'd scared him, I might have laughed. Instead, I climbed off him and returned to my side of the bed.

"I'm sorry. I shouldn't have touched you like that," I said, rubbing my hands over my face. "Even though you started it."

He began laughing. "And you think I'm the kid in the room."

I turned my head to glare at him, but the sight of him laughing stopped me in my tracks. He was breathtaking. "I thought I'd scared you, and now you're laughing," I muttered, leaning over to turn off the lamp. "You're a very strange man. And the fact I'm sharing my bed with a complete stranger is just..." I sighed and lay back on my pillow.

"Exciting? Sexy? Routine?"

I bit back a laugh. "Certainly not routine."

"Well, that's a shame. You should try it sometime. Hm. I guess you are. But I mean, you should try it in the good way. The sexy way."

"I see how well that worked out for you."

Cal was quiet for a minute, and I worried I'd touched a nerve. I still couldn't stand knowing he'd slept with Prescott.

"It did work out well for me," Cal said smugly. "I'm lying next to a bajillionaire on thousand-thread-count sheets aboard his multimillion-dollar yacht looking at a sweet all-expenses-paid week of vacation in the British Virgin Islands. I'd say that's a pretty good reward, all in all."

I turned my head to look at him. Only the shadow of his profile was outlined in the dark room. "And you said you didn't want to be Julia Roberts."

He sighed. "I'm trying to make lemonade out of lemons, Jon. It's called focusing on the silver lining. Maybe you should try it."

No one had ever called me Jon before, besides my mother when I was very little, and I had to admit, I kind of liked it. Not that I would ever tell him that.

"Go to sleep, Cal."

As he shifted in the bed, I caught a whiff of my shower gel on his skin. I bit back a groan and turned my back to him. I'd originally bought the shower gel for my ex. I'd wanted to bring Mason a little something from a business trip to Vail, and there'd been a men's boutique just outside the resort where I was staying. Every time I'd passed the open door of the boutique that week, I'd smelled the incredible scent coming from inside. I'd finally popped my head in to find out what it was. But when I'd brought the bath stuff home, he'd refused to use it, asking me if it was some kind of veiled message about the way he smelled.

After the split, I realized that I should have bought it for myself if I liked the smell of it. Maybe I should have bought Mason something more impressive like the latest model of Patek Phillipe watch or tickets to an exclusive, sold-out event. As if that would have made a difference. There was never enough showering of affection in any form to make Mason happy. I'd canceled work plans to spend time with him, I'd arranged surprise parties for him, and I'd spent hours hanging out with his friends when he'd said that was the single most important thing I could do to show him I cared about him. But none of it was enough unless it also came with a proposal, joint bank accounts, and a half stake in my family business.

I wasn't even sure the proposal had been all that important.

I closed my eyes and let out a breath. Enough thinking about the past. I was here to relax, supposedly, and perseverating on Mason wasn't exactly conducive to that.

"You want to talk about it?" Cal asked softly from behind me.

"You sail for a living?" I asked. "I mean, that's what you want to do with your life?"

The only answer for several moments was silence until I felt him shift again. "Yes."

"What's your favorite sailboat?" I was trying to distract myself from memories of my ex as well as my attraction to this sexy stranger by talking about a safe topic, one I knew we had in common.

"A Sunfish or maybe a Dart 16."

The answer surprised me. Those little boats only cost a few thousand dollars. They were the kind of watercraft summer camps used with kids. I flipped around so I could see his shadowed profile again. "No, I mean your dream boat."

He shrugged. "My dream is to teach kids to sail, so a small, easy-to-sail beginner boat *is* my dream boat."

I came at it from another direction. "If you had all the money in the world, which boat would you buy?"

He turned his head toward me. "Jon. If I had all the money in the world, I'd buy a fleet of Sunfish or Darts. I'd start a sailing school."

His passion intrigued me. "There's a story there."

Cal sighed. "Maybe. But it's a depressing one."

"Well, you're clearly not ready for sleep, and I'm a good listener if I try really hard." I lay on my side wishing I could see his facial expressions better.

"There's a woman named Annie Jackson who runs a sailing school back home. It runs almost year-round, but in the summer she also puts on an elite sailing camp for kids from all over the country. She has a hundred acres of waterfront land on the lake. It has cabins, a big rec hall, sports fields, and walking trails. It's awesome. I took sailing lessons there when I was around eight years old. I can't even remember why since none of my siblings were interested. It didn't matter, really. I fell in love with it. I liked it so much, I spent every spare minute I could there until I was old enough to get hired on. I worked on the boats as many hours as she'd give me, and when she couldn't pay me for more, I did it voluntarily."

He shifted to face me, the whites of his eyes flashing in the dark space between us. "I had a plan to stay there forever, but it just wasn't meant to be."

"Why not?"

"Annie was like a mother to me after my own mom moved overseas. We got really close over the years. Once I'd worked there for a while, she started hinting at putting me in charge one day so she could retire and travel. She said I'd need a business degree, my captain's license, and a certain number of hours logged on the water in order to gain the trust of the parents whose children attended the camp. She takes the program's reputation in the sailing community very seriously. It's why I came to the Caribbean in the first place." He sighed. "But then Annie's nephew and wife showed up asking to take over. Which is fine. I understand family is everything. Hell, family *is* everything to me. But it kind of..."

"Took the wind out of your sails," I said gently.

"Yeah. And he's big on 'family values' which is basically dick-speak for being a homophobic asshole. So now I'm kind of... avoiding the issue, I guess you could say. And trying not to picture that immature jackass, who never once tried to sail his own boat the two summers he came to camp, in charge of Annie's beloved program."

"Can you buy it off him?" I asked, falling back onto what I knew best. Investment and acquisitions.

Cal let out a soft chuckle. "Yeah, Jon. Let me just write a check. I think I might have a couple hundred bucks in my account right now, and my spotty work history at Buoy Dan's is exactly the kind of consistency and stability the banks like to see when loaning a twenty-three-year-old money."

He was right. No one would give him money for something like that, even if he had the business degree and could account for his professional sailing experience.

"I'm sorry." It was all I could think to say.

He took a breath. "It's fine. My grandpa always says, 'Sometimes golden opportunities are covered in horse shit and kicked to the back of the stall. If you don't know how to work hard and get your hands dirty, you ain't never gonna find 'em.'"

"He sounds like a good man."

Cal swallowed. "The best. Shot down in Vietnam and made it out. Both of them, Doc and Grandpa. It's how they met and fell in love."

"When you mentioned your grandfathers earlier, I didn't realize they were a couple. That's amazing. They were able to keep it secret?"

"Oh. No. They weren't... I mean, while they were active duty, Doc was still married to my grandmother. It was after they got out and Grandpa came to work on Doc's family's ranch that they fell in love. After my dad and his sisters were born and my grandmother had passed away."

He told me more about his large family and the ranch in northern Texas. I could hear the affection in his voice for his grandfathers, his siblings, and the land he grew up on. As the comforting rhythm of his voice washed across me, I realized I'd relaxed into the mattress and fallen half-asleep. For some reason, I didn't want to fall all the way asleep and miss a minute of hearing his stories.

"What about you?" he asked. "How did you get into sailing?"

"My father belonged to a yacht club on Lake Michigan. I don't even know why since he never took the time to go there very often. But he signed me up for sailing lessons when I was a young teen, and I fell in love. Unfortunately, they didn't have sailing at the boarding school I went to, so I never got back to it until college. Thankfully, at Northwestern they have a sailing center. I was able to take more classes, rent boats, go on group trips, and pretty much sail whenever the weather was good enough. It was my go-to stress reliever, especially during finals in the spring."

"That sounds amazing. I sailed for Texas A&M's rec team, but I also took eighteen credit hours every semester so I could graduate early. It didn't leave as much time for sailing as I'd hoped."

That explained how he could be so young and already have so much professional sailing experience. "Did you get a business degree?"

He made an affirmative sound. "Management, specifically. In hindsight I shouldn't have focused so much on small business. Maybe I can get a job in yacht sales in Galveston. It's worth a shot."

I tried to lighten the mood since this story had obviously reminded him of a lost dream. "But then you'd have to pretend your favorite boats weren't five-thousand-dollar Sunfish," I teased.

He huffed out a soft laugh. "What about you? If you hadn't been *gifted* this yacht, what dream sailboat would you want?"

"The J-Class Rainbow by Holland," I said immediately. "I've been obsessed with it since I saw a YouTube video of it two years ago. Gorgeous ship."

Cal chuckled again, and the warm laughter relaxed me farther into the bed. "Dude, that's worth less than this monstrosity. Why not sell this and get that?"

"No one I know wants to sail on it with me. My brother and sister don't like the way a sailboat tilts. Plus, it's a completely different experience. I like being on the water, and you have to admit, this is a nice way of doing it. Diving is easier off a boat like this, and it fits more people in comfortable staterooms." I thought about our current situation. "Although still not enough for this trip," I added with a smile.

"If only you could afford both," he teased. "Can you imagine? *'Which luxury yacht shall we take out today, Brendan, the motor or the sail*?' Talk about first-world problems."

"Who's Brendan?" I asked, to steer us away from the topic of money. He clearly had no idea who I was and what I did for a living, and I suddenly discovered I wanted to keep it that way. If he knew I could afford both, and both of the shipyards where they were crafted as well, there was no telling what he'd think. "My pretentious fictional boy toy is named Chauncey."

Cal chuckled. "But can we call him Chaunce when we're in a hurry?"

"I frequently do. *'Chaunce, be a dear and fetch me the chablis tout de suite'* is a phrase that is often heard around the hedge maze when I'm parched."

He laughed some more, and I idly wondered how much of my fortune I'd be willing to give up to hear his laughter continue.

But these were dangerous waters, and I'd already given myself one stern reminder about the fact Cal was essentially an employee which meant he was off-limits. Flirty joking was fine. Imagining him naked and impaled on my cock was not fine.

After a few minutes of silence, Cal yawned. "Thank you for letting me stay," he said in a sleepy voice. "I'm sorry for... all this."

I made a sound of acknowledgment and forced myself to turn away from him again so I wouldn't be tempted to reach across the smooth sheets to touch his warm skin. As tense as I felt right now, lying so close to someone this alluring, I knew I wouldn't be able to get any sleep at all. I'd most likely get up in the morning with my muscles tied in knots from trying to hold myself on the very edge of the mattress.

But that's not what happened.

At some point I must have fallen asleep, because I awoke in the morning wrapped around Cal Wilde like a very possessive boa constrictor. His face was mashed into my chest, and our legs were tangled together like pretzels. Every breath I took was scented with the combination of his sleepy skin and the faint traces of my shower gel. At first, I thought I was still asleep and dreaming, but when Cal arched his morning wood into my upper thigh, I knew I was very much awake.

And I realized inviting this tempting man to stay on board with me this week was going to be more challenging than I'd expected.

5

CAL

I WANTED TO CLING ON TO THE DREAM A LITTLE LONGER. WORTH WAS A pirate, and he was about to do something very, very naughty to my booty. But when I realized we were no longer on a creaky, triple-masted ship, I catapulted out of the bed so fast, I hit the wall and bounced right back onto the bed, mildly stunned.

"What just happened?" Worth sat up and shot me a look of confusion mixed with annoyance.

I rubbed the lump on my forehead with my fingers while my cheeks heated in embarrassment. "It's like a gymnastics dismount. I was trying to impress you."

Worth's eyes lowered to my very obvious erection tenting out the pajama pants I'd borrowed. "Can't say I'm all that impressed," he teased, making my cheeks heat even more.

"Fuck you," I muttered, standing up again and making my way to the bathroom. I wondered if he'd let me borrow some shorts and a T-shirt just long enough for me to duck over to the marina shops and pick up some basics.

I brushed my teeth and washed my face, stalling in my morning hygiene routine in hopes he'd be gone by the time I came back out. No such luck. Worth was exactly where I'd left him, and of course he looked sexy as fuck in the rumpled sheets. The imprint of his arms and legs still lingered on my skin, but I refused to acknowledge it.

"Your turn," I said, plastering on the chipper face of someone who hadn't just thrown himself face-first into a wall after clinging to the man like one of those stickers on produce that refuses to budge.

"I put some clothes over there for you," he said, gesturing to the sofa. "Feel free to head up to the galley for breakfast. Julo makes banana dumplings you don't want to miss."

As he walked over to the bathroom, I couldn't help but stare at Worth's muscular legs. He had the calves of a cyclist even though he'd mentioned living in Chicago. I wondered if he went to spinning classes in some posh boutique spin gym or if he was rich enough to have his own spin bike in a special gym in his house or apartment.

I rolled my eyes as I pulled the clothes on. Of course he was rich enough to own an exercise bike for god's sake. The bedding in this room alone was probably worth more than a fancy Peloton bike.

Hopefully there would be strong coffee waiting for me when I got upstairs. I was sick and tired of thinking about Jonathan Worthington, and I needed some caffeine to help me make a plan for the day. I also needed to call Doc and Grandpa at some point and let them know I'd gotten another job and would be staying down here a little longer.

After changing into the clothes and mentally thanking Worth for picking a pair of athletic shorts with a drawstring for my skinny ass, I grabbed my phone and headed up to the galley. It was still early. As soon as I got to the top of the stairs and had a view outside, I saw the light, rosy pink remnants of sunrise. It was probably around half past six which was my usual waking time when working on a boat, but I wondered if Worth was still on Chicago time and feeling the effects of the hour difference.

Stop thinking about Worth.

I bit back a groan of frustration. I didn't need a man to fuck. I needed a job, an excuse to stay down here and away from Hobie as long as possible.

A tall man with a thick ponytail of dreads and a big, friendly smile greeted me in the galley. Soft steel drum music played from somewhere nearby, and the warm breeze crossed through the room from all of the glass walls that were now open to the outside. "You must be Cal. I'm Julo. What're you hungry for this early morning?"

He had an island lilt to his voice that helped me relax. When I'd first moved to the Caribbean, it had taken me a while to slow down and stop taking myself so seriously. Being around so many laid-back locals had helped a ton.

"Worth says you make some kind of dumpling I need to try. And I'd kill for some coffee if you'll point me to the machine."

Julo nodded at a carafe already set up on a nearby tray with mugs and fixings. "Help yourself there. I'm making apple fritters today. Will get you some dumplings tomorrow. You want egg casserole too? Kinda spicy."

"God, that would be great. Thanks." I began pouring myself some coffee. "I'm from Texas. Our definition of spicy isn't the same as others'."

"Man after my heart, then," he said, turning to make me a plate.

I sat down at the counter opposite where he was working. "Where are you from, Julo?"

"St. Elizabeth Parish. Jamaica. Mostly Black River, but I was born inland closer to Lacovia. You been to Jamaica?"

"Only Kingston. I had to pick up a catamaran and sail it back to Tortola for a job."

He placed an overloaded plate in front of me before crossing his arms over his broad chest. "Freya said you were a guest of Mr. Worth. You work on boats?"

I nodded and took a bite of the fritter. "This is amazing. Yeah. I captain charter boats for Buoy Dan's. You know it? They have boats in St. Mitz, Tortola, and Grand Cayman."

He nodded. "My buddy Robbie works for them too, on the docks in Tortola. Repairs and stuff like that."

I vaguely remembered a young man who'd replaced a few broken halyard cleats on a boat I'd brought in. "Short guy, lots of muscles, and calls everyone 'cuz'?"

Julo's laughter was deep and vibrant, filling the space between us just as Natalia appeared at the top of the stairs. "Yah, that's the one."

"Good morning," I said to Nat before taking another deep slug of the coffee. "You're going to need to change into something with an elastic waist before breakfast," I warned.

She reached for a mug on the coffee tray. "I learned my lesson early on the last time I was here. Wait till you taste his—"

"What the fuck?"

I spun around on the stool to see Prescott appear at the top of the stairs. He stared at me like he was seeing a ghost. His mouth opened and closed a few times while his brain tried to catch up to the fact I was still on board this ship. Finally, he narrowed his eyes at me in warning and opened his mouth to say something.

Before he had a chance to get out a single word, Worth came up behind him with caution flashing in his eyes toward me. "Good morning, everyone."

"Hey, baby," I blurted before I could even think to stop myself. I had no idea why I said it, but maybe I couldn't stand the idea of Prescott Resnick standing there thinking he was better than I was. In that moment, I didn't want to be the cheap piece of ass he'd picked up and dropped like I was nothing. I wanted to get back at him for treating me like trash. And maybe my subconscious knew that acting like there was something between me and the wealthy owner of this boat would drive Prescott up the wall.

Everyone in the room froze as blood began roaring in my ears. I'd just fucked up royally. Worth was going to demand my removal, and I'd be stuck in Turshall Cay without my passport, my credit cards, or any way of returning to St. Mitz. And even if I could find my way back, I'd be jobless and finally have to face returning to Texas.

Slowly, as if he had all the time in the world and no care at all, Worth walked up to me and cupped my face in his hands. I wanted to whisper an apology, but I was too shocked at his expression. He looked at me like I was the rarest treasure in the world, and my stomach fell into the deepest depths when I realized he was leaning in to kiss me.

I sucked in a breath as soon as his lips touched mine and then continued to explore them at his leisure. When he finally pulled back and locked eyes with me, I felt light-headed from lack of oxygen.

"Good morning, beautiful. I'd ask how you slept, but I'm afraid I didn't let you sleep much at all, now, did I?" He turned to Julo and asked what was on the menu this morning as if he hadn't just shocked every single person in the room, including myself.

What the fuck had I just done?

Prescott spluttered, clearly struggling to find some words to ask what I was doing there and who I was but finding it difficult considering any attempt to claim knowing me would be met with questions.

He was saved by the appearance of another man. The new arrival was a younger, bespectacled version of Worth and also bore a striking resemblance to Nat, so I assumed this was Lucas. I couldn't help but feel immense guilt after having slept with his fiancé, even if it was unknowingly.

Nat's eyes sparkled at me. "Uh, Worth, did you maybe want to introduce everyone to Cal and this time include a bit more detail than you did last night?"

I suddenly fell in love with the smell of my coffee and held my face down toward my mug while clinging onto it tightly with both hands. Maybe he was going to wait until we were alone to kick me out. In the meantime, I was going to savor the flavor of his kiss and the memory of that hot mouth on mine.

Worth stepped next to me again and put his arm around my shoulder. "Of course. Everyone, this is Cal Wilde. He'll be staying on board with us this week as my own personal guest. Cal, you've already met Natalia and hopefully our renowned chef, Julo, as well. This is my brother, Lucas, and his fiancé, Prescott."

I shot laser eyes at Prescott and clinched my chest in mock surprise. "*Fiancé*? The two of you are engaged? To be married? How *amazing*! How absolutely thrilling." I didn't take my eyes off the little weasel, and I enjoyed every squirm of his discomfort. "You'll have to tell me *everything*, like where you met and what made you fall in love. I can't wait to hear—"

A muffled snort came from the direction of the chef while Nat's eyebrows furrowed.

Worth lowered his hand and pinched my side to shut me up before continuing with his introductions. "Yes, we're certainly planning on celebrating their... union... this week. Meanwhile, Nat's husband, Jin, is probably still asleep. He was in California for work, so I'm sure he's plenty jet-lagged. Have a seat at the table everyone. I'm sure Julo is going to take good care of us this morning before we hit the shops and pick up Nat's friends."

"Yes, sir," Julo said with his easy smile.

We all took a spot at the big dining table. Just as I was about to take the seat farthest from Prescott to avoid any awkward conversation, Worth nudged me right between Pres and Lucas before taking his spot at the head of the table.

"Thanks, *cupcake*," I said, plastering on a fake smile.

"I know you like to feel the sun on your skin. Besides, I'm just so happy you're finally able to meet my family, *darling*," he shot back with a real smile. "Remember, the reason you're here? My family?"

Oh. Right.

I smiled at Lucas and completely ignored the asshole on the other side of me for now. Even though I was technically supposed to be working on him, I didn't have the mental fortitude quite yet.

"So, Lucas, Jon tells me you like to—"

Natalia snickered. "He calls you Jon, that's so sweet."

I felt my face heat, and I refused to glance over at the man in question to see his response to her teasing. I wasn't even sure why I'd called him that. The first time I'd done it, it had been to tease him, but then he'd seemed to soften a little, so I kind of wanted to do it again. "*Worth* tells me you like to dive. Do you have any specific sites you want to dive this week?"

Before Lucas could answer, Prescott jumped in. I'd been waiting for him to lose his patience.

"So, *Cal*... what do you do for a living?"

I turned to face him and steeled myself. "I discipline old men on boats."

Worth choked on his eggs, and Nat stopped her coffee mug halfway to her lips. Prescott's jaw dropped.

I laughed and shook my head. "Sorry. I haven't had enough coffee yet this morning. I meant *instruct*. Not discipline. And, obviously they're not *all* old men, but most of the people who charter the big sailboats down here are wealthy older guys. I think maybe they've always dreamed of being taken for a ride..." I took a sip of my coffee. "... on a nice big sailboat, and now they finally have enough money to do something about it. Depending on the client, I'm either an instructor or a charter captain. What about you? What do you do when you're not spending time with your charming *fiancé*?" I lifted an eyebrow at him before taking another sip.

His nostrils flared. "I practice law at a firm that—"

"He's a paralegal," Worth inserted under his breath.

Lucas shushed him with a glare.

Pres shot Worth a look. "Paralegals practice law. Who do you think does all the actual work? Certainly not the attorneys. I practice at a firm that specializes in commercial real estate."

I gave him my biggest smile and my most genuine support. "Hopefully all that practice will pay off one day and you'll be able to do it for real. Good for you."

I turned to Lucas without waiting to see Prescott's reaction. "What about you, Lucas?"

Lucas's eyes flicked to his older brother as if searching for permission or approval. I wondered what that was about.

"I recently graduated from veterinary school."

That surprised me. "Really? That's fantastic. My brother West is a doctor, and my brother Hudson raises rare breed sheep. Hudson's so annoyed West didn't become a vet instead of a physician, so he's always teasing him about his 'lesser' medical degree. It's gotten to the point I think our sister Sassy might actually go to vet school just to shut them both up."

Lucas smiled. "It's a lot of work just to quiet a family feud."

"Nah, she'd be a great vet. She's always been a natural around animals, but she's scared. School wasn't easy for her, so she's convinced she can't handle graduate school. My grandfathers have been leaning on her pretty hard to at least try."

Lucas crinkled his brow. "That's tough. Maybe she'd rather be a vet tech. Much less schooling, and she'd still be able to help your brother a ton."

"That's what I told her, and there's a program close to home at the same place she's taking her prerequisites."

We talked a bit more while we ate breakfast. As expected, the food was amazing. Every time one of us groaned in pleasure or complimented Julo, he simply chuckled and continued working on whatever it was he was doing on the other side of the galley counter.

I ignored Prescott as much as possible, but I could feel his laser stare on the side of my face. When he finally got a chance to interrogate me again, he asked, "Cal, how did you and Worth meet, exactly?"

"Exotic dancing," I said at the same time Nat said, "Sailing school," and Worth said, "I helped him come out of the closet."

I snorted and clapped my hand over my mouth before I was able to shower everyone in coffee.

Lucas's laugh was light and sweet, and I knew right away I wanted to wrap him in bubble wrap and protect him at all costs. I'd only been sitting next to him for half an hour and I could already sense his genuine interest in and care for others. He seemed so different from Worth, which was especially strange since I didn't know Worth at all either.

Grandpa had always told us kids to "go with your gut" about people, and I had a sense that Lucas was a good person. A kind person. Which made me feel even worse for having slept with his fiancé. Worth was harder to pin down. I trusted him—whether I should or not remained to be seen—but I didn't consider him sweet and kind in the way Lucas was. Jonathan Worthington seemed more sharklike. I just didn't know if he was a fairly harmless reef shark or a cutthroat great white yet.

I met Worth's eyes across the table and felt the apple fritters take a tumble in my stomach. Fuck, he was sexy. He hadn't shaved this morning, and his scruff made him look more human. The breeze ruffled his hair, and his blue eyes danced as his laughter died down. The laugh lines next to his eyes reminded me of one of those deliciously older movie stars like Hugh Jackman or that guy from *Mad Men.*

"Cal, darling. Are you ready to go shopping? I have plans to spoil you this morning." Worth was clearly shocking the hell out of his brother and sister because they both gaped at him.

My lips felt numb under the unexpected affectionate attention. No man unrelated to me had ever spoken so dearly to me before. "Um... I... I'm not sure the stores are open yet?"

"I called ahead to Van Cleef and Arpels and they've agreed to let us in by appointment. I wanted to see if you like the Midnight Planétarium watch everyone's been talking about."

I didn't know what the hell that was, but Prescott must have. He made a muffled "eep" sound and stiffened next to me.

I frowned and tried to head this bullshit off at the pass. "Baby, remember when I lost my Rolex and you bought me the Omega Seamaster to replace it? I love that thing. I don't need a new one."

"That's just for the water. I want you to have a nicer one to wear out to dinner." He stood and came over to rest his hands on my shoulders. "Thanks, Julo, for another incredible meal. Sorry to eat and run, everyone, but I want to make sure we get our shopping in before Mia and Jade get here. Captain Vin would like to depart Turshall Cay early this afternoon if that's okay with everyone."

I wondered if Worth could feel me shaking under his fingertips. My big mouth had gotten me into some ridiculous scrapes in the past, but this took the cake. There was no telling what his reaction would be behind closed doors. I'd rather get chewed out in private than on the streets of Turshall Cay where someone could overhear me begging him not to ditch me.

Everyone around the table nodded and started to get up and disperse. Julo came over to clear the table, and I instinctively started helping him.

"Cal," Worth said softly so only I could hear him. "Let Julo do it, please. That's what he's here for."

I glanced between him and the chef. Julo winked at me and said, "He's right. If you cleaned up your own plates, I'd have to go back to working at the Blue Turtle and wearing a uniform. I think it's much better here if you don't mind."

He laughed again while he cleaned up. He wore black shorts and a red tank top that looked amazing against his dark brown skin. Clearly there was no strict dress code to work on the *Worthington*. It surprised me, honestly. I would have thought a rich guy like Worth would want everyone dressed just so.

While Worth had his back to me, thanking Julo again for breakfast, Pres grabbed my arm and tried pulling me out onto the deck. Thankfully, my foot caught the leg of a nearby dining chair, making a sound loud enough to get Worth's attention.

"What are you doing?" he asked in a voice loud enough to make Pres tighten his hand on my arm. I pulled my arm out of his grip but decided there was no time like the present to try and earn my keep.

"Pres just wanted to show me around a little, I think. You don't mind, do you?" I tried giving him significant eye contact, since he seemed right on the verge of pulling me away from Prescott.

Worth plastered on an apologetic smile that didn't reach his eyes. "I do, actually. But only because I don't want to be late for the jeweler. Pres can show you around as soon as we get back, I promise."

I shrugged and gave Prescott the most genuine look of regret I could manage before stepping closer to Worth. "Sorry, Pres. We'll see you back here in a bit."

Worth took my hand and held it firm. I couldn't decide if it was a grip meant to intimidate me before booting me off his boat or make sure I didn't run away from this cockamamie scheme we'd—okay, *I'd*—hatched.

And, honestly, I wasn't sure which I was hoping for.

6

———————

WORTH

W𝐇𝐄𝐍 C𝐀𝐋 𝐇𝐀𝐃 𝐂𝐀𝐋𝐋𝐄𝐃 𝐌𝐄 "𝐁𝐀𝐁𝐘," I 𝐂𝐎𝐔𝐋𝐃 𝐇𝐀𝐕𝐄 𝐄𝐀𝐒𝐈𝐋𝐘 𝐁𝐑𝐔𝐒𝐇𝐄𝐃 𝐈𝐓 off as a friend's teasing. Maybe roll my eyes and sarcastically reply, "Morning, snookems." But I hadn't. I'd spent the entire time in the shower wishing I could do more than sleep chastely next to Cal's young, fit body. I'd quickly justified my wayward thoughts by realizing my plan to reveal Prescott as a cheater would work better if Pres thought he was getting something of mine.

So when Cal had given me the opening, I'd taken it.

"You know I don't have much money, right?" Cal whispered as we climbed aboard the tender to take us to the marina. "I mean, on me. I only have what I took to the club that night. Everything else is back on St. Mitz, including my passport. And, well, that would also mean that I can't... I can't, um, travel from here back to St. Mitz with anyone who might need to see a passport since I don't have one, and it's not that I don't respect your need to get rid of me as soon as possible, I do. I really do. I shouldn't have said what I did, but I'd really appreciate it if I didn't end up in a Turshall jail cell because—"

"Stop," I said calmly, glancing up at the captain, who was patiently waiting to run us over to the island. "Take a breath."

I realized Cal hadn't met our captain yet, so I took the opportunity to introduce them. "Cal, this is Captain Vincent Clarke. Vin, this is Cal Wilde. He's a licensed captain himself, so if you find you need an extra pair of hands this week, he's more than willing to step in."

Cal looked between me and Vin, realizing from my words that I wasn't getting ready to throw him overboard. He finally took a breath and smiled at Vin. "Nice to meet you. Worth is right. I'm happy to help, and I love to work."

Vin's rare smile glinted against his dark skin. "As if I'd put a friend of Mr. Worthington's to work. Welcome aboard."

Cal immediately began asking him questions about where he was from, and when he learned Vin was from Barbados, he praised something called a ham cutter and off the two of them went on a conversation about their favorite foods from around the Caribbean.

It wasn't a surprise to hear Cal having such an easy time meeting and talking to new people, but I still envied it. Both my father and grandfather had been stoic men who'd cautioned me regularly about trusting strangers. They'd conveyed story after story of instances where people had attempted to use them for handouts or manipulate them in business dealings. Even knowing all of this, my father had been taken advantage of by four different wives, my mother included. I guessed the advice had only applied to men.

"Keep yourself to yourself, Jonathan," my father had told me in his stern voice a few weeks before he died. "They're all out to get something from you. Just remember that."

And time after time, I'd seen their warnings come true. When I was younger than ten, I'd played baseball in the summers. One of my teammate's dads had come up to my father after a game and gushed about how well I'd pitched. I'd stood there basking in the kind of praise my own father had never given me. But then the man had gotten around to asking Father if he could take us out for pizza because he had some business ideas he wanted to ask about. It was one of many, many times people had used me to get to my father.

And it hadn't always been about my father or money either. When I was in boarding school, my roommate had begged to spend one Christmas with me so he didn't have to face his tedious family. As soon as he'd settled in at my house, he'd gone in search of my stepmother, Nat and Lucas's mom, to try and seduce her. I'd remembered immediately how stupid he'd gotten over her when she'd come to visit earlier in the semester.

People were users. That was simply how it was, especially when you had something they wanted.

I wondered if Cal was taken advantage of because of how easily he trusted people. Maybe he was too young to have learned life's harsh lessons yet.

"You're being awfully quiet," he said when Vin reached the dock and began tying the tender to the cleats.

"You shouldn't trust people so easily," I said.

His eyes widened in surprise, but he didn't say anything until we'd climbed onto the dock and began walking toward the shore.

Cal turned back with a wave and smile for Vin. "Thanks for the ride, Cap!"

Vin chuckled and shook his head before untying the tender to return to the ship. When we reached the boardwalk leading to the shops, Cal turned to me. "Are you saying you don't trust your own captain?"

"What? No. Of course not. Don't be ridiculous."

Cal tilted his head. "Then what's this about? Are you talking about me trusting *you*?"

I shot him a look. "Maybe. You don't know me from Adam and yet you've agreed to let me haul you around the Caribbean no questions asked."

His easy smirk dropped into the beginnings of annoyance. "Fuck you, Jon. In case you forgot, I don't really have a choice."

I wanted to tell him not to call me Jon when he was mad at me, but I bit the words back since they were stupid.

"What's this really about?" he asked, leading me toward a discount $5 T-shirt store. I steered him back toward the higher-end dive shop I'd been heading toward. I hadn't made special arrangements, but I knew dive shops usually opened early and this one was big enough to have everything.

"Never mind." It shouldn't have mattered to me if Cal was a trusting person or not. "And I will pay for your clothes and gear. Don't worry about it."

"I'm sorry," he said after a minute. "About the whole 'baby' thing. I didn't think. Sometimes I just say stupid shit."

"No kidding."

"Are you... is it... I mean..."

I didn't like hearing him unsure of himself. "It's fine," I said quickly. "This is better, actually. Prescott will want you even more if he thinks you're mine."

Cal stopped and studied me for a minute. "Okay, but... can you... can we just forget the payment, then? I really don't want it to be a *Pretty Woman* thing."

"We're not having sex," I hissed. "But if you don't want to get paid for this, we can just consider your gear the payment, all right?"

"Fine. But I can pay you back for it when we get to St. Mitz."

I opened the door and held it for him. "I'm ignoring you."

Cal sighed as we entered the store, but I couldn't help but notice his eyes light up when they landed on the dive gear off to the left. I couldn't remember the last time I'd dated a guy who enjoyed scuba diving. One guy I'd hooked up with in college had a diving bumper sticker on his jeep, but otherwise, most of the men I'd dated preferred drinking on the beach or a party cruise to staying sober enough and hydrated enough to get to depth.

It was tempting to encourage him with some high-end gear, if only to ensure I'd have someone to dive with all week.

"This is the kind of shorty I have, and I can recommend it," I said, pointing to a round rack of short wetsuits.

"Oh, that's fine. I don't need a shorty. I'll just dive in trunks."

"Cal. If we go on a deep dive or a wreck, you'll want the protection. Besides, you can't have enough body fat to stay warm on a second or third dive."

He narrowed his eyes at me, but his lips still curved up in a slight smile. "You making little-guy jokes at me again?"

I held up my hands in surrender. "After getting beat up in bed last night? I don't think so. Pick out a suit though. Please?"

"Fine." He found the right-size wet suit and thrust it against my chest. I guessed I was his shopping cart now. "I do need trunks though. Or... actually, it's probably better if I wear a teeny Speedo."

Okay, maybe it was a good thing I had the thick neoprene suit in front of me. As soon as my brain supplied an image of his tight body in a scrap of swimsuit, I got a little light-headed. "No need for that," I said before clearing my throat. "Trunks make more sense in the water."

Cal's expression called me on my bluster. "Mm. Methinks I struck some kind of nerve. Let's see what they have..."

He led me over to a display of men's suits and picked the tiniest one.

"I think that's a headband," I muttered.

"It's a thong."

"No."

"It is, I promise."

I cleared my throat. "No. I mean... you're not getting that one. Pick something else. What about this one?" I grabbed the nearest pair of trunks and shoved them at him.

He glanced at the material and back up at me. "These are board shorts. They'd be pedal pushers on me."

"What the hell is a pedal pusher?"

Cal hung the trunks back up and pulled out a much shorter pair. "I would have thought you'd know since you were probably alive in the fifties. What about these? I'm going to try them on." Without waiting for my answer, he ducked behind the slatted door of a nearby dressing room.

When he opened the door again, I felt my entire body start to tingle. Cal Wilde stood there in the tiniest pair of boy shorts with absolutely everything else on display. His tanned skin set off by the navy suit, the curves and bumps of his trim muscles along his abs, chest, and arms, and the gorgeous swell of his tight ass as he spun in a circle to show off the suit.

"Gnfh," I croaked.

His eyebrows lifted, and his lips widened into a cheeky smile. "Winner?"

"Too small," I managed. "Too tight."

He turned his back to me again and wiggled his butt. "Isn't that the point?"

I clutched the wet suit in front of me to maintain whatever scrap of dignity I still possessed. "Try on the board shorts. You'll be more comfortable in them."

He walked a few feet away to another rack and sifted through it before grabbing a few more suits and returning to the dressing room. For some reason, I was having trouble breathing. The store's air-conditioning was probably broken.

The young woman behind the register walked over after finishing ringing someone up. "Does he need any help?"

"He seems to be doing just fine on his own," I muttered. "Won't listen to a word I say."

She laughed and looked toward the closed dressing room door. "My dad says the same thing about me."

It took me a few beats to realize what she was implying. "He's not..." I didn't get the chance to finish telling her Cal wasn't my son before the door opened again, revealing him in an even smaller suit. His dark happy trail wandered down into the top of a rainbow-colored Speedo that was more than happy to inform everyone in sight distance what his parents' views on circumcision were. The rounded bulge in the front of that suit made my mouth fill with saliva.

"Mother of pearl," the woman breathed.

"Jesus fucking Christ," I said. "Absolutely not. *No*. Take it off."

"Don't listen to your dad," the saleslady said. "That suit is hot on you. It was made for you."

Cal snorted at the word *dad* and then looked at me with eyes sparkling. "But *Daddy*, I want it." He full-on pouted, and I had to bite back a laugh.

He turned around again and shook his ass. The woman next to

me let out a sigh of longing, and I wanted to tell her I completely understood. Instead, I barked at him to hurry up. "We still have to go find you a damned Omega Seamaster when the jewelry stores open up."

Cal's smile died. "What? No. What?"

I shrugged, enjoying seeing him wrong-footed. "You told everyone you had an Omega Seamaster, so we need to find one."

"But... that's a four-thousand-dollar watch. Just tell them I lost it like I did the other one. We'll play the dumb-blond card."

"If we're not going to get the other one I mentioned, then we need to get you something." I made a hand gesture to remind him to hurry up, but he continued to stand there.

"Okay, but... you'll keep it when we're done, right? You'll use it or give it to someone else as a gift?" He clasped his hands together and fidgeted. "And what if I lose it for real? Can I get insurance on it just in case? How much do you think that costs?"

"I can't talk about this with you while you're naked." I turned around and busied myself picking out some other gear he needed for diving. They carried the same dive computer I had for myself, so I grabbed one of those along with a mask, split fins, booties, and a snorkel. I selected a few T-shirts in his size as well as a hoodie in case there were cool nights on the water. As the stack on the front counter began to grow, Cal came out of the dressing room and added the suits he'd selected to the pile.

"What's all this?"

"You need clothes and gear. What kind of BC and regulator do you use?"

He looked very uncomfortable. "Is there any extra gear on board? I can just use that."

"If you're my... whatever it is we're calling you... then you need decent gear. I'll pick the same ones I use, and you can tell me if those work for you."

When I reached for the Poseidon regulator, Cal knocked my hand away. "Please," he said in a low voice, flashing me pleading eyes. "Do not spend this much money on gear. I can't afford to pay you back. I'll stay back on the boat. I don't need to dive."

I couldn't decide if he was trying to manipulate me or not. If he was playing some kind of long game with me, he was damned good at it. He truly looked pained by the amount of money I was spending on him.

"I will get this dive gear as an extra set for the ship, and you can use it this week. Okay? And since when do you call it a boat? There's an easy way to tell the difference between a boat and a ship, you know…"

He elbowed me in the side. "Jackass," he muttered. "But, um… thanks. That would make me feel better."

With the issue settled, I was free to indulge in the high-end gear I wanted to select anyway. Once we had a giant stack on the counter and the saleswoman's eyes were bugging out, I pulled out my phone to dial Vin so he could meet us with the tender.

We checked out and loaded everything in the ship before thanking Vin and heading back into the marina shopping area.

"What's next?" he asked. "I need to get some basics like underwear and toiletries. I think there's a drugstore this way."

I followed him down a narrow side road to the pharmacy indicated by a big green cross on the front of the building. After he purchased what he needed, we made our way back to the main drag and looked for a store that sold high-end men's watches.

"I still think this is stupid," he said under his breath. "You should have listened to me and gotten a wrist dive computer instead of the gauge one. Then everyone would have known why I was wearing that instead of a fancy watch."

"I prefer the gauge type. The wrist ones are bulky and uncomfortable." That was true, but I also had a petty ulterior motive in getting him an expensive watch to wear. Part of me wanted to see Prescott's reaction. And, okay, fine, part of me wanted to see Cal's face light up as he discovered the features of a watch like that. I could also picture how it would look on his tanned wrist.

I spotted the jewelry store and led him inside. "Indulge me,

Calgary," I said in a low voice as we entered the cool quiet of the store. "If you let me get you this watch, I'll let you spin as many bullshit tales about me to my siblings you want."

His face lit up. "You mean it? I can tell them about the time you and I went naked skydiving?"

The salesman and the client he was helping both turned their heads toward us, and I realized Cal wasn't speaking in the same low voice I was. I felt my face heat. Even though it was still morning, the store had several clusters of customers already. "I changed my mind. Let's go." Before I could turn around, Cal grabbed my elbow.

"Sorry," he said with a laugh. "I'll be good. I promise. Maybe I'll just tell them about the quiet nights at home in front of the fire."

"They wouldn't believe that either. Lucas and Nat know me well enough to know I don't get home from work in time to indulge in a quiet night in front of the fire."

His smile dropped, but before he could chastise me the way my siblings would, a man who'd been browsing one of the jewelry cases did a double take. "Cal, is that you?"

He was tall and slender, looked to be in his midthirties, and positively reeked flashy wealth. He might as well have been carrying one of those Louis Vuitton bags that had the logo repeated all over it in neon yellow to make absolutely sure everyone knew how much he'd paid for it.

Cal's hand slid down from my elbow to my hand and gripped it tightly. I tried to read the expression on his face, but all I could sense was discomfort. I had no idea why. "Kincaid. Hi, how are you?"

"Oh, darling, it's lovely to see you again. Come, give a kiss," the man said as he leaned in to give Cal double cheek kisses. Cal's hand tightened in mine, and I squeezed it back to let him know I wasn't going anywhere.

"What are you doing in Turshall Cay?" Cal asked as if making polite conversation. "Have you chartered another boat?"

Kincaid's eyes flicked between me and Cal. "Yes, the BVI again. I tried to get you as our captain, but they said you weren't working there anymore." He pushed his lip out in an exaggerated pout. I wondered what I could do or say to move this exchange along.

Cal shifted on his feet. "I work out of St. Mitz now." The man shot me another curious look, so Cal finally caved and introduced me. "Kincaid Price, this is Jonathan Worthington."

At the sound of my name, the man's eyes lit up with recognition and his entire body language changed. He reached out a hand to shake which meant I had to let go of Cal. "Nice to meet you," I said politely.

"It's an honor to meet you, Worth," he gushed. "I've heard incredible things about your firm. My friend Terry owns Ansoft. I believe you helped them with their most recent round of funding."

I slid my arm around Cal's waist and pulled him against my side. "I did. How do you know Terry? Are you from Boston as well?"

He nodded and went into a small-talk frenzy of name-dropping. I finally lost my patience. "I'm so sorry to cut off our conversation, but I promised Cal we'd pick up his new watch before meeting my family back on the ship. Maybe we'll see you on one of the islands this week?"

Kincaid's eyebrows lifted. "You'll be in the BVI too? How wonderful. Let's do dinner one night."

Cal's hand clutched at the hem of my shirt in a very clear message of *no fucking way*. I shot Kincaid my biggest smile. "We're here celebrating my brother's engagement, so I'll have to leave our plans up to him, I'm afraid. Have a wonderful week on the water."

I pulled Cal over to the first free salesperson I saw on the opposite side of the store. Thankfully, she brought us the watch selection we needed right away, and we walked out of the store fifteen minutes later with a Seamaster gleaming on Cal's wrist.

He was clearly self-conscious about it and kept thrusting that hand deep into the pocket of his shorts to hide it. It was kind of endearing.

"Who was that?" I finally asked once we'd left the shop and wandered several shops down to a place we could get a coffee.

"Total creeper. He and his snotty friends seemed to think that I was more than the ship's captain. At some point during the week of their trip, I think they all tried it on with me. He was the worst though. He snuck into my room one night drunk off his ass, acted like I'd been encouraging him, which I assure you, I hadn't been."

I stared at him. "You're kidding? What did you do?"

Part of me wanted to turn right around and confront the asshole —teach him a lesson about abuse of power—but then I remembered this wasn't the Wild West and I wasn't Cal's protector.

He sighed. "I blamed it on my boss. I told him I was dating someone and I'd also get fired if they found out I'd slept with a customer. Which wasn't necessarily true, but it was all I could think of in the moment. I didn't want him to get angry and pull his business from the company I worked for. He tried to assure me no one at my work would find out, but I was finally able to convince him I was in a monogamous relationship. I told my boss about it when I got back, in hopes of not having to work with Kincaid's group again, but I don't think my boss believed me. That's when he transferred me to St. Mitz, and it's probably why I was the first captain let go at the end of the high season."

"That's unacceptable," I said angrily. "That's illegal. It's a hostile working environment."

Cal shrugged. "Well, they control my work permits, and as long as I was still employed on the water, I was happy. The guy wasn't going to force me physically or anything. He was just super pushy. It happens."

We placed our orders at the counter for iced coffee and stood to the side to wait. "What an ass."

Cal chuckled. "Actually, it was kind of nice running into him while I had you with me. Made my story about being in a relationship more believable."

We got our coffees and made our way back outside. I found a bench for us to sit on with a view of the water beyond a small park near the edge of the marina. After a few sips, Cal sighed. "That's good. Thank you. And thanks for letting me use you back there."

I leaned back and put my arm behind him on the bench. "Do a lot of charter clients come on to you like that?"

Cal took another sip of his drink. Maybe he was stalling. I wasn't sure.

"I mean, define a lot. Most of the groups I take out are families or groups of couples. On those trips, I've had lots of people flirt before but only two guys actually try to do something with me. One was the husband of this super-snotty family from Alabama. He'd had too much to drink and asked me to suck him off late one night when everyone else was asleep below decks. He was so drunk, I just replied in French as if we'd been speaking in French all along. It confused him so much he finally gave up and went to bed."

I laughed. "That was clever."

"I can't take the credit. My brother Otto told me that trick from the time he worked on a submarine. One of the sailors on his sub slipped into his native Portuguese when he was tired, and he'd get frustrated when the other guys didn't understand him."

We watched a toddler across the marina park squawk with delight at the sea birds swooping low. Cal continued his stories. "Then the other time it happened, the guy was just lonely and closeted. I felt bad for him. Plus he was hot as shit. So I fucked him."

The words struck me in the gut, creating a strange mix of disapproval and desire. Was I the creepy guy in this week's boating trip for him? Did Cal see me as the lonely client who needed a little attention?

"Not all lonely men want to be fucked," I said peevishly, looking out across the water to avoid seeing his reaction.

7

———————

CAL

I'D TOUCHED A NERVE. WORTH'S REACTION MIGHT AS WELL HAVE BEEN A warning flag. I tried to stay calm rather than feeling defensive about my own history. "No. They certainly don't. But the man in question had been harboring a crush on his sister's husband for fifteen years. And he was stuck on a small boat with the two of them for a week. We both needed a release, and we'd spent hours leading up to it in great conversation. I made a judgment call."

Worth sniffed and took another sip of his coffee. "Mpfh."

He was kind of cute when he slipped back into haughty mode. I laughed, enjoying sitting there in the sun with a nice cold drink and a sexy man's arm around me. I couldn't think of a place I'd rather be in this moment. "I'm not a saint, Jon. Besides, when I worked in the BVI, it wasn't easy finding hookups. The locals are very conservative. I was young and horny. Still am." I winked at him. "But the best trips are the ones with a boat full of gay guys. I've had several of those trips, and they are tons of fun. It's basically an orgy at sea. I never drink while I'm working, but on those trips, I've definitely snuck in some sex play with clients. That's the kind of trip Kincaid's charter was, but I knew right off the bat those guys were way more likely to report me to my boss. If I'd been a woman sleeping with clients, my boss wouldn't have had a problem with it, but a man sleeping with male clients? Meh."

"Typical hypocrisy," Worth muttered.

I nodded. "It's been better in St. Mitz because there's a gay club and another place that's more of a beachside sports bar owned by a gay couple. You'd probably like Ron and Tim. They retired down here from Wall Street and opened up the place."

We continued sipping our coffees while we watched the tourists and locals around us. I told Worth a little more about St. Mitz and how I'd enjoyed it more than Tortola even though it had paid less. He asked about how the charter trip jobs worked and where we sailed. By the time we'd finished our coffees, I'd completely relaxed from the run-in with Kincaid.

I began to stand up, planning on tossing my coffee cup in a nearby trash can, but Worth's arm tightened around my shoulder, keeping me on the bench.

"I'm sorry," he said quietly. "For sounding like I was judging you. I dated an employee once, so I'm not one to talk."

I looked over at him. He appeared troubled. I was surprised he was lowering himself to admit any failings to the likes of me.

"Do you want to talk about it?" I asked.

"God no. I just wanted you to know that I live in a glass house. And apparently I like to throw a stone or two from time to time."

He peered at me from the corner of his eye, and then we both laughed. "Noted," I said. "When you mentioned hypocrisy before, you were referring to yourself. Got it."

Worth stood up and reached out a hand to pull me up too. I reveled in the solid warmth of his grip. Every moment of holding hands in the jewelry store had been branded into my memory like a particularly enjoyable game of pretend.

He dragged me to some of the fancier shops and bought more clothes for me despite my strong objections. I got a secret thrill from watching him turn a little snooty about how any man on his arms would need certain "accoutrements" in order to be believable. I guessed "accoutrements" was rich-guy speak for silk shirts and linen pants because I noticed him sneak some of those into the bags even after I'd insisted him dressing me up like Douchebag Barbie was a hard limit.

"Shoes," he muttered at one point, pressing his hand on my lower back to steer me toward yet another boutique.

"I have shoes."

"You have rubber flip-flops. Not the same thing."

"We'll be on a ship. I don't need shoes on a ship."

"If we go onto an island for a restaurant meal, you will need something other than those." He peered down at my dollar-store shower shoes with disdain. I could admit they weren't making their best appearance at this moment, considering there was a bite out of one of them and the other had been worn almost paper-thin at the heel.

"The dollar store is over this way," I said, trying to turn us around. "I can replace them with a brand-new pair."

Worth shuddered. "Certainly not. I will compromise on a nice pair of leather flip-flops if need be."

I looked down at the well-worn but still impeccable canvas slip-ons he wore. It kind of surprised me he didn't have on a pair of tasseled leather driving mocs from Coach or Cole Haan or something.

"Yeah, okay. Leather flip-flops, I can do. But then please put me out of my misery and get me back out on the water. I wasn't made for this shopping bullshit."

"No kidding," Worth said under his breath.

We entered the store and ran right into Lucas and Prescott. I wasn't surprised to see them since the marina shopping area was fairly small, but I was surprised to see Lucas looking so flustered. The edges of his hair were damp with sweat, and his face was flushed. Deep creases ran between his eyebrows. He sat on a bench surrounded by mountains of shoeboxes.

Worth stepped toward him and squatted down in front of him. "Are you okay?"

Lucas's eyes flicked between me, Prescott, and Worth. "Yeah. I'm just trying on shoes and getting frustrated, that's all. How are you? What've you found? Anything good?"

Worth looked worried, so I decided to try and lighten the tense mood. "Worth made me get a skimpy bathing suit, but I don't know if I'm brave enough to wear it," I joked. It was a lie, both because he hadn't made me get it and also because I couldn't wait to wear it and see Prescott's reaction. Okay, fine. I couldn't wait to see Worth's reaction too.

Lucas smiled. "I'm sure you'll look great in it. You'll put the rest of us to shame."

I waited for Prescott to say something nice about Lucas's body, but when he didn't, I jumped in. "Are you kidding? You're in great shape. The only thing I have on you is a tan from being in the islands longer, but a little St. Tropez will fix that right up." I winked at him and glanced at the shoeboxes all around him. "I hope you're a size nine because that's going to make my shopping go a lot faster."

I moved past Prescott and squeezed onto the bench beside Lucas. "Jon, I am yours to accouter."

Worth's nostrils flared with a suppressed laugh, and his eyes lightened. "And I am ever at your service, Your Highness."

When Worth stood back up to browse for what he wanted, I leaned over and bumped shoulders with Lucas. "What are you looking for in here today? Seems like you're not finding it very easily. Maybe your brother can help fetch."

Lucas opened his mouth to answer, but Pres beat him to it. "He needs new running shoes at the very least. He forgot to pack his and won't be able to keep up his running program without them. I also think he needs a pair of leather mocs in case we decide to go out to eat at a resort while we're down here."

I saw the words hit Worth's ears because his entire body tensed. He turned around and caught my eye. It was clear he realized Pres had sounded exactly like he himself had. "You know what? I think we're good. If you're happy with what you have, I'm happy. Let's go."

Lucas's eyebrows creased in confusion. "Why'd you come in here if you didn't need any shoes?"

I ignored his question and asked one of my own. "Where are you going to jog on a ship?"

Lucas looked up at Pres. "That's what I asked him. Even the islands we're visiting don't have paved paths or roads. That's why I didn't pack my running shoes."

Pres said, "I just know how important your exercise is to your mental health. That's the only reason I thought you might like to have them."

Worth stepped closer until I could feel his body heat against my shoulder. "We'll be swimming and diving every day. That will give you plenty of exercise."

I grinned at Lucas in hopes of helping him relax. "And if not, I'll break out some dance music on deck at night and we can shake our booties till the wee hours."

Lucas smiled back. "I do love to dance."

"Perfect," I said before turning to face Worth. "Now find me a pair of leather thongs quick so we can get back on the boat and change into my new swimmy ones."

Worth's face flushed as I shook my hips, and Lucas laughed. Within a few minutes, we were able to find a pair of shoes that worked for me. Lucas found a pair of leather boat shoes Pres seemed to find passably acceptable, and the four of us made our way back to the tender. Once on board the ship, Worth and I went straight to the stateroom to put our purchases away.

As soon as the door closed behind us, I whipped around and hissed at him. "Don't ever make me shop again. That was excruciating."

Worth rolled his eyes and set his shopping bags down on the long desk surface built in along one wall of the room. I noticed his laptop was set up which meant he'd probably checked his email or something this morning before joining us for breakfast. It reminded me that he had a life outside of this vacation. According to Kincaid, Worth was some kind of investment person, but I didn't know enough about any of that to even pretend to know what his computer work would entail.

"Hardly. At that last place you got to sit and play social butterfly while I did all the work."

I sat on the end of the bed and threw myself back on the soft duvet, stretching my arms overhead and making a snow angel on the cool cotton. The room had been cleaned in our absence, and I wondered who on board had that job. Probably Julo but possibly Freya. I didn't feel comfortable having someone clean up after me, but I reminded myself they were cleaning up after their boss. I just happened to benefit from it.

I sighed. "It was hard work, but I muddled through. I think surviving it deserves a fruity drink."

"You're in luck. Julo makes a rum punch that'll make you forget your own mother. He'll break out the drinks and snacks when we get underway. Nat should be back with her friends in a few minutes."

He sat down at the desk and opened his laptop, turning his back to me. I rolled onto my side and rested my head in my hand. "Do you think Prescott pressures Lucas to work out or something? What was that about?"

Worth's shoulders tensed. "I don't know. But the sooner Lucas sees what an ass he is, the better."

I rolled onto my back again and studied the ceiling. "Your brother is super sweet and cute. He could do so much better than Prescott Resnick."

Worth swiveled around to face me. "Like you?"

I deliberately misunderstood him. "I could do much better than Prescott too. Yes."

He huffed and turned back around. "Don't put the moves on my brother," he warned in a low voice. "That's not why you're here."

That pissed me off. "Fuck you, Jon. You think I'm going to fuck Prescott, sleep with you, and then try and put the moves on your brother? Jesus."

"We're not sleeping together," he said with his teeth clenched.

"We are literally sleeping together. I just mean I'm not going to let Lucas think I'm with you at the same time I'm putting the moves on *him* and hoping Prescott puts the moves on me. Christ, it's like one of those plays where the characters are running on and off stage and everyone is keeping a secret."

He faced me again and yanked a hand through his hair. "So you *are* planning on putting the moves on him, just after some kind of etiquette grace period?"

"No! God, you're infuriating. Do you think I'm that desperate that I need any of you fuckers?"

Worth tilted his chin down and shot me a look that was meant to remind me of my shitty dalliance with Pres.

"Shut up," I muttered. "I was desperate for a job, not a piece of ass."

"Well, if your way of trying to get hired is by sleeping with the boss, you might want to reconsider."

He was so fucking annoying. I'd had enough of his hoity-toity attitude. I needed a drink whether it was time to leave port or not. And maybe if I could go ahead and unmask Pres as a giant cheater quickly, he'd leave and I could get to the portion of this deal that might actually lead me to gainful employment.

"Don't worry," I said, moving off the bed to rifle through the shopping bags. "I've definitely learned my lesson." I found the tiniest swimsuit I'd purchased and flounced toward the bathroom to change. "I'll get out of your hair so you can work."

Worth's back was still facing me when I finished changing, but it didn't matter. The tiny Speedo was meant to tease Prescott, not Worth. Besides, he was right. Sleeping with someone wasn't the way to get hired, and I needed the job way more than an orgasm.

As I took one last look at Worth before closing the stateroom door, I also realized he was probably one of those guys who came all the way to the Caribbean to get away from it all, but never actually left the work behind. I had no interest in a man who couldn't relax from time to time, especially someone who chose to spend time with his computer instead of his siblings. My father was the same kind of workaholic, and I'd learned early on not to expect something from a man who valued his career over family.

It was one thing if there was a work emergency, but quite another if you were simply addicted to your devices. In addition to watching my own father's ambition pull him away from his family, I'd seen many people on my charter trips lose their minds when confronted with uninterrupted family time. The number of times I'd been asked for the Wi-Fi information on a small charter catamaran was laughable.

But since we were on a luxury yacht with plenty of satellite Wi-Fi support, Worth could work as much as he wanted. And, honestly, it was none of my business. I wasn't his boyfriend, and I wasn't actually even his friend.

I grabbed my sunscreen, sunglasses, a few other odds and ends, and a beach towel I'd found in a cupboard in the bathroom and headed upstairs to find a seat in the sun.

Thankfully, Julo already had the island music turned up, and I could hear the blender going somewhere above us. He was busy prepping lunch in the galley, so I didn't disrupt him. Natalia's laughter rang out on the top deck, so I followed the sounds until I found the party. The roof was open, and the sun streamed down to a group of women sitting around a table with drinks and snacks. Lucas and Prescott were in the hot tub with another man I hadn't met yet.

"Cal!" Nat said, standing up and waving me over to the table. "I want you to meet my friends." She introduced me to an adorable woman named Mia with short, pixie-cut hair dyed purple and twin dimples in one cheek when she smiled. The other woman was sleeker-looking—like a panther—with silky black hair tied back in a twist and elegant features. Her name was Jade which was easy to remember because her eyes were a striking green that glittered with mischief. Something about these three women together reminded me of my sisters, and I knew they were going to be tons of fun on the ship this week.

Jade looked me up and down in a way that made me grateful I'd thrown on one of Worth's button-down shirts as a kind of cover-up. "You're delectable, aren't you?" I assumed it was a rhetorical question.

Nat ignored her friend and said, "Oh, and that's my husband, Jin."

She pointed to a man with similar long silky dark hair, but his was pulled up in a messy bun to keep it out of the water of the hot tub.

The man looked up and smiled, lifting his cup of punch in a toast gesture. He was gorgeous and reminded me of an actor from a fantasy movie I'd seen recently. As I looked around, I realized every person on the ship was beautiful. It was like being on the set of a fashion shoot, and it made me feel uneasy. I didn't belong here. I was a farm boy from a tiny town in Texas. Sure, I talked a big game, and I'd met lots of people from all over the world thanks to my job, but when it came down to it, I didn't know how to even have a conversation with these people. They'd all presumably gone to fancy schools and lived in big, exciting cities and had active social lives with their other wealthy friends. The closest I'd come to knowing what big-city life was like was when I spent time at my sister Hallie's place in Dallas.

Jade craned her neck to see behind me. "Where's Worth? Didn't he come up with you?"

"He's working," I said absently, making a beeline for the pitcher of rum punch I spied on a nearby table.

Nat sighed. "Why did I even ask? I hoped he'd be different with you here, but I guess not." She was clearly annoyed, and I wondered if I should have kept my mouth shut.

"I'm sure he'll be up soon. In the meantime, have you guys ever played Liar's Dice?"

My attempt to distract them from Worth's absence was successful. I pulled out the bag of dice I'd picked up at one of the shops and ran downstairs to beg some Solo cups off Julo. Once I was back at the table with the three women, we started playing.

As Captain Vin steered us slowly out of the Turshall Cay area, the hot sun, cold drinks, and easy company worked their magic. Pretty soon we were laughing and teasing each other like we'd been together for years instead of hours. I was doing a fairly decent job of ignoring Prescott's pointed stares while at the same time preening a little bit to see if he'd take the bait. The whole situation made me nervous which made me drink faster. By the time Worth finally poked his head up on the top deck, I was feeling just *fiiiiine.*

"There's my boo," I said. "Come lie with us. Wait, that didn't come out right. Come liar with us. No. Come dice with us." Mia and I started giggling.

Worth's furrowed brow smoothed out, and he grinned. "Seems I'm a little late to keep you from overconsuming Julo's special punch."

"There's some kind of magic in that shit," I admitted. Natalia snorted, and Jade held out grabby hands toward Worth.

"Come say hello, big guy," she purred.

Instead of walking around to her side of the table, Worth leaned across me to drop a kiss on her cheek. I got a face full of delicious Tom Ford cologne and felt Worth's hand trail along my shoulder as he leaned in. I shuddered. Damn this man for being so sexy.

After he leaned the other way to kiss Mia's cheek, he turned back to me. "Having fun?"

I nodded. "I taught them Liar's Dice, but then they all kicked my ass."

He laughed and ran his fingers through my hair. I lapped it up like a dog finally being pet by his favorite human. "I was wondering if you wanted to go up on the bow for a little while." He was looking at me with such feigned affection, it made my stomach wobbly.

"Um, yeah. Okay."

He reached out his hand for mine, pulling me up from the bench at the table. As soon as he saw the suit I was wearing, his eyes widened. I still had the button-down on, but it was open, flapping a little in the breeze.

"I thought you decided against that suit," he said. His eyes were lasers attached to the scrap of rainbow-colored fabric.

I took the opportunity to remove the shirt and twirl around in a circle, ostensibly showing it off for Worth even though Worth would know I was trying to tempt Prescott. "Nope, that was you. I like it."

"Me too," Lucas said from where he sat on the edge of the hot tub. "It's sexy."

"No kidding," Jin said with an easy smile. "I'm not even gay and I can appreciate your man in that suit."

Worth made a little growling sound under his breath. I noticed

Prescott's eyes track my every move, but he smartly kept his mouth shut.

Natalia teased her brother. "Is that why you're taking him away from us? You want his hot little bod all to yourself?"

Worth slid his arm around my waist. The sensation of his smooth palm against the bare skin of my hip was intoxicating. I wanted to turn toward him and bury my face in his neck to inhale more of his scent and feel his arms tighten around me. "Something like that. But you're all welcome to join us on the big sun bed. I wanted to enjoy the view as we approach the islands. We should be able to see the tip of Virgin Gorda soon."

As he led me toward the stairs, Worth slid his hand lower on my hip until it brushed my ass. I wasn't sure if it was intentional or not, but it sent a buzz of need through my body. This tiny swimsuit wouldn't be forgiving if I spent too much time noticing Worth's touch, so I busied myself running through mast light combinations in my head.

Red over red, this boat is dead...

"You okay?" Worth asked in a low voice when we got down to the main level of the ship. When he spoke in that voice that only I could hear, it went straight to my lower belly. I nodded, afraid if I opened my mouth, I'd blurt something stupid like a demand for him to take me to bed and pound me into the mattress.

Red over green, sailing machine...

"Maybe we should grab you some ice water," Worth said, heading toward the galley. I noticed he'd changed into his own swim trunks which were snug on his very nice ass.

Green over white, trawling tonight...

It wasn't like I was hard up. I'd had sex with Prescott yesterday, for Pete's sake. But there was something about this man, this gruff and grumbly stiff suit of a guy, that made me wonder what it would feel like to be naked against him. Was he as controlled in bed as he was around other people? Was he dominant with his partners? Did he command obedience the way he would with a client or employee? Or did he change into a desperate, needy sub who begged to be taken care of?

Worth's eyes narrowed at me as he handed me the bottle of water. "Why so quiet?"

White over white, short tug in sight...

I busied myself with the water, taking huge gulps and sputtering a little when the word *tug* echoed in my brain. Worth finally sighed and reached for my hand, pulling me out to the deck and up to the bow. A giant sun bed dominated this part of the ship, and I gratefully climbed onto it and sprawled out like a starfish on my back. The sun blasted down on my skin, sapping any residual energy right out of me.

"This is heaven," I said on a sigh. "Remind me to write your boyfriend a thank-you note."

Worth settled next to me, only he sat primly with his back against the cushions and his long, elegant legs crossed at the ankle.

"What boyfriend? And why the thank-you note?"

"You have elegant legs," I said. He needed to know.

"Thank you. But you didn't answer my question."

I waved my hand around at the ship. "This. Whoever gave you this—and let's be honest, it had to be someone you were fucking—is god's gift to mankind. They must love you enough to want you to spend some time relaxing in luxury. This is my dream. Being out on the water, soaking up the sun, not having to worry about real life or anything else..." I took a deep breath of the Caribbean air. "Heaven."

Worth's fingers found their way into my hair again, and I closed my eyes with a contented sigh. I wondered if he realized he was doing it. We were in a strange alternate reality where I couldn't be sure what he did to further the ruse of us dating versus what he did out of any genuine motivation. Right now, I didn't much care. I just wanted his hands on me any way I could get them.

"Ex-boyfriend. Yes. But I'm fairly certain he acquired the *Worthington* for his own enjoyment rather than mine."

I tried not to think of him with a gorgeous, rich boyfriend. "Maybe he was trying to get you to stop working long enough to relax. Nat said you're a workaholic. Maybe your ex was trying to tell you something."

I stretched in the sun like a cat and heard a choking sound come from Worth. "Maybe you were right about that suit. Even I can't keep my eyes off you, and I'm not interested."

I opened one eye and glared at him with it. "Thanks for that. I can't begin to tell you how good it makes me feel knowing you don't find me attractive."

At least he had the wherewithal to look contrite. "I do find you attractive." His voice had deepened again in that way that endangered the elastic barriers of my swimsuit. "Of course I do."

He cleared his throat and continued. "It's just that... I don't... I mean, I... Well, you see..."

I opened both eyes and sat up. Worth had only gotten this flustered one other time in front of me, and it was the only other time we'd discussed his dating history.

His eyes were hidden behind his sunglasses, and his face was angled away, gazing off the port side of the ship.

"I find you very attractive, Cal. But I won't be seducing you this week. My quota of sleeping with and/or dating men in their twenties should have topped out ten years ago."

He was such an ass. "You're ageist. What's wrong with men in their twenties?"

One eyebrow peaked over the top of his sunglasses frame. "You don't know what you want."

I wanted to tell him I knew for damned sure what I didn't want, which was a stodgy old workaholic stick-in-the-mud, but before I could say any of that, I heard Lucas and Prescott coming toward us. I turned over and crawled toward Worth on all fours, letting Julo's rum punch lead the way. "Oh, believe me, Mr. Boring and Mature, I know exactly what I want."

8

WORTH

I WAS OUT OF MY DEPTH.

I'd pulled Cal aside after realizing we'd never gotten on the same page about our story. As soon as Prescott started asking Cal questions about me, we'd be toast. But every time Cal and I were together, my brain seemed to short out before I had a chance to discuss our situation.

This young man was in his physical prime. Every defined muscle was covered in tight, perfectly tanned skin, and the bulge in his tiny swimsuit had been making my mouth water since I'd first spotted him on the top deck. Why was I trying so hard to deny my desire to toss him down on the nearest surface and make him come?

Why not just fuck him and enjoy yourself?

Before I could argue with the devil on my shoulder, Prescott and Lucas came around the corner, followed by everyone else.

"We're crashing your make-out session," Natalia said, plopping down on the giant chaise.

Cal slowed his crawl and winked at me. I could almost see the machinations going on in his rum-soaked brain. His face turned into a lazy smile, and he draped himself across my chest, resting his head on my shoulder and snuggling all of his sun-warmed bare skin against me. I wrapped my arm around his back and began to trail my fingers along his spine.

If Prescott was there, I needed to play the part.

Keep telling yourself that.

Nat moved closer to me to make room for Mia. Jade perched on one of the side benches so she could set her drink down on a nearby table and have her hands free for texting.

Nat sat cross-legged facing us. "So, Cal, tell us more about you. What do you do when you're not sailing?"

I wasn't surprised by her inquisition since she knew I'd sworn off dating when things had crashed and burned with Mason. She had to be extremely curious about what kind of man would have changed my mind.

Cal kept his head on my shoulder but angled it so he could see her across my chest. "I've been learning origami. So far I can make a boat and a crane, but I have the instructions for a turtle next."

Nat stretched her neck around to seek out Jin. "Jin! Cal's been learning origami. Tell him about the ones your baba makes."

Before I could worry this was just another of Cal's tall tales, he sat up excitedly and reached out with a *come here* gesture toward Jin. "Do you know how to do it? I really want to be able to make one of those multicolored cubes. My family all exchange handmade Christmas ornaments each year, so that's what got me into it. I want to make origami ornaments. I only have a few months left to make a gazillion of them."

Jin sat down on the edge of the big chaise next to Cal. "Yeah, so my grandmother is crazy good at those things. She can make the kind of birds with all the folds for feathers in their wings. Whenever someone has a new baby, she makes a mobile to hang over their crib with multicolored birds—all different kinds—and they're like works of art. She wants everyone to use the mobile over the crib, but no one will. They take lots of pictures and then display it in a glass case or whatever, to keep it for the baby when they grow up."

Cal's face lit up as he listened to Jin's stories. When Cal asked Jin where he was from, he'd gotten even more excited.

"I've always wanted to dive there. My brother Otto said he dove in Okinawa when he was in the navy and loved it. He has a ton of friends who've been stationed there long-term. They rave about it. Did you love growing up there?"

Jin laughed. "Yeah, I was spoiled, but then we moved to Indiana when I was fourteen and it was a total culture shock."

Cal nodded. "Ugh. No shit. I remember coming back to Texas after my first trip to visit my parents in Singapore, and it was like seeing America through new eyes. I can't imagine what it was like for you."

They continued chattering on while Natalie nudged my shoulder. "He's adorable. And so sweet. How'd you really meet him?"

I didn't want to lie to her, but at the same time, everyone was within hearing distance, and I wasn't about to tell her the truth. "I really did meet him on a boat," I said. "It was a bit of a whirlwind. I'm still not quite sure which way is up."

All true.

Her eyes flicked between us, and a little wrinkle formed between her eyes. "But... after Mason... I thought..."

I hated looking like a fool and feeling like a hypocrite. I'd made such a production about what a mistake it had been dating a younger man that I couldn't blame her for calling me out on it.

"What can I say? I'm a glutton for punishment." I'd tried to say it lightly, but it was hard to sugarcoat the truth. My entire relationship with Mason had been punishment, and judging myself afterward for allowing it to happen was a second round of punishment. A double whammy of regret and stupidity.

"Maybe. But I can already tell he's different from Mason," she continued.

"How can you say that? You've known him less than twenty-four hours." I didn't add that *I'd* known him less than twenty-four hours.

"I can tell. It's in the way he talks to people. He shows genuine interest in them by asking questions, and then he pays attention to their answers. I remember introducing Mason to Mia the first time at a fundraiser. As soon as he heard her last name and realized her family owned the cafe chain, he went off on a twenty-minute bitch session about the time he went into the cafe and had to deal with the horror of getting someone else's coffee by mistake. Apparently, he was allergic to dairy which is weird since he ate the hell out of that gourmet ice cream we had at Spike's."

I knew the story well. He'd passively implied it had been my fault for making him late that morning. How his being late had resulted in being served the wrong coffee was beyond me. At the time, I'd thought his constant chatter about what had gone wrong during his day was part of his charm. Like a comedic monologue or something. It had taken Lucas's quiet comment after a night at the theater to wake me up to the reality of it. "It must be difficult making him happy, brother. I'm sorry."

I'd stood there in the late-night drizzle staring at Lucas while his words tumbled through my brain, landing with heavy thunks over all of the excuses I'd made through the years Mason and I had been together. That night at the theater, Mason had complained about us being stuck with the understudy, he'd bitched about the woman's jacked-up hair in front of him, and he'd asked me at least three times why I hadn't sprung for box seats so we didn't have to sit so close to other people. I'd seen Mason as adorably high-maintenance when everyone else around us saw him as a selfish asshole.

"He's not allergic to dairy," I muttered. "He just told people that to explain why he was such a coffee snob. Anyway, can we not talk about Mason, please? I was actually beginning to relax."

"You need a drink," she said with a grin. "Let me grab you one. Stay right here."

When she climbed off the chaise, I tuned back in to the conversation Cal was having with Jin about Jin's vintage car collection.

"But you don't drive them?" Cal chuckled. "Why collect them if you never take them out of the garage?"

It was something I'd often wondered too.

Jin swallowed the sip of his punch and laughed. "Everyone asks me that. If you had a collection of something super valuable, would you risk wrecking it? Do you collect anything?"

Cal shot Prescott a look before reaching out and placing his hand around my thigh possessively. "Older men with fancy boats. But I promise you, I ride them as often as possible. I find it's good for them. Keeps their creaky old parts in working order."

Prescott sputtered, but the rest of us laughed. "Gee, thanks," I said drily. "I'll remember that later. Maybe my old parts need to go in for a tune-up if they're not passing muster."

Cal draped himself across me again and brushed his nose along my cheek. "I didn't mean you. Your parts are top-notch. They're Daytona 500–level professional. They purr like a kitten."

My skin broke out in goose bumps, but I ignored it. "Like a ferocious lion, I think you mean." My voice sounded weird in my ears, rough and low. I rubbed a hand up and down his back, feeling the smooth, warm skin I wanted more of.

Cal pressed a kiss to the edge of my mouth. "Sure, baby. A manly lion. Mmhm."

I steeled myself against a full-body shudder. I wasn't about to lose control of myself just because Cal Wilde was a particularly good actor. I turned and met his lips with mine, taking the opportunity to taste him softly. His eyes widened in surprise for a millisecond before he closed them and hummed his approval.

Nat's voice jerked me back to reality. "You know Jade is filming this for Instagram, right?"

Cal pulled away and tucked his face in my neck. "Sorry," he whispered. I pulled him tighter against me. I didn't much care what people on Jade's social media account thought of me, and I'd been out for over twenty years. But that didn't mean it would be fair for Cal's reputation to be seen kissing a random older man on a boat in the Caribbean. I opened my mouth to warn Jade against tagging him but then stopped myself. Cal was a big boy. If he didn't want to be tagged in a social media post, he could speak for himself.

"It's fine," I assured him softly. Then I glanced up at Nat and reached for the drink she offered. "Thanks."

I took a sip of the cold punch and nearly groaned when the sweet and spicy flavors hit my tongue. "Perfect." Cal straightened up and pulled the cup out of my hand to take a sip. I watched his Adam's apple bob as he swallowed. He handed it back with a cheeky grin and then turned to Prescott. I felt his body tense, but his face stayed happy and easy.

"So, Prescott and Lucas, do you collect anything? Jin collects vintage automobiles, Nat collects old concert tickets, Mia collects vinyl which is weird since she admits to not owning a record player, and Jade implied earlier that she collects parking tickets."

I could tell Nat was besotted with Cal. What he didn't know was, while she did collect old concert tickets, her most valuable collection was the group of friends and family she attracted and held close to her heart. I could already see Cal was her newest acquisition, and that realization made my heart speed up in fear. I didn't want to let her down when she learned the truth.

Lucas looked over at Pres, deferring to him for a response.

Prescott's nostrils flared. He was clearly annoyed by Cal's presence, and it wasn't like I could blame him. Had I been in his shoes, I'd have been very uncomfortable right about now.

"I collect wine," he said. "Lucas doesn't much care for it, but I've been trying to educate him on the benefits of having a varied selection on hand for any occasion."

Lucas blushed and looked a little flustered. "I prefer craft beer, so I really don't need a selection of wine on hand." He glanced at Prescott. "Except for you, I mean. Which is why I installed the temperature-controlled wine thingy."

Prescott sighed. "It's called a wine cellar, Lucas."

"But that doesn't make any sense since it's not in the basement. It's more of a fridge, I think," Lucas said, shooting Cal a wink. I was surprised by it. He was obviously acknowledging Prescott's snobbery in some way. Either that, or he was simply feeling playful and teasing. Either way, I liked seeing him joke around, and I wanted to see more of it. If he could hold his own around Prescott, maybe I didn't need to worry quite so much about him.

"It's still called a wine cellar, Lucas," Pres muttered. It wasn't until then that I realized Pres was drinking wine and not punch. His loss.

Cal shifted against my side, sliding one lightly haired leg against mine. I closed my eyes to focus on the feel of it but then quickly snapped out of it and tried to focus on taking another sip of my drink.

Cal's fingers meandered across my chest as he spoke. I was grateful to be wearing a shirt since it was the only thing keeping me from groaning out loud at his touch. "My grandfather has a special storage solution for his wine. It's a shelving system built from scrap two-by-fours, and it can hold up to fifty boxes of Bota or thirty boxes of Franzia. We tested it when we had my brother's wedding. We're kind of a family of Bota Box sluts, so we stocked up." Cal reached for my cup and stole another sip. "When I get married, I'm flying Julo in to make this shit for my wedding party. It's incredible."

Prescott coughed into his hand. "Where did you say you were from, again?"

Cal sat up and stretched, raising his arms above his head and then twisting side to side. I couldn't take my eyes off him, and neither could Prescott.

"Hobie, Texas. Teeny place kind of northwest of Dallas and closer to Oklahoma."

"How did you get into sailing growing up in a place like that?" Lucas asked.

Cal pulled his knees up and wrapped his arms around them. My eyes went straight to the bulge between his legs, but as soon as I realized what I was doing, I looked up at his face. He bit his bottom lip to hold back a smile, and his cheeks were pink from more than the sun. Clearly he'd caught me staring at his junk. I huffed and looked out to sea.

His voice was light with laughter when he spoke again which drew my eyes right back to him like industrial magnets. "Hobie sits on a large lake with tons of pleasure boats. There's a sailing camp on the lake, and the woman who runs it also rents sailboats to tourists. I fell in with her when I was little and never looked back."

I could tell by his closed-up body language he wasn't interested in sharing more details. I felt oddly special that I knew the story of Annie's camp and how important it had been to Cal's future. Without thinking about it, I reached over and took his hand in mine. He glanced up at me and gave me a soft smile of thanks.

Thankfully, the moment ended when Mia gasped and pointed to something in the water. We all stood and moved over to the railing on the starboard side where a flying fish zinged about a foot above the surface of the water several yards off the side of the ship. As soon as it reentered the water, several more popped up farther off the edge of the ship to take their own flights through the air.

"What are those?" Mia asked.

Cal's face lit up as he explained about flying fish, describing something about a neural arch and vertebrae allowing them the structure needed to lift themselves out of the water and into the air. He told Mia about the different theories for why they leapt out of the water, and within moments, everyone was paying rapt attention while he described other aspects of the reef ecosystem and how it was impacted by Hurricane Irma a few years ago.

"There's a coral nursery here in the BVI that was wiped out by the hurricane, but they've been helped by the Coral Reef Consortium which has made a big difference in getting them back online as quickly as possible." He went on to describe the process of growing new coral in protected areas and then installing the branches in the reefs. Jin mentioned a similar reef conservation program in Japan, and the two of them continued talking happily as we motored closer to Virgin Gorda where we'd be mooring for the night.

As soon as we approached the mooring ball Vin had selected, Cal couldn't help but scramble around to help Freya with the hook. I had to admit, even though Freya was in great shape, I felt better seeing Cal leaning out over the bow than the heavily pregnant chief mate.

Freya stifled a laugh when Cal flicked water from the hook on an unsuspecting Jade. I caught Cal shooting Freya a wink, and my stomach swooped as if he'd winked at me. I needed to get a damned grip.

I took the opportunity to move inside the ship and find a glass of cold water. Julo was still prepping food, softly singing along to the music playing from the ship's speakers. I assumed he was working on the crew's dinner since the rest of us had reservations at the restaurant on the island.

"You're welcome to join us at CocoMaya," I told him as I reached around him for the pitcher of ice water on the counter. I'd invited him to join me for dinner many times whenever I went to a restaurant on shore, but he never accepted. It didn't mean I'd ever stop trying. "You could try the parsnip puree I told you about."

His deep laugh always made me smile. "And give Pat the satisfaction of cooking for me? No way. Besides, my conch fritters gonna make Freya cry tonight."

"I heard that," Freya said, hustling in from the deck and heading to the bridge. "It doesn't take much these days, so that's nothing to brag about."

Julo met my eyes. "You go have fun with your family. They missed you. And maybe you give that new man of yours some pampering while you're at it, yeah? I think it's been a long time since that one has tasted a twenty-dollar salad."

I took a seat on a stool in front of where he was chopping green and red peppers on a well-worn board. "He's not my new man," I said softly so no one else could hear. "That's just…"

Suddenly, I thought of something. "Were you around that night? When Prescott brought him on board?"

Julo kept his eyes on the peppers, as if they might run off at any minute. "Mpfh," he muttered.

I leaned in and lowered my voice even more. "Not fair," I hissed. "You and I both know what happened with that prick, and after all the time spent on this ship after the Mason situation while I moped around like an asshole, I would have hoped you'd have some kind of loy —"

He held up his hands in surrender and took a look around to make sure we were alone. "Fine. But I think he's a good one. You might want to give him a chance."

"Who?" I asked stupidly. Thankfully, Julo didn't dignify my question with an answer.

"Di topanoris brought your boy 'round late at night." He took a minute to toss the pepper pieces into a bowl while looking up at me through his dark lashes. "Acted like it was his ship." He shrugged and set the bowl aside before wiping his hands on a nearby towel and then crossing his arms in front of his chest. "I didn't know it was Lucas's man. When you told us his name and he was a guest coming early, that's all I knew."

I blew out a breath. Even if he had known, it wasn't like Julo was going to say anything to a grown man about who he could and couldn't sleep with. Still, it rankled me. Not only had Prescott cheated on my brother, but he'd also treated Cal like shit, leaving him to find his own way off a stranger's ship. Not to mention the lying the little weasel had done in the meantime.

Julo grinned at me. "That one makes you angry, I can see."

Now it was my turn to grunt which only made Julo laugh.

"I want Prescott gone, Julo," I said softly so no one else could hear. "He's not good enough for my brother."

Julo had a strangely knowing glint in his eye. "I'm not so sure your brother is as helpless as he seems. You might be surprised yet."

Before I had a chance to remind him that Lucas was practically still a child and had been used this way many times before by gold-digging users, Nat and Jade came around the corner from the deck passageway, laughing about something and waving an empty drinks pitcher at Julo. He teased them about being lushes.

"Isn't it supposed to be a workday for you ladies?" he asked as he began to mix another pitcher of punch. "I didn't think swimwear models got a day off."

They lapped up his easy charm, and I took the opportunity to head back outside to rejoin the group at the bow. Before I stepped onto the deck, however, Julo called my name.

"Worth, hold up."

I turned back around in time to catch the cold bottle of water he tossed at me. "For your man, Cal," he said with a knowing grin.

I shot him the bird.

9

CAL

Prescott finally got me alone late that night after dinner. Worth had asked me to escort Mia back on the first tender while he waited to settle the bill. Mia's head had started hurting halfway through dessert, and Worth had told us to find Julo when we got back on board for his magic headache tonic.

Whatever Julo put in that disgusting drink must have worked wonders, because Mia fell right to sleep as soon as I got her to her room. When I stepped out of her room and pulled the door closed quietly, I almost stepped right into Prescott. The doors to their two rooms were right next to each other in the same hallway as ours. As *Worth's*.

"Shit, sorry," I said automatically before realizing who it was. "Oh."

"Fucking finally," he hissed. "What the fuck are you doing here? What the hell happened? Did you seduce me on purpose? Was this some kind of test? Who the hell are you?"

I was so bombarded with his questions, I didn't even know where to start. When *I* seduced *him*? Hardly. When I didn't answer right away, he grabbed my upper arm. "Don't fuck with me, Cal, or I will tell Worth exactly what happened between us."

I spoke at full volume, hoping Lucas wasn't in earshot. "You mean how you begged me to fuck your face? Or how—"

He slapped his hand over my mouth which stung like a bitch and surprised me enough that I bit my own lip by accident. I tasted the copper tang of my blood and flared my nostrils in annoyance.

"Shut the fuck up. I don't know what little game you're playing, but the minute you tell anyone what happened between us, things are going to go just as badly for you with Worth as they will for me with Lucas. So I'd advise you to keep your mouth shut."

His nasty, clammy hand was still covering my mouth, so I grabbed his wrist and yanked his hand away. I wanted to tell him to go fuck himself. I wanted to give him a good junk shot with my knee. I wanted to do any number of things to give him a piece of my mind, but that wasn't why I was here. I was here to seduce him.

I softened my tone. "Listen, I'm sorry. I didn't know..." I struggled to come up with a plausible story. "I didn't know that you and Worth were like family. And I didn't know the name of the ship that night. I was distracted by..." I attempted to give him a shy up-down, as if the ugly Hawaiian shirt he sported was the hottest thing a man could possibly wear. "Other things."

His forehead wrinkled in confusion for a microsecond before smoothing out in a knowing smirk. "Understandable. But I—" He stopped for a beat when we heard footsteps above and shoved me away from him. "Are you open?"

It took me a minute to understand what he was asking. "Me and Worth?"

He made a sound of frustration. "Yes. Is that why—"

The footsteps came down the stairs as I desperately tried to determine which answer would work better to keep him interested. I decided to play coy.

"You'll just have to find out, won't you?" I winked at him and stepped farther down the hall toward Worth's stateroom door just as Worth hit the bottom step and saw both of us in the tiny hallway.

His eyes skipped back and forth between Prescott and me before landing on me. "What happened to your lip?" His voice sounded deep and growly, enough to make me worry what he'd do if he knew Pres had touched me in anger.

"I bit it. It's fine."

His nostrils flared, but he stayed calm. He turned to Pres. "Lucas is upstairs talking to Nat and Jin on the deck behind the living room. Cal and I are headed to bed. See you in the morning."

After dismissing Prescott, Worth approached the door to his stateroom. I expected him to move past me into the bedroom, but he stopped and reached for me, grasping me around the back of my neck and pulling my face toward him. My heart rate jacked up anticipating a kiss on the mouth—something showy to make Prescott jealous maybe—but he veered to the side and pressed his lips to the side of my face near my ear.

"Come to bed, sweetheart," he said in a low voice. It wasn't low enough for Prescott to miss it, which I assumed was the point. But it was certainly low enough to make my dick lean toward him in an effort to hear more.

"Mmm," I managed back.

As he stepped past me, Worth trailed his hand down my chest to my stomach, lighting up nerve endings I hadn't known I possessed. Saliva pooled in my mouth.

Once Worth had disappeared into the room, I realized Prescott had stepped closer to me. "You know he's using you, right?" His voice was too low for Worth or anyone else other than me to hear it.

I barked out a laugh. "Even if that were the case, I'd be happily complicit."

"He's never going to give you his money. This is what he does, Cal. He seduces young men with stars in their eyes and then drops them the minute they want anything serious. If you don't believe me, ask anyone on this boat about Mason."

It was on the tip of my tongue to correct him about the boat/ship thing, but I kept my mouth shut. I was afraid that if I opened it to say anything, I'd admit that it didn't matter if Worth was using me since this was all temporary and for show. For *him*.

"So, enjoy his largess while you can," Pres continued, moving away from me back toward the stairs. "And don't be surprised if he drops you the minute the *Worthington* docks back in St. Mitz." He chuckled as he started up the stairs.

I couldn't help but get in the final word even though I probably should have kept my mouth shut. "I don't want his money, Prescott. Just his big, thick cock down the back of my throat."

Feeling smug, I turned around and caught Worth watching me with a raised eyebrow and smirk. Shit.

"Don't flatter yourself," I muttered, stepping into the room and closing the door behind me. "It's not like I've actually seen your cock."

I wanted so badly to add the word *yet* to that sentence, but I controlled myself. I still had a bad taste in my mouth after the encounter with Prescott, so I wasn't exactly in the mood to see anyone's dick.

"What did he say?" Worth asked. "And did you really bite your lip, or did that asshole put his hands on you?"

"I really bit my lip." He didn't need to know the details, not if I was ever going to succeed in my mission to tempt Pres.

I tilted my head from side to side and rolled my shoulders to get rid of the tightness. I hadn't realized I'd held myself so stiffly when I was talking to him. "He's such an ass. He thought I'd 'seduced him on purpose' for some nefarious reason," I said, using air quotes. "Gross. He also thought maybe it was some kind of test, like you'd set me up to lure him into an infidelity trap. Oh, and he threatened to tell you all about my whoring ways."

Worth looked amused which annoyed me. I growled at him.

"Cal, you have to admit he was right. I am setting you up to lure him into an infidelity trap."

"He's disgusting. I can't believe I was desperate enough to—"

"Stop. I do not want to be reminded of you naked with that man." I chose to interpret his gruff tone as possessive, even though it was more likely due to his disgust with Prescott in general rather than any particular interest in protecting my virtue.

"Me neither," I muttered, reaching for the button on my shorts.

I'd eaten so much at the restaurant, the waistband was digging into me. Maybe it was a good thing Worth and I weren't having sex since I felt like a blowfish right now.

I stripped out of my shorts and hung them up in the closet since I'd only worn them for a few hours at dinner. While I was in the closet, I took a deep breath of the familiar scent I'd gotten super cozy with the day before. Still sexy as fuck.

"The good news," I said over my shoulder while hanging up the shirt next, "was that he asked if you and I were open which hopefully means he's still interested." I realized how that had sounded, and I turned around to elaborate. "Sorry, I just mean... he's still the cheaty jerk we knew him to be."

Worth glanced up from where he'd been leaning over the bed arranging his pillows a certain way. When he saw me standing there in my underwear, he did a funny kind of double take.

"Uhn," he said. "That's... good."

I couldn't quite tell if he was talking about Prescott's cheater status or the way I looked in my boxer briefs. Either way, his cheeks looked pinker, but it could have been a trick of the dim lighting from the bedside lamps.

It didn't matter. I took my turn in the bathroom, marveling not for the first time at how fancy everything was. The bathroom was sleek and modern with two sinks, marble counters, and a giant, glass-enclosed shower. I brushed my teeth and washed the salty air off my face and neck before making sure the bathroom was as clean as I'd found it.

When I stepped back into the stateroom, I found Worth typing away on his laptop. He'd changed into sleep pants and was noticeably, deliciously shirtless. Since his back was to me, I was able to drink my fill as I fumbled my way into bed. The sound of his fingers clicking away on the keyboard lulled me into a half sleep.

"Something important going on at work?" I murmured when I realized he was doing more than just checking email.

"Hm? Oh, yes, well... there's an interesting company I've had my eye on for a while. My assistant messaged me an update about the company getting closer to needing another round of funding. If so, I'll have to decide if I want to pull the trigger on investing in them or not."

"Any reason not to?"

He swiveled around in the chair to face me. My eyes were immediately drawn to his hairy chest and the soft, barely there swell of his belly. Why did I look like a drunk blowfish after a big meal while he looked like a sexy, cuddly teddy bear? It was hardly fair.

Worth sighed and ran fingers through his dark hair. "I'm not sure the world is ready for this technology yet."

"What's the technology?"

I could see the excitement in his eyes. "It's a company that's almost perfected electronic paper."

I blinked at him, surprised by the information he'd shared. I knew from a quick Google search on my phone earlier this afternoon that Jonathan Worthington owned a successful venture capital firm called Spinnaker Capital, and I also knew from my brother Hudson what that meant. "What's electronic paper?"

Worth clasped his hands together and leaned forward until his forearms were resting on his thighs. "It's kind of like if a Kindle was a thin sheet of paper. You would read the newspaper on it, then it could change to your utility bill or the contract you need to sign for work or your child's homework assignment. Imagine sitting at an attorney's office to sign a stack of legal paperwork related to a real estate closing and there was only one piece of paper on the table. This technology would replace much of the paper we use over time. The concept is brilliant. It has the ability to change the environmental impact of the paper and pulp industry, and I want to be a part of it. It's why I've been watching and waiting for them to get to this point."

I turned onto my side to face him. "Then go for it. What do you have to lose?"

He cracked a smile. "One hundred and eighteen million dollars."

I almost choked on the amount. "Oh," I squeaked. "Oh, right." This discussion was officially over my pay grade, and I wanted out. "Well, then. Something to think about, I guess. But maybe do your thinking tomorrow. The brain gears are awfully loud on your side of the room right now, and I need my beauty sleep."

He stood up and stretched, displaying the bare front of his body in a way that made me want to whimper and beg. Just one touch. Just one taste. That was all I needed.

"We're diving tomorrow, then checking out the Baths," Worth said, moving around to the bathroom. "Any particular sites you'd recommend?"

I thought about what we were close to. "Yeah, actually. Mountain Point is a good one. It's on the lee side of the island and has lots of sharks and eels. Big-ass lobster. There's also the Invisibles. That's the one with the rocky peak that juts out almost to the surface of the water. You can usually spot turtles there, and I can show you a cave full of glassy sweepers."

He chuckled as he entered the bathroom.

"Why are you laughing at me?" I called after him.

He turned back around and grinned at me. "You offered to show me a cave of glassy sweepers. It reminded me of last night when you kept talking about euphemisms."

I groaned and threw my head back on the pillow. "As if I'd ever invite you into my cave," I muttered to myself.

"I heard that," he said between the sounds of toothbrushing. "And if I wanted in your cave, it wouldn't take much to get you to invite me in, sweetheart."

I hated he thought he knew me that well. I hated that he thought I was so easy simply because I'd slept with jackass Prescott. More than anything, I hated that he was right.

The following morning found the two of us twisted around each other again like a pair of hot noodles. It felt so good, I immediately pretended to still be asleep. All I wanted was to indulge for a few minutes. I'd never had the kind of relationship where I could wake up in another man's arms like this. I'd been so busy with work and sailing and always seeking logged hours on the water that I'd mostly gotten off with one-night stands and casual connections. Even when I'd been able to stay the night with someone, I'd avoided it. The fear of falling for someone I couldn't have always kept other men at arm's length. And I couldn't have any of these men whose only time in the Caribbean was a week here and there before they flew back to whatever corporate life they led in a landlocked city.

So I was hungry, *starving* for this skin-on-skin indulgence. I wanted to know what it was like to be the man who got to wake up in Jonathan Worthington's arms. I wanted to know what it felt like to pretend to be cared for like that. When I'd first met him, Worth had seemed like the standoffish type, the kind of man who wouldn't treat his partner with tender affection. But now I strongly suspected I'd been way, way wrong.

Even when he was annoyed with me, his touch was gentle, and in this bed, both early mornings so far, the way he held me... *gah*. It was like... I couldn't even describe how sweet it was. One of his hands cupped the back of my head with his fingers threaded through my hair, and the other hand rested so low on my lower back, I felt it brush the top of my ass. I wanted him so fucking badly, and I refused to feel guilty for it. I refused to feel cheap simply because I was starved for physical affection.

Starved for physical affection?

The thought stopped me in my tracks and made me rethink the past year of my life. I'd been busting my ass working for Buoy Dan's, taking charters out one after the other with as few breaks as possible between. I remembered five specific times in the past two years when I'd found someone to hook up with. Twice it was a shared quickie blowjob with someone I'd picked up at the club in St. Mitz. Once was the client I'd fucked on a charter, once was a quick frot with a guy in Dallas when I was home for Doc's birthday last year, and the final time was the unfortunate encounter with Prescott.

None of them had even included any kind of kissing or make-out session first.

I sighed. That was crappy. It was fine to have fun with guys like that, and I certainly didn't have big regrets about the way I'd spent the past couple of years. I was proud of the work I'd done to further my career, and even though my dream of taking over Annie's sailing school had been trashed, I still had a strong resume for that kind of work. Just because I was no longer going to manage the program in Hobie didn't mean I couldn't run a sailing school somewhere else. I needed to focus and make a plan.

I pulled away from Worth and scrubbed my face with my hands. So much for enjoying a morning cuddle. Now that the job situation was in my head, I was fucked.

Worth rolled over and reached for my hand. He wasn't fully awake, but he was alert enough to wrap his index finger around my pinky.

"Can we talk about the elephant in the room?" he mumbled sleepily squeezing my finger, "Because I can't say I'm hating it."

I looked over at him, noticing his eyes were still closed and there was a pillowcase wrinkle on his cheek. The nest of dark hair on his head was shot through with strands of silver as if a magpie had deliberately woven tinsel into its home.

"Is the elephant your breath? Because if so, *I'm* hating it." I teased.

"Get back over here and snuggle me. We will tell no one of this."

This Jonathan Worthington was someone I could quickly get on board with. I scooted over and smushed my body up against his side, laying my head on his chest without realizing my own nest of bed head was enough to choke him.

He made a disgruntled noise and tried to flatten out the part that tickled his nose.

"Why don't you have a boyfriend?" I asked because apparently my brain filters were still dead asleep.

His fingers continued to toy with my hair as he let out a breath. I'd been joking about his breath before. Like everything else associated with Worth, it was miles away from putrid.

He shifted his hand down to my back, and the feel of his smooth fingertips along my skin made me shiver. "I broke up with someone about six months ago. Well, longer now, I guess. It was just after New

Year's. So... more like eight or nine months. It made me gun-shy, to say the least."

"Why?"

He exhaled. For a minute, I thought he wasn't going to elaborate, but he surprised me. "Because the kind of man I find myself attracted to is not the right kind of man for me."

"What does that mean?"

Worth's fingertips trailed up and down my spine. "Mason wanted my money. More specifically, he wanted my business. And not even my business. He wanted my father's company, or what was left of it."

I remembered reading online that the Worthington family was originally involved in making grain harvesters in the early 1900s. That had led to a larger business centered around agricultural manufacturing, but I wasn't sure if that was the company his family still owned.

"Is the venture capital firm your father's company?"

He shook his head and moved his hand back up into my hair. Even if he started talking about agriculture futures or combine harvesters, I'd lie here happily as long as he kept his hands on me.

"No. That's my company. I started it when my grandfather died and left me some money to invest. It was my final year in college, and I was taking an economics class from a woman who ran a successful venture capital firm. Several of the examples she used in class were based on her own experiences with funding start-ups, and it really piqued my interest. I approached her with a ton of questions, and she connected me to a professor in the Software Engineering department, who introduced me to a group of friends that had developed an app for a class project. They were trying to get the app off the ground. After lots of back-and-forth and getting to know the group, I decided to back their efforts. The company grew from there. Faster than I ever imagined since that little app was bought by a tech giant five years later for $850 million dollars."

I sputtered and craned my head to see if he was pulling my leg. He wasn't. "Holy fuck. That's amazing."

He cracked a smile. "It was. You should have seen these guys' faces when they got the offer. It was definitely one of my best memories since going into business. We've had a lot of celebrations and incredible acquisitions, but those guys... it was definitely something special. So you can imagine how much that helped me to fund other businesses, and it's snowballed since then."

"But that wasn't the company Mason wanted? Why the hell not?"

Before he could answer, my stomach let out an embarrassing growl. Worth smirked at me. "It's a long story. Let's get you up to Julo before you waste away. You must not have eaten enough at the restaurant last night."

I groaned and rolled out of his arms. "How is that possible? I ate every marine animal in the islands and enough dessert to put my grandpa's sweet tooth to shame."

But he was right. I was starving, and I could tell from the edges of the window coverings that the sun was already up.

I stood and stretched, not missing the caress of his eyes along my body. "Okay, but promise me you'll tell me the story when we get upstairs?"

Even though I was desperate to know more about what had happened, I wasn't exactly looking forward to hearing about Worth in a relationship with someone else. Maybe it was because I knew it didn't end well and I was waiting for the part where someone got hurt. Or maybe it was because I'd started to give a shit about this guy who was turning out to be more than I'd expected, more than I'd given him credit for.

Worth narrowed his eyes at me. "You're not diving in that skimpy suit, are you?"

I extended the stretch and waggled my hips a little. "Why? You scared it'll distract you from all the pretty coral?"

I expected him to scoff, but instead, he scraped his bottom teeth along his top lip before saying, "Maybe. I can't deny you're sexy as fuck."

My face suddenly felt warm. "Thank you. But I'll remind you about the fancy wet suit you bought. So, yes, I'm going to wear the

Speedo because it's much easier to pull the shortie over it than trunks. But you won't be able to perv on me while we're diving."

I turned and headed to the bathroom, feeling the heat of his stare on my ass. It may have been my imagination, but I thought I heard him mutter about still being able to perv on me even in a wet suit.

10

———————

WORTH

I HADN'T BEEN KIDDING ABOUT CAL. THE MAN WAS IN PRIME SHAPE from working on boats and most likely spending plenty of time in the water and sun. He was healthy and vibrant, the opposite of someone like me who spent most of their time in a climate-controlled high-rise.

In addition to that, he was charismatic and sweet. Natalia had been right when she'd pointed out how attentive he was. All through dinner, he'd asked open-ended questions of Nat's friends to learn more about them and then listened carefully to their answers.

It was still early, so we were the only ones up. Julo greeted us with coffee served on the aft part of the main deck.

Cal stretched out on the sofa cushions and hugged his mug to his chest. "God, how can you ever leave this to go back to Chicago?"

I looked out at the aquamarine water and the white sandy beach in the distance. Sea birds flapped lazily here and there, and the soft sounds of the water lapping against the hull made the perfect accompaniment to the soft island jazz Julo was playing in the galley.

"Sometimes I don't," I admitted. "After Mason and I parted ways, I came down here intending to sell the ship, but the sun was like a drug on my winter skin. I ended up staying for two months."

Cal's jaw dropped so comically, I wished I'd had my phone to snap a picture of it.

"You *what*? That doesn't gel at all with the way Nat describes you. What about work?"

I took a sip of the hot coffee and groaned in relief. It was perfect. "I still worked. The ship has Wi-Fi as you know. I just couldn't face returning to the biting cold. Julo, Vin, and Freya were good company."

He studied me as if seeing me in a new light. "That breakup must have thrown you for a big loop. Does Nat know you spent two months down here?"

I looked around to make sure she wasn't sneaking up on us. Little sisters were notorious for hearing everything. "No. I didn't tell the twins because I wanted to be alone. I was afraid if they knew I was down here wallowing, they'd show up to help."

Julo appeared with a couple of trays full of breakfast finger foods like the banana dumplings I couldn't get enough of, crepes wrapped around eggs and sausage, and more fresh fruit on skewers.

Cal practically drooled. "Julo, I think I'm in love with you."

He shot me a wink. "Well, you'll have to fight Freya for me, and I'm afraid she hits below the belt."

Cal's eyes widened in surprise. "You're together? Congratulations on the baby, man. I had no idea."

"Luckiest bum alive," he said with a wink before returning to the galley.

Cal turned his sparkling eyes to me. "How exciting for them. And what a dream to work and live together on a ship like this. I have a million questions for them now, but I refuse to get sidetracked. What happened with Mason?"

"Julo and Freya met when Vin hired them both two years ago. It's a good story."

"Stop changing the subject," he said, taking a bite of a banana dumpling. "Oh Christ on a cracker. This is better than sex."

Sitting on the deck next to an attractive man and feeling the warm Caribbean breeze across my skin while I ate one of my favorite breakfast treats was a little bit of heaven. I didn't want to ruin it by going into detail about my embarrassing choices.

I flapped my hand. "What's the expression you young people use these days when something is long and boring? Tee dee el are?"

Cal snorted and sat forward when some coffee dripped out of the corner of his mouth. "TL;DR," he corrected. "Back in the day, people called it the CliffsNotes version. At least, that's what my mom told me one time."

I leaned my head back and groaned. He was so young. "Anyway, the bottom line is, I hired an executive assistant to help me manage my responsibilities at Dad's company after he died since I was still busy managing my own firm and didn't want anything to fall through the cracks. After several lunches and late-night meetings, I made the mistake of sleeping with Mason. Then I started dating him. It took me three years to learn that he'd been more in love with the company shares than with me. To add insult to injury, I was dealing with my stepmother at the time, Lucas and Nat's mom, who—it turned out— had been having an affair during my father's battle with lung cancer and had only stayed with my father to inherit half the company when he passed. It was a mess, and it left me feeling very jaded about relationships to say the least."

"I'm sorry, Jon," he said softly, taking my hand in his. "My brother-in-law Augie comes from big family money and has had similar issues. I know it left him feeling like he could never trust anyone."

I shrugged. "Sometimes it's easier being alone."

Cal rolled his eyes. "You're an idiot. No it isn't. Augie adores my brother Saint and vice versa. Both of them are a thousand times happier than they ever were alone. You're being a drama queen, and if you're going to be that way, you at least need to dish the tea about how you finally sent him packing."

Nat must have heard us talking because she plopped down in the chair next to me and grabbed a dumpling. "Can I tell it? Please?"

Cal rubbed his palms together. "Hell yes. You'll do the story justice. Bring it."

I groaned and reached for my coffee.

Nat leaned forward to grab another dumpling. "After Worth broke up with him, Mason made a scene at the company holiday party like it was some kind of *Real Housewives* show. He accused my brother of sexual harassment, threatened to sue him—quote, in open court, unquote—and then finally let it slip that if Worth didn't want him, surely Robert from accounts receivable would."

Cal started giggling and couldn't stop. "Tell me there's video. Please baby Jesus."

Nat moved over to sit on the chair closer to Cal. "No, but get this. It turned out that Robert is straight and married, *and* he has a knack for forensic accounting. He was so pissed after being dragged into this that he ended up uncovering all kinds of shady expense reports and financial transactions in which Mason had forged Worth's signature. After that, Mason had to go away quietly or risk legal action."

I remembered how embarrassed I'd been when he'd aired our personal dirty laundry in front of employees, some of whom had known me since I was a teenager coming to work with my father. But I'd deserved it for being stupid enough to date an employee in the first place.

I stood up to get a coffee refill inside. Lucas was sitting on a stool at the galley counter sipping juice from a small glass. "Morning," he murmured. "We diving today?"

"Absolutely. Cal has some special spots he wants to show us. Once everyone gets up and fed, we'll get the tender out and load it up with the tanks."

Julo handed me my refilled mug. "Captain Vin already loaded it up for you. Good to go whenever you're ready. Jin just took a cooler of water and fresh fruit down there for the surface interval."

I thanked him and took the stool next to Lucas. "How are you doing?"

He rolled his shoulders and grunted. "I think I sleep ten times more deeply on this boat. I haven't decided if that's a good thing or not, but it'll be good to get in the water and stretch out."

Lucas took another sip of coffee and eyed me over the mug. "You look awfully chipper this morning."

I shrugged. "I'm excited to get down there and see what we see. It's gorgeous outside."

Julo nodded as he transferred more food onto a decorative tray. "Gonna be a good one today."

Lucas sat back and stretched his legs out. "Tell me about Cal. I didn't know you were bringing someone."

I felt like an ass considering the only reason Cal was even on this ship was because Lucas was engaged to a philanderer and his own brother was bound and determined to ruin his engagement. Suddenly, when faced with lying to my brother in order to protect him, I realized how wrong it all was. But I wasn't a good enough person to call it off.

"It's nothing serious," I said, clearing my throat. "Just thought some company would be nice this week since you have Pres and Nat has Jin. That's all."

And when the words came out of my mouth, I realized they were almost true. It wasn't that I enjoyed being alone. On the contrary, I actually really liked being in a relationship. But it would be a long time before I'd allow myself to reach that level of trust with someone else again.

"I like him," Lucas said. "He's funny as hell, and he was so sweet last night when Mia was talking about her niece struggling to learn how to ride a bike."

I thought back to the advice he'd given her about trying a balance bike or using her feet to scoot first. He'd sounded like an experienced dad, but then he'd told a story about his little sister having all kinds of trouble learning and his older siblings had been a nightmare about it. By the time he finished telling the story, Jade was laughing so hard she was crying and Nat had nearly choked on her drink.

"He's a people person," I said.

"You're drawn to men who are entertaining. I think you enjoy being able to sit back and watch so you don't have to be in charge of keeping the conversation going."

I wasn't sure I'd ever been described that way. Was it true? But more upsetting was the comparison between Cal and Mason.

"Isn't everyone drawn to people who they find interesting?" I asked.

"I guess you're right. But I think you're drawn to performers. Maybe Cal is a Leo. We should ask when his birthday is."

"When whose birthday is?" Cal asked, walking through the open slider doors from the deck.

"Are you a Leo?" Lucas asked, instinctively reaching out to clap my mouth closed before I could scoff at him about horoscope nonsense.

Cal nodded. "My birthday was three weeks ago. Why?"

Lucas started laughing, so I swatted his chest. "That doesn't prove anything," I muttered. I tried not to think about how he was *barely* twenty-three.

"No reason," Lucas said. "I was simply speculating on why you were so fun to be around. Leos are the life of the party."

Cal's cheeks turned pink. "Oh. Um... thank you?" He stepped closer to me and asked in a lower voice, "Have I been talking too much? I tend to take over a conversation. It's a problem that's been pointed out to me in the past."

I sensed Julo stiffen, but he kept his mouth shut. Meanwhile, I slid an arm around Cal's waist and pulled him close. "Never," I said as sincerely as I could manage without sounding angry. "I could listen to you talk all night, and anyone who feels otherwise is welcome to take a long walk off a short plank."

Lucas leaned around me to see Cal. "Not at all. I meant it as a compliment. I'm sorry if it came out another way. I really enjoyed getting to know you better last night, and I'm happy you're here with us."

Cal swallowed and glanced at me before meeting Lucas's eyes again. I could tell he was uncomfortable with Lucas's praise. "Thanks. That means a lot."

Nat wandered in to meet Jin, who was finally emerging from downstairs. "Let's get this show on the road. Someone wake Prescott up. I'm ready to get underwater."

The dive was perfect—clear visibility, plenty of marine life, and almost no current at depth. The six of us paired up naturally as couples and explored Mountain Point. Cal pointed out a moray eel hiding under a rock with his toothy mouth open like a highly attentive mouth breather.

Toward the end of the dive we spotted a sea turtle swimming lazily in the distance. Lucas swam closer and took the opportunity to spin around with his arms and legs out, stretching the way he'd mentioned wanting to. A long-forgotten memory of taking him to an inflatable play place when I was in college popped into my head. I remembered Lucas jumping and doing flips, reveling in the enjoyment of stretching out his body in the air. He'd chatted excitedly the whole way home, begging for me to take him again the next time I came home on a school break. Nat, as usual, had brought friends along, and they'd giggled happily in the back seat while Lucas had described every jump, flip, and slide he'd perfected in the two-hour visit.

My dive computer beeped a warning, jolting me back into the present. I was ascending a little too quickly, so I stopped and waited for Cal to catch up. When I saw his face, I noticed the furrows of concern aimed at me. I flashed him the okay signal to let him know I was aware of needing to slow down, and we made the rest of the ascent to the fifteen-foot safety stop together.

When we finally got back on the tender, the first thing out of his mouth was a lecture. "You can't zone out when you're ascending, asshole!"

"I know. I'm sorry."

"I tried to grab your leg to stop you, but I was too far away."

"My computer beeped anyway, and I stopped immediately," I reminded him, refusing to think about what would have happened if I hadn't been diving with a computer and had continued up without thinking.

"The last thing we need is to find a fucking hyperbaric chamber." He continued griping as he stripped off his BC and dropped the tank into the clip to hold it against the side of the tender. "Do you have any idea how claustrophobic those fuckers are? And you're in there for hours."

I reached out and grabbed his arm. "Cal, I was hardly at risk for the bends. We're talking about me going up maybe five or ten feet of depth too fast, not fifty. Calm down."

The boat rocked as Jin climbed aboard. Cal reached out automatically to help but didn't stop bitching at me in the process. "It doesn't take much, and if you'd gotten hurt on my watch, I would have..." He stopped to focus on getting Jin's tank off and untangling him from his regulator and octopus tubes. Once his tank was in a clip, Jin clapped a thanks on Cal's shoulder and moved over to help Natalia up.

I took a seat behind the wheel to get out of Jin's way, and Cal sat down on the bench next to me to do the same. "I was scared you didn't know," he said more quietly.

I put my hand on his leg and squeezed lightly. "I promise I know what I'm doing. I may not be an instructor like you, but I have my advanced certification and have been on many, many dives."

He let out a breath. "Okay. Sorry. I just..."

I turned and faced him, automatically tunneling my fingers in his messy wet hair to get it off his face. "I get it. You've probably had to babysit enough newbies underwater to think most tourists are one stupid mistake away from being the Dave."

Jin took a seat on the bench behind us while Nat rifled through the cooler for a bottle of water. "What's the Dave?" Jin asked.

"Dive accident victim," Cal and I said at the same time before grinning at each other like fools.

When Lucas popped up at the ladder, Cal moved to help take his gear for him. I could tell from his smooth movements swapping out tanks and resetting the equipment that he'd done this hundreds of times. My eyes devoured the muscles moving under the tanned, smooth skin of his back where his shorty had been peeled down to his waist. His shoulders and biceps tightened as he lifted and moved air tanks, and by the time all of the equipment was set up for our second dive, I wasn't the only person mesmerized.

Prescott was practically drooling over Cal even as his own arm was resting on my brother's shoulders. Lucas was talking to Nat about the fish they'd seen, so he didn't seem to notice his fiancé's lecherous eyes.

When Cal made his way back to the bench after untying us from the mooring buoy, I stood and gestured for him to take the wheel. "You probably know where we're going better than I do, so why don't you drive?"

Cal sat and started the engine while I kept my eye out for other divers in the water nearby. Once we were safely away from the dive site, he picked up speed.

I watched him as the wind whipped his dirty-blond hair dry and the edges of his eyes crinkled under his sunglasses. His muscled fore-arms flexed as he turned the steering wheel and adjusted the throttle, and the tempting trail of hair that led from his belly button down into his wet suit looked like something I wouldn't mind exploring with my tongue.

It was easy out here under the late summer sun, skipping along the surface of a water blue enough to make my eyes leak, to imagine maybe I could take this beautiful man to bed and let myself enjoy him at least once. What would be the harm in that? If he was amenable to a temporary arrangement and could agree it was simply physical, it wouldn't have to mean anything. And more than that, I wouldn't need to worry about trust issues or him using me for my money.

"Why are you staring at me?" Cal asked with a smirk. "Do I have something on my face?"

I told him the truth. "You're gorgeous."

He did a classic double take at me, his smirk sliding off when he realized I'd meant what I'd said. "Um, thank you."

I faced into the wind and laughed loud and free. Throwing Cal off his stride was more fun than I'd expected until his elbow got me in the gut.

Oof.

"Stop being so smug," Cal warned. "And go back to being the stodgy old workaholic please. That guy was at least predictable."

Nat looked back from her spot near the bow and winked at me. She must have heard our flirting. I watched the way Jin kept a casual grip on her inner thigh as the tender bumped across the water. They were good together. I remembered the first time she'd brought him to meet our father at a family dinner. Jin had been polite and attentive to all of us, including Nat, but when she'd tripped down the final stair of our father's brick patio and scraped her hands and knees, Jin had lost his calm demeanor and fussed over her like she was the queen mother.

He was forthright enough to argue with her about issues he disagreed with, but if she was ever feeling fragile, he dropped everything to coddle her. She treated him with the exact same love and reverence. I loved seeing how happy they made each other.

Then there was Lucas and Prescott.

"We're here," Cal said, pulling back on the throttle. "Can you take over at the wheel while I grab the hook and get us tied up?"

We switched positions and maneuvered the boat to the mooring ball. Once Cal had tied us off, Nat passed out fruit and waters to anyone who hadn't already gotten some. The taste of fresh pineapple after a mouthful of salty regulator was heavenly.

"God, there's nothing better," Cal groaned. A drop of juice balanced delicately on his lip until it lost the fight with gravity and slid down his chin.

Everyone else went back to talking about what they'd seen on the dive, except Prescott. When I turned around to reach for another slice of fruit, I saw Prescott's eyes locked on Cal. Pres had stripped off his wet suit for the surface interval and right there, plain as day, was an obvious Cal-boner in the front of his trunks.

At first, I thought maybe he was hard for his own fucking

boyfriend, but then I realized that Lucas was one row behind him, adjusting something with his gear. No, Pres was clearly hot for my boyfriend just like we'd planned.

Only now it didn't feel nearly as satisfying as I'd imagined it would.

11

CAL

I was in my element on a dive boat. The equipment and procedures were second nature, and the camaraderie that naturally happened on a group dive was one of my favorite social situations on earth. There was so much to talk about after being under the water, and shared experiences tended to bring people closer together.

I looked around at all of the happy faces and relaxed body language. I was grateful to be in a group of experienced divers since it meant a lot less chance of trouble, even something as minor as seasickness now that the water was getting a little rougher as the day progressed.

We hadn't gotten as early of a start as we'd hoped due to an unexpected gossip session Nat had to have with her friends when Jade came across some gasp-worthy photo of a friend of theirs on Instagram. One of the upsides to being on your own ship was being flexible, so we'd all just lounged around on the deck with more coffee and breakfast until she was finally ready.

But now as I watched the chop increase, I wondered if that was such a good idea.

"What's wrong?" Worth asked softly. "You're frowning at a dolphin."

I blinked and looked more closely but didn't see any fins. "I don't see any dolphin."

"I was kidding about the dolphin. But you are frowning."

I surveyed the water around us and noticed three other boats tied to mooring buoys nearby. If the professional operators were still in the water, it was a good sign.

"It's getting choppy. That could mean current below the surface. Is everyone here strong and fit enough to swim hard if we need to?"

Worth explained that everyone on board exercised regularly, and they'd all run in a charity 5K over Memorial Day weekend. That was way better than the odd mix of fitness levels I usually had with charter clients. "Okay, good," I said, letting out a breath. "Then I'm going to check everyone's gear one last time, and we'll get in the water in about fifteen more minutes."

I made sure we each had fresh tanks connected to our gear and everyone's air was turned on and showing at least three thousand psi. After that, I downed another few gulps of water and sucked on some orange slices until everyone seemed about ready. Once everyone started pulling back on their wet suits, I gave a mini dive brief about the site.

"The Invisibles has a submerged pinnacle that's home to a ton of fish, sponges, and soft coral. Basically, it's a giant rock formation with lots of cracks and crevices which means plenty of hiding places to spot shy fishes like fairy basslets, blennies, and gobies. But there are also bigger fish like jacks, queen angelfish, and barracuda. There's some current here, so watch your depth since it's a second dive. We don't want to go too deep. There's also some fire coral on this dive, so be careful what you brush up against and try to make sure all of your gauges and hoses are tucked in."

I caught Natalia's cheeky grin. "Yes, dive master. Whatever you say, dive master," she teased.

I felt my face heat. "Sorry. Old habits."

Lucas reached out and patted my shoulder. "Nah, it's great. Sometimes I get nervous diving, so I like having a dive master with us."

I glanced at Worth, who was smiling approvingly. As long as he was happy, I was happy.

Jin helped Nat into her BC and over to the edge of the boat. "Last one in's a rotten egg!"

Once she was ready, Nat rolled backward off the side of the tender and splashed into the water. Jin went next while Prescott and Lucas used the other side of the boat for their entries. Worth and I took separate sides of the boat to make sure they all gave the okay signal. Once it was just Worth and me left on board, I had this odd impulse to kiss him. He just looked so happy and relaxed, he was hard to resist.

Nonetheless, I resisted. He wasn't actually my boyfriend, so I'd have to reserve any kisses to the times we were forced to play the boyfriend role.

"Let's stay close to Lucas on this one," I suggested. "We don't know how strong the current will be and—"

I didn't even have to finish before Worth nodded and murmured it was a good idea. The two of us got geared up and rolled back into the water.

The dive was excellent. We saw tons of fish and even a small nurse shark dozing under an overhang. I was relieved to get through it without the current causing any problems. It was a little hard getting everyone back in the boat with the increased chop, but everyone pitched in and stowed gear quickly so we could unmoor and motor back to the yacht.

Thankfully, the yacht was moored in a calmer spot, so when we got back on board, we sat down to a nice big lunch without having to fight the wind and waves. In the meantime, Mia and Jade had finished the online scuba class I'd set them up with and begged me to take them in the water after lunch for a taste of what it was like using the BC and regulator. I asked them several questions and was surprised to learn they'd taken the lessons seriously and retained the most important information.

"Okay, but let's wait for me to digest this incredible meal first," I said, pushing my plate forward in hopes that would make me stop eating. Julo had served grilled chicken skewers and a special Jamaican veggie slaw that was out of this world. I hadn't been able to control myself. "I might need a siesta."

Mia groaned and leaned back in her chair. "I both hate and love Julo."

Worth chuckled. "Agreed."

Nat's eyes sparkled at her brother. "It's nice to see you relaxing, Worth. Lucas and I were worried about you this summer. It seemed like you never left the office."

I wondered if he would ever tell them about spending so much time down here earlier in the year. It wasn't any of my business, but I thought maybe it would give them some peace of mind to know he took so much time to himself to try to get over the Mason situation.

"I was working on the CloudCorr deal," he explained calmly. "It required lots of work since the company was acquired only two weeks after completing the funding round."

Nat and Lucas both shot him looks. I didn't want to see the conversation turn into an intervention, so I tried to change the subject.

"My brother once snuck onto a yacht to steal a Delacroix painting," I blurted.

The table went silent, and all the heads swiveled toward me in slow motion.

"Um, he's... well, he *was* an art thief. Ahem, allegedly. And when the authorities brought him on board to help take down another art thief, they needed him to steal a painting from this guy's yacht in the Mediterranean."

Worth sighed. He didn't believe a word I was saying, which made me feel oddly giddy. It wasn't a believable story, but it was a hundred percent true.

"Sneaking onto yachts must run in your family," Prescott mused.

Oh no he didn't.

I snapped my head around and glared at him. "I was invited on this yacht," I said pointedly, wanting desperately to point out that he had been the one to invite me.

"I was only kidding," Prescott said. "Lighten up."

Worth stiffened in the seat next to mine, but I latched onto his thigh under the table and squeezed to keep him from saying something he'd regret.

"Maybe I'll take that siesta after all," I said, standing up. "Mia, Jade... how about two hours and then we'll head over to the Aquarium? It's a nice shallow site which is great for beginners. Whoever else wants to come is welcome to join us as long as your dive computer says it's okay."

Nat grabbed my arm. "Wait, I want to hear more about the art thief."

"That was just a teaser. I'll tell the whole story at dinner when there's alcohol involved."

I smiled at everyone and cleared my dishes to the galley despite Julo's judgmental look at me doing any cleanup. Freya was standing between the galley and the doorway to the bridge where I could hear Captain Vin talking. I stepped up to poke my head in and ask if it would be okay if I took the tender to the dive site later. I was sure it was, but I didn't want to make assumptions with the captain of the ship.

He agreed easily, and I made my way downstairs to the stateroom. Worth was already there.

"Prescott Resnick is an ass," he grumbled.

"Yep." I threw myself down on the cool duvet and bunched up a pillow under my head. "Sorry to bail, but I really did eat too much. Julo is a stealthy weapon if you ever need to incapacitate an enemy."

Worth laughed softly and made his way over to his laptop to do some work. Why didn't that surprise me?

"Don't do stupid work. Snuggle me," I whined. "It's cold in here with the air on. What's the point of having a fake boyfriend if I can't use his body for my comfort and pleasure?"

Worth turned and pinned me with a heated stare, almost like a promise. My words echoed softly in the room like a dare. For a split second, I wondered if he'd actually come over here. But then he stood up and slid open the porthole window to let in the warm ocean breeze. "There. Get under the covers if you want to warm up more. I need to check my email and respond to my PA about a few things."

I was more disappointed than I'd expected. After sleeping two nights in his bed and feeling his hands on me around the others... I'd begun wanting something I knew I couldn't have.

After a few minutes of listening to the soft click of his keyboard and watching his sexy forearms, I couldn't take it anymore.

"You know... if we're sharing a bed anyway..."

"No." Worth didn't even turn around.

"I'm just saying, no one would need to—"

"No."

I huffed and flipped over, showing him my back even though he wasn't paying any attention to me. I was twenty-three and horny. There was no need to spend this entire week chaste when two consenting adults with needs could help each other out really easily.

After a few more minutes, I turned back over. "Hear me out."

The quiet rumble of his laugh made me even more anxious to get him naked. The sound went right to my dick. "You're just bored," he said. "Maybe read a book."

"All this relaxing you're doing, which is impressing your siblings by the way, would be totally leveled up if we added a blowjob to the mix."

Worth shifted in his chair but didn't respond. He went back to clicking away.

"Or," I continued, sitting up to make my case, "a dick in your ass if you want to go a little further. It might be the cure for what ails you."

He closed his eyes and rubbed his face before turning to me. I didn't miss the adorable flush on his cheeks.

"First of all, I don't bottom. Secondly—"

I cut him off. "Ever? Why? Because you're old and set in your ways or because you've never tried it and experienced the pleasure of your prostate?"

"Introducing sex to this ridiculous situation would only complicate matters."

Suddenly, I could picture him in a stuffy corporate boardroom

droning on about boring nonsense like dynamic synergy and lever-
aging paradigm shifts for optimum output.

I threw myself back onto the bed with a groan. "God, you're a
boomer."

"Not."

"Okay, you're Gen-X. And you want to know how I know? You use
the word 'not' as a complete sentence."

He chuckled softly as he turned back to his work. "And you're a
horny teen. Or close enough."

"Are you saying you're not horny?"

"At the moment? No, I'm not horny. I'm working. Or trying to,
anyway."

I tried to catch a glimpse of his crotch, but it was hidden under
the desk. "Okay, but this morning I woke up with an old-man boner
trying to fornicate with my belly button, so you have had moments of
horn. Admit it."

He scrubbed his face again. "You exhaust me."

"I'd like to exhaust you," I muttered, flipping over onto my stomach. I must have succumbed to the lull of the gentle rocking of the
ship and the delicious lunch because the next thing I knew, Worth
was shaking me awake.

"The ladies are asking about their dive." He sat next to me on the
bed in a glow of afternoon light.

I blinked awake. "Huh? Shit. What? Did I fall asleep?"

He brushed his fingers through my hair and looked down at me
with a soft expression. "Yes. Right in the middle of a tirade about
what a sex god you were and how you were going to rock my world
with your power moves."

"Shut up," I mumbled, moving closer to him without thinking. I
threw an arm over his lap and spooned his leg.

"Now you're humping my leg."

"I'm cuddling your leg, and you clearly don't know what shut up
means."

Nat's voice came from somewhere behind me. "Get your lazy ass up. Mia and Jade finished another unit in the online lessons and want to get in the water."

I dragged my hand down Worth's leg until I got to the hem of his shorts, and then I snuck my hand up inside the shorts along the bare skin of his hip. He sucked in a breath which made me feel slightly smug. At least he couldn't claim to be unaffected by me. "You're not wearing a suit," I complained.

"I'm staying here. Lucas, Nat, and I need to go over some legal documents while we're all together. I think Jin wants to go with you though."

Nat patted my leg and moved back toward the door. "I'll tell them ten minutes, okay? Jin is already loading the equipment and tanks."

As soon as I heard the click of the stateroom door, I crawled up Worth's body until we were nose to nose. "Come with me."

He ran his hands through my hair again. "Can't."

"Won't," I corrected.

Worth's hands moved down to my shoulders and then my back. I never wanted his touch to end.

"Tell you what," he said with an indulgent smile. "If you go teach those two how to manage themselves underwater, I'll let you be in charge of the entertainment after dinner tonight."

My eyes widened in surprise as I imagined the two of us naked and sweaty in this bed.

"Not that," he said with a laugh, pushing me off him. "I meant games or whatever. Liar's Dice like you mentioned before."

"Fine. But I'm only going because I need to swim off that lunch so I can gorge myself again at dinner." I moved to the closet to find a pair of dry swim trunks. I selected the navy boy shorts and shimmied my clothes off before slipping them on.

Worth made a strangled noise behind me. "You... you can use the bathroom if you want."

I turned around right as I pulled the suit up so he was only left with a tease. "Oh I will. Thanks," I said before sauntering over to the bathroom.

Once I closed the door, I let out a breath. This was a problem. I really and truly wanted him. And it wasn't just physical. He was turning out to be a little bit more kind and attentive than I'd originally given him credit for. And generous.

Because I was a nosy asshole, I'd discovered that the legal documents he was referring to comprised an agreement concerning his father's company, Jacoy Agribusiness Corporation. I was no attorney, but a quick glance at the cover sheet seemed to say the purpose of the agreement was to transfer ownership of JAC from Worth to Lucas and Natalia. It wasn't like I'd gone searching through his stuff, but he'd left the folder open on the desk when he'd gone up to lunch.

He was handing over their father's business to Lucas and Natalia completely.

That kind of generosity reminded me so much of my own brothers, it made my eyes sting and my heart thump with a strange kind of homesickness. I'd picked up a few pieces of Worth's family history here and there, mostly at dinner last night, to learn that Worth's mother hadn't been Worthington Sr.'s first wife, but she'd been the first to have his child. When Worth was only nine, she'd left her husband and son to follow another man to California. It sounded like Worth didn't keep in contact with his mother, and I wondered how much it bothered him.

The twins were born to wife number four, an eighteen-year-old cocktail waitress Worth's father had met on a business trip to Kansas City. He was the king of prenuptial agreements, but for some reason, he'd died leaving half the business to his young wife, Lucas and Nat's mother. Both Lucas and Nat had expressed horror and regret at "what she did" to Worth after his father's passing, and I guessed it had something to do with her meddling in JAC affairs at the same time Mason was doing the same.

So to see Worth handing over a business he'd worked so hard to protect was not only surprising but impressive. If I was interpreting the situation correctly, it meant he wasn't the bucket full of rich-guy stereotypes I'd pegged him with on first glance.

I sighed and finished up in the bathroom before making my way back out to the stateroom. The last thing I needed to do was get lovesick over a man who would never want someone like me, a dead-broke charter captain without a boat, a plan, or a future.

"You all set?" Worth asked from his spot back at the desk.

"Yep. I'll see you back here in a bit. Good luck with the family meeting."

I left and made my way aft to where Jin and the ladies were waiting. Once checking my own equipment and the ladies' equipment to make sure we had everything we needed, I untied the lines and tossed them to Freya, who gave us a big push with her foot.

"Happy diving," she called with a wave. "Julo will have punch and appetizers ready when you get back."

We found a mooring ball at the Aquarium and tied up. Before putting on our gear, I sat Mia and Jade down to go over several things.

"One of the most important things to remember is not to panic and not to go up in the water too quickly," I reminded them. All of this had been covered in the online class they'd taken, but I needed to make sure they realized the importance of staying calm. "We're not going too deep here, and since it's your first time down, you won't have much to worry about in terms of nitrogen buildup in your blood. However, Jin and I do since we've already been on two deeper dives today. That means that if you go up too quickly, Jin and I can't go with you or help you. So it's really important to stay close to us and never ascend quicker than your bubbles, okay?"

They both nodded.

"Okay, another thing is to watch your air gauge and your depth gauge. I don't want you going deeper than about forty-five feet, and I don't want your psi to read under a thousand. Once you reach a thousand psi, we'll start ascending. At this shallow depth, it will give us plenty of time to explore. Any questions?"

"What if we see a shark?" Jade asked.

"We will probably see a shark. There are a ton of them here, but they're not something to panic over. Most of them are reef or nurse sharks and have no interest in harming you."

Mia nodded. "Except my cousin has a friend who got attacked by a hammerhead once."

I gritted my teeth. That wasn't the best way to calm a nervous diver. "We're most likely not going to see a hammerhead. If you do, you'll have major bragging rights. If you're worried about anything you see down there, just stay close to me and we'll stay away from them."

Mia continued. "What about barracuda? They have super-sharp teeth."

I nodded. "They do. And they're kind of creepy because they swim up above you in your blind spot. But, again, they're not interested in you if you leave them alone. Eels are the same. They look toothy and scary, but they're usually hiding and trying not to be noticed."

As we began to put on our BCs, I explained the equipment. Once we were ready, I did one more review of hand signals before helping each of them sit up on the edge to do a back-roll entry. Jin had hopped in the water first to help anyone who needed it, but they did great, and within moments we were descending to forty feet.

After testing the ladies' buoyancy, we cruised around to look at some of the surrounding coral. It was fun to see Jade's face light up when she saw a spotted eagle ray flapping lazily through the water in the distance, and when Mia discovered the grass along the sandy bottom was actually a field of garden eels standing in their little holes, she made a high-pitched squeal through her regulator.

They had a great time and handled themselves perfectly.

In the end, the danger came from an unexpected source after we'd done our safety stop and were climbing back into the boat. Jin climbed into the boat first, and then Jade followed him. Just as Mia grabbed the little ladder and began to unbuckle her BC to hand it up, Jin slipped and accidentally knocked his tank and BC overboard, right into my face. The metal tank knocked me on the head, something sharp scraped my forehead, and the bulk of the whole thing ripped the regulator from my mouth and the mask off my face. I had just enough time to mentally laugh about Jin being the Dave after all before sinking down into the water in a breathless shock.

12

WORTH

In the end, I hadn't gotten much work done while Cal had napped in my bed. I'd sat and stared at him, noting every inch of his face and body. Even though I knew he was only interested in something physical, I wasn't sure I could say the same anymore. He was sweet and kind, interesting and funny. And the fact he was willing to teach my sister's friends to dive for free was just one example of what seemed to be his usual generosity.

How was it possible I was falling for another young man? Did I have a type? I hadn't thought so, but maybe there was something about it that called to me. Or maybe I was simply drawn to men who didn't take life as seriously as I did.

I couldn't deny he was a good influence on me, and when I sat down on the deck with my brother and sister, they immediately began saying the same thing.

"You're happier now than you ever were with Mason," Nat began. I ignored her and opened the folder with the contracts.

"He's cute too," Lucas said with a smirk.

"Mpfh." I slid the copies out and distributed one to each of them before reaching into my pocket for the pens I'd brought.

"It's too bad his family wants him to marry that girl," Nat said.

I fumbled all three pens and watched them skitter in different directions on the wooden decking. "What? What girl?"

Lucas frowned at us. "I believe the proper term is woman. Geez, Nat. Since when are you such an anti-feminist?"

Nat nodded. "Sorry, you're right. That *woman*."

"What woman?" I barked. "What woman are you talking about?"

My heart was thundering, but it was probably just from reaching down to scramble for the pens. I pegged my sister with a look that meant business. She responded with nothing but sweet affection.

"You really like him."

"What. Woman," I demanded through clenched teeth. "He's gay. I can't believe his family would push him into... wait. Isn't half his family gay?"

Lucas chuckled. "More like eighty percent."

"So then why—"

Julo set down a pitcher of lemonade beside us on the table. "She's yanking your chain," he said in a low voice. "Naughty sister."

I shot Nat a look. "You're making this up? Why?"

She reached out and grabbed my hand, threading our fingers together in a way she hadn't done since she was in elementary school. "I want you to stop resisting this."

Lucas looked between the two of us. "What do you mean resisting? Aren't they dating?"

Nat let out a breath. Clearly she suspected something. "He's keeping Cal at arm's length. He's scared of another Mason situation."

"Can we move on to the legal portion of this discussion, please?" I begged.

"Legally, you're old enough to be his father," Lucas teased.

"Legally, what I heard you two up to last night wasn't allowed in the state of Florida until 2003."

I snapped my head around. "We slept. Since when is sleeping illegal?"

"Technically," Lucas said, "she didn't say it was illegal. She said the opposite."

Julo chuckled from the side of the deck where he was hosing something off.

"Are you saying you're not sleeping with him?" Nat pushed.

I didn't want to lie to her, but if he and I were together, how could I tell her we weren't sleeping together? Suddenly, I pictured myself wrapped around his sleeping form and realized I didn't have to lie. "I am sleeping with him. Of course I am."

Nat sat back with a satisfied grin. "Good. That's all I wanted to know. It explains why you're so damned relaxed."

I wish.

"Back to the contract," I said, pointing to the paper. "This is the exact copy your attorney was given and we all agreed on."

Lucas shook his head. "We never agreed. In fact, Nat and I fought against this quite hard."

Nat leaned forward. The sun slanted across her dark hair, bringing out chestnut-brown highlights that reminded me of her mother. Thankfully, she'd inherited Angela's beauty but my father's analytical mind. "He's right. We don't want to inherit the family business without part of our family. And that's you, moron."

"We've been over this. I'm staying on the board and will make sure to have a hand in operations. Father should have never left it to me, and your share shouldn't have been given to your mother, no offense. I don't need the money, and I want to make sure the two of you are set for life. Please sign these agreements. If you want me to be happier and more relaxed, you'll do this for me."

Nat grumbled about me not playing fair, but they both signed the documents. Captain Vin signed as the witness, and I shuffled the originals back into the folder just as Freya called out from the bridge.

"Cal's hurt! They're coming in on the tender and need help."

My breath caught in a hard ball in my chest, and black spots pricked at the edges of my vision. I raced down the stairs to the aft deck where they'd pull up. Sure enough, in the distance I could see the tender hauling ass, leaving a thick white wake behind them. Jin was at the wheel, his dark hair flying around his face. I couldn't see much else until they got closer, and then all I noticed was the blood.

It was smeared on the white hull of the tender in several places, and I could see equipment scattered around in the boat instead of being stowed properly. Mia and Jade seemed to be caring for Cal, who was slumped on the floor of the boat.

"It's not as bad as it looks," Jin called out as Julo tossed him a line. "He's okay. Just might need stitches."

I wanted to vomit over the side. "What happened?" I asked, hopping on board the tender as soon as it was close enough. I pulled Mia's shoulder back so I could see Cal. Blood streamed from a cut near his hairline, and a bruise was blooming on one of his cheekbones.

"Baby, shit," I said, crouching down and reaching for his face. "Are you okay? What happened?"

I pulled off my T-shirt and used it to wipe the blood away from his eye. Cal reached for my wrist, and I noticed his hand was trembling.

"I'm okay. Just got knocked around a little."

Mia was crying. "He almost drowned. I almost couldn't reach him in time."

He glanced at her and smiled weakly. "It was only thirty-five feet deep. I would have gotten my shit together in time. I promise. It just surprised me for a minute, that's all."

"Let's get your wet suit off so you don't get cold," I said, reaching for the zipper pull. "Everyone else hop off the tender and give us some room please. Someone ask Lucas to get the first aid kit."

I helped peel the suit from his skin before pulling him up and getting an arm around his back.

"Sorry," he said. "I'm fine. Just a little shaken up and waterlogged."

"Don't apologize," I said gruffly. "C'mon, let's get you on the ship and get you cleaned up."

His hands clutched at me like he was afraid he was going to trip and fall. I took it slowly and made sure we were steady before stepping from the tender onto the ship. Julo's strong arms reached out to help.

"Lucas is waiting inside, and we have towels and a blanket," he said. "Freya is making him a hot drink."

"I'm fine," Cal muttered.

"You're not fine," I said. "You're literally bleeding from your face."

We made it up the steps to the main deck, and I practically carried him inside to the sofa where a nest of towels and blankets waited.

"This is too much," Cal said. "It's just a cut. Give me a Band-Aid."

I ignored him and led him to the towels, helping him down since he was clearly still unsteady.

"What happened?" I asked Jin, who stood there looking guilty and concerned.

"It was my fault."

Cal interrupted. "It was an accident. Don't be ridiculous."

Jin continued. "A flying fish landed in the boat and surprised me. I jumped and slipped and accidentally knocked my BC overboard right onto Cal's head. The tank was still attached."

"I didn't know about the fish," Cal said with a weak smile. "That explains things."

Jin allowed himself to grin. "Jade scooped it out and tossed it back in the water, if you can believe that."

Cal snorted softly. "No way."

I could tell he was trying to play off his pain and exhaustion, so I asked everyone but Lucas to give him some space. Even though I couldn't settle enough to sit down, I kept hold of his hand while Lucas took a look at him.

"Just a reminder, I'm a vet, not a physician," Lucas muttered, dabbing the cut on Cal's face with an antiseptic pad.

"You were an EMT in college," I reminded him.

"Only so I'd have an excuse to stay at school with my boyfriend for the summer." He shined a penlight in Cal's eyes and seemed relieved by whatever he saw. After asking him a few questions, he concluded, "If you have a concussion, it's mild. We'll wait and see how you feel after a little while. If you get dizzy or have a slow reaction time, we'll reassess. Meanwhile, this cut on your face will prob-ably be okay with butterfly bandages."

"Maybe we should take him to the hospital in Tortola just in case," I suggested. "Or I can fly him to Miami."

Cal's cheeks turned pink which was ten times better than the pale face he'd arrived with. "I don't need a hospital. I just need to lie down for a few minutes and catch my breath."

As Lucas worked on the cut, I helped Cal take a few sips of the drink Freya handed me. "It's a warm lemonade. Julo's mom swears by it."

Lucas finished and sat back. "You're going to have pain from that bruise on your cheek. I'd recommend taking ibuprofen and keeping with it till morning at least. You might try an ice pack too."

"I'm fine. Thank you for bandaging it." He moved to stand but was clearly still shaky.

"I'll help you downstairs," I said, sliding an arm around his waist and helping him down the stairs and into our stateroom.

As soon as the door was closed behind us, he turned in my embrace and planted his face in the crook of my neck, holding on to me in a surprising hug with a death grip. "Just for a second," he whis-pered. "I'm sorry."

I wrapped my arms around him and held tight. "Shh, it's okay. For as long as you need."

"Just scared me, that's all. I thought I'd pulled Mia down with me. Thank god she's okay." His voice was muffled against my skin, but it still sounded so young. He was only twenty-three. How many times would he have had a scary moment like this in his past? Probably not many.

"It scared me too, and I wasn't even the one it happened to," I admitted softly. "When I heard you were hurt, I almost threw up."

He pulled back and sniffed. Tear tracks smudged the tops of his cheeks, and I wiped them away carefully with a thumb.

"At least I'm the one it happened to instead of Mia or Jade. They probably wouldn't have ever gone diving again."

His hair was stiff with salt, and he still had crusty spots of blood on his neck and hands.

"C'mon, let's get you rinsed off in the shower, and then you can get in bed." I took him by the hand and led him into the bathroom where I leaned into the large marble shower to turn on the water.

"I think I swallowed a gallon of seawater. I feel like I ate dead plankton." He reached for his toothbrush and started brushing while the water heated up in the shower. "I've taken my mask off underwater a million times. I've lost my regulator plenty of times. I've even done classes where all of our kit was removed and we had to find it all and redress at depth."

He rinsed and spit in the sink before turning to face me. "But I've never lost my mask and regulator while also bleeding and swallowing a stomach full of water. I honestly thought I would have handled it better."

I tried to reassure him. "It doesn't sound like you panicked. Mia said by the time she reached you, you'd found your regulator."

"Yeah, but I lost the damned mask, and it was brand-new. Might need to head back there tomorrow to look for it. I think we were only in thirty-five feet of water. Should be able to find it." He stepped closer to me and put his thumbs in the waistband of his boy shorts. I noticed his hands were still shaking.

"Forget the mask," I snapped, reaching out to pull him close again. "I don't care about the mask. I care about you."

Cal's eyes widened. "I'm fine. I told you. Accidents happen."

He was right. Thankfully, he didn't verbalize the fact I was overreacting, but I still felt the truth of it in the room like a heavy fog. I was overwhelmed with feelings of panic and the need to protect him— feelings I had no business or interest in having. Why did my heart always race ahead of my brain?

"Right, well..." I cleared my throat and let go of him, making sure the towel was within easy reach for when he finished. "Wash up and call me if you need me."

Cal gave me a sweet smile. "Need you to wash my back, maybe?"

Yes, please.

"This marble floor can be slippery," I said gruffly like a mean old custodian. I exited the bathroom before saying anything else ridiculous or inappropriate.

While he showered, I pulled out some clean boxer briefs and a T-shirt for him to wear. I closed the window blinds and lowered the lights. Nat knocked on the door to check on him and bring us some bottles of water and a little basket of candies.

"Thanks," I murmured. "He's taking a shower."

"Julo says sugar is good for shock." Nat's eyes were full of worry. "Mia said the accident was really bad. He started sinking like a rock, and Mia swam like hell after him hoping to at least grab his leg or something. I guess he finally got his regulator enough to take a breath, but then he made Mia go slow back up. Jin hopped in the water to see what was taking them so long. He thought the worst had happened, and he's still shaken up."

"Tell him he didn't do anything wrong. And he did great keeping a level head and getting everyone back here safely."

She nodded and let out a breath. "That's what I told him. He said poor Cal was pale as death and vomiting up seawater. When he saw the blood too, Jin almost panicked."

"But he didn't. He handled it well."

Nat bit her lip. "Is he okay? Really?"

I pulled my sister into a hug. She was a kind person who cared about others. Even though she hadn't gone into a caring profession like Lucas, she had the same big heart. "He'll be okay. I think once he naps for a couple of hours, he'll be able to join us for dinner on schedule."

"Okay, but if not, we'll bring you guys a tray. Don't push it."

Once she left, Cal poked his head out of the bathroom. "Can I come out?"

I handed him the stack of clothes, and he ducked back in to get dressed. When he came back out, I noticed a red scrape on his leg I hadn't noticed before.

"What happened here?" I asked, smoothing my hand along his calf.

"Oh, I'm not sure. I think I might have brushed up against a coral formation on the way down. Hopefully it wasn't fire coral."

I pulled back the covers and followed him into the bed.

"You giving me a pity snuggle?" he teased in a voice heavy with fatigue.

"Mm-hm. I want to hold you to make sure you don't get into any more trouble for a while."

He chuckled. "Mm, sounds good. I like snuggling with you. And this bed is the best."

Cal drifted off before he even finished talking, and I was grateful for it. I hoped like hell he'd feel better when he woke up, but in the meantime, I enjoyed every minute of holding on to him.

He smelled like my shower gel again, and his wet hair stood off his scalp in damp spikes that tickled my chin. I rubbed my hands up under his T-shirt and along the smooth skin of his back, feeling the tiny bumps of his spine and the bony wings of his shoulder blades.

I wanted to protect him. I had a fierce, visceral need to wrap him up and keep him safe. Just thinking about him taking in a mouthful of water while sinking underwater made me feel jittery and fearful in a way I'd only ever felt before one time. A nanny had left Nat and Lucas alone at a park once when they were four. A stranger had found them and called the police, and the police had somehow tracked me down at boarding school after Nat had told them that their brother, Jonathan Worthington, went to a sleepaway school that had a sign with an orange bell on it.

Thinking of my brother and sister alone in a Chicago park had overwhelmed me with fear and the constant, buzzing anxiety of "what if" thoughts. Thinking of Cal sinking down on the reef without his mask or regulator gave me the same sense of impotent worry. What if it had ended differently? What if they'd been moored over a deeper spot? What if there hadn't been anyone left in the water to go after him? What if he hadn't been so well trained on helping himself?

"I'm fine," he murmured in his dozing state. "Stop."

"You reading my mind?" I asked softly, running fingers through his drying hair and kissing the top of his head.

"Your body is so tense." He didn't open his eyes, but he snuggled even closer. "Relax with me."

"I..." I wanted to tell him I was having feelings. I wanted to ask him to be more careful. I wanted so badly to ask him if I could just hold on to him a little longer until I felt steadier again.

"I'm relieved you're okay," I said instead. "*So* relieved." My voice sounded odd in my ears.

His eyes blinked open, and his forehead crinkled as he peered up at me. His face looked sleepy and sweet. The bandage near his hairline made my heart flip around like I imagined the flying fish had when it had landed in the boat. "Jon?" he asked.

I couldn't think straight. My brain was swirling with a million thoughts, and my lips itched to press against his like maybe it was the only thing that would reassure me he was here with me and fine.

"I..." I said again, stupidly. My throat was thick with indecision. "Can I... can... *fuck*."

I leaned in and tasted him, trying to keep the kiss soft and light so as not to hurt him. Cal let out a soft sound of surprise but didn't move away. Instead, he inhaled through his nose and surged forward, deepening the kiss and bringing a hand up to cup the back of my head.

We kissed like we were desperate for it, like one of us was the sun and the other a sunflower stretching its neck to get as much warmth as possible.

Within seconds, Cal was squirming on top of me, shifting over until his knees landed on either side of my hips and the hardening ridge of his dick pressed into my stomach.

"You're hurt," I said against his lips.

"Don't you dare," he warned, tightening the hold he had on the back of my head.

I stopped fighting it and let myself feel. The weight of his body on mine. The scratch of his whiskers against my cheek. The gentle thrusts of his cock against my stomach.

And the utter certainty that this was going to end in disaster.

13

CAL

I couldn't believe Worth had kissed me, had let his moment of weakness actually turn into something physical. After all of the walls and barricades he'd erected, he'd actually succumbed to this obvious attraction that had been sparking between us.

It was un-fucking-believable. Every brush of his lips against mine made me want more... harder, deeper... just... *more*.

"Please," I heard myself beg. I'd take anything from him. *Anything*.

Worth grabbed my ass and squeezed. Soft curses fell from his lips between kisses. Finally, he pulled back and sucked in a much-needed breath.

"You're hurt," he said again.

"Not hurt," I argued. "Horny." It wasn't an accurate description of what I was feeling, but I hoped it at least got the message across.

Worth cupped the sides of my neck. "You need to rest. We should—"

I didn't want him going down the responsible-adult path. "We should fuck. I sleep so well after an orgasm." Score one for me for being so reasonable.

Worth's eyes widened. "You could be concussed."

"I'm not. Besides, what better way to celebrate being alive than with sex?" I countered.

"This would complicate things," he warned. "We weren't... we weren't supposed to..."

We stared at each other while a million words seemed to pass unsaid between us.

"Please," I whispered again. "I want you. I want you to touch me and kiss me and put your fingers inside me and then fuck me hard. Or soft. Or both. I've wanted you from the moment you got bossy with me that first night."

He continued to stare at me as my words sped up his breathing. His face finally cracked a smile. "Why doesn't it surprise me that you enjoyed being bossed around?"

I leaned in and kissed him again, moving from his lips down to the square angle of his jaw and down his neck. "Let me suck you off."

"No," he said firmly. "You're going to lie back and stay still."

Worth nudged me off him and onto my back on the rumpled duvet. I had to admit to myself that sinking back into the mattress felt amazing. He turned on his side and slid a hand under my T-shirt. I sucked in a breath. My dick tented my boxers until the elastic waist was almost pulling away from my skin. When his hand skimmed along my stomach, I groaned and leaned back, closing my eyes and savoring every touch. I didn't know much about Jonathan Worthington, but I knew for certain he would come to regret hooking up with me. So I needed to enjoy every moment of his attention while I had it.

He pushed up my shirt and leaned in to drop an openmouthed kiss along my happy trail. I gasped and pressed my hips up, but Worth's arm came down across my hips to keep me still.

"No moving." His voice was gruff, and it made me a little giddy.

"Oh god," I breathed as his chin brushed the tip of my cock through the cotton. "Oh god, please. Please."

"Shhh. Patience. There's no rush."

Part of me wanted to ask him why he was suddenly open to having sex with me. Surely, it wasn't the diving accident, was it? Why would that have made him more interested in having sex with someone he'd already judged as too young, too beneath him?

His hand came up to brush against my balls, and I realized I didn't care why. Only *when*.

"Touch me," I begged. "Now."

"Mm" was his only answer. He continued teasing me with one hand while pushing the shirt up with the other and kissing along my chest until he reached my nipples. I suddenly realized I could help, and I ripped my T-shirt off, nearly knocking him in the chin.

"Fuck, sorry." Before I waited for his response, I shimmied out of my boxer briefs too, just in case.

Worth's eyes nearly bugged out of his head. "Jesus fuck."

I settled back on the bed again. "Better without the clothes. Go back to what you were doing."

He tilted his head at me. "Who's in charge here?"

"Oh, right. You. Super you. Go. Go back to taking charge." I winked at him. "I'll allow it."

He grumbled as he leaned down and buried his nose in the crevice between my sac and my thigh. I put my hands on his head and felt the silky thickness of his hair. If sex Jesus was listening, I hoped he thought I deserved a treat.

I bit my lips to keep from begging again. I'd begun to think maybe that slowed Worth down, and I wanted to figure out what sped him up.

He nuzzled my balls and then dragged his beard scruff along my skin. I could already smell the faint traces of his sweat from earlier in the day, and I wanted more of it. I wanted to inhale his armpits and lick every inch of his chest hair. He was the sexiest man I'd ever hooked up with, and I wanted everything with him.

His voice was rough, and I felt his hot breath against my dick. "You're so fucking sexy. Sleeping with you every night and not being able to make you come is killing me. I want to put my hands on you, strip you naked, and put my tongue on you." He licked a hot trail up my dick and brushed a finger against my hole. "I lie there every night and imagine fucking your ass into the mattress. I think of what it would feel like to have this tight hole squeezing my cock."

Old man had dirty talk game. I swallowed a puddle of drool. "Uh-huh. That. Let's do that."

He chuckled before sucking my dick into his mouth and wrapping his tongue around it like a vine.

"Holy fuck! Yes. Fuck, *fuck*." I howled, gripping his hair harder than I'd intended. "Oh suck that dick. Please. Fuck. Suck it. Just like that." The man was a miracle worker with his mouth. I couldn't remember the last time someone had made me feel like swallowing my own tongue.

Worth's hands explored everywhere while his mouth took me apart. He plucked my nipples, squeezed my shoulders and biceps, kneaded my ass cheeks, and finally, he pressed a long finger into my mouth before working it into my hole and using it to push me over the edge.

After an embarrassingly short time, I shouted out my release and came in his throat. When the spots disappeared from the edges of my vision, I was still heaving in breaths like I'd run a marathon.

Worth's head rested on my thigh, and he was shaking like he was laughing. Just before I complained to him about making fun of me, I realized he was jacking off. I jackknifed up so I could watch. His fat, ruddy dick shuttled through his hand, and the muscles in his back and shoulders flexed under his skin. Within seconds, some of his hot spunk landed on my foot and leg.

"Shit that was hot," I whispered.

Worth angled his head to face me. The dazed look of satisfaction looked so good on him. I tried pulling him up for a kiss, but he shifted my arms away so he could push up on his own.

"Lie back down," he said. I obeyed immediately. Worth leaned down and kissed me more deeply than before. The muffled sounds of our mutual pleasure, hums and soft gasps here and there between swollen lips, filled the room for a long while.

When Worth finally pulled away, he stared down at me. This was probably the moment when he would gently admit what a mistake we'd made by hooking up.

"I just came harder than I have in months, and yet... I still want to fuck you like a damned animal."

I blinked at him. That was unexpected.

"Okay?" I did a mental survey of my anatomy to assess my preparedness. Oh, who was I kidding? I was game at the drop of a hat. This hot daddy could have me whenever and wherever he wanted. "That was supposed to be, 'okay.' Statement, not question," I clarified.

The laugh lines deepened next to his eyes, making him impossibly more handsome. "Good to know. But this time I really am going to insist you rest."

"But you'd like to add a rain check to that statement? Okay. I accept."

Worth leaned down and kissed me again, softly this time. I cupped his face and held him there, afraid that he'd pull back and end my lazy exploration of his mouth too soon.

"I can't get enough," he whispered.

"Keep trying," I teased. We continued making out until I finally drifted off to sleep with my face on his chest and his fingers dragging up and down my spine.

When I woke up a little while later, Worth was on his computer again.

"That's a buzzkill," I said before I could stop myself.

He swiveled in the chair and looked me over as if searching for a health status meter like the kind on video game characters. "How are you feeling?"

"Much better. Did you and the twins have your meeting while we were gone?"

"What? Oh, yes. Fine. But, listen, I was doing some research about concussions and wanted to ask if you have ringing in your ears, blurry vision..."

As he continued to name other symptoms, I stared at him in disbelief and a strange kind of dawning horror.

I liked him. Like... really, really liked him. Troublesome levels of like.

My brother's words pinged around in the distance behind the roaring in my ears.

If you never listen to another word I ever say, at least remember this: never trust a rich older man trying to get into your pants. They're manipulators and users.

Surely he didn't mean Worth though. Right?

"It's happening, isn't it?" Worth asked, crinkling his forehead in concern.

Yes. Yes, it was happening. I was falling for a rich older man against my better judgment. And if he wanted in my pants, I wasn't sure I cared why.

He stood up. "The ringing in your ears. I'm going to tell Vin to take us to Tortola. Hang tight."

It took me a second to realize what he was saying. I squawked, "No! No ringing. I promise."

"Okay, but... you kind of look like something's wrong in your head."

If he only knew.

"Maybe," I admitted. "But it's not a concussion. I promise."

He studied me for a beat before blowing out a breath. "Okay. We'll keep observing you. The websites all said symptoms can occur in the first seven to ten days."

"I wasn't hit hard enough for a concussion."

"You have a horrible bruise on your cheek. You were hit square on the face."

The little divot of worry between his eyes made me irrationally happy. He cared. About *me*.

"I promise. Can we get back to the part where you had your hands and mouth on my dick, please?"

Jonathan Worthington blushed. "That was nice."

I barked out a laugh. "That's like saying this multimillion-dollar ship is nice."

His expression turned to one of teasing as he came closer. "It is though, isn't it?"

I nodded. "Yep. Super nice. *Really* nice."

He leaned over and kissed me. My lips were raw from all of the kissing we'd already done as well as the scrape of his stubble, but I wasn't about to let it stop me from getting more of his kisses.

"It's getting close to dinnertime. Do you want to eat with everyone upstairs or stay in our room?"

Was it silly that I kind of loved hearing him call it our room? Maybe I had a Cinderella complex of some kind, but that was okay. I'd allow myself to live the fantasy for the rest of this week without second-guessing it too much.

"Let's go upstairs. I don't want everyone to think I'm worse than I am." I shot him a pointed look, and he scoffed.

"Fine. But no alcohol."

"Yes, Daddy," I said. And I enjoyed every bit of the growl he gave me in response.

"I'm just saying, it's awfully convenient that—" Pres stopped talking as soon as I appeared at the top of the stairs. He and Lucas sat at the dining room table while Julo bustled around behind the galley counter.

Lucas's face lit up when he saw me. "How are you feeling?"

"Much better, thank you."

Worth moved around me to pull out a seat at the table. I noticed this time he didn't choose to seat me near Prescott. Instead, he put me right next to his own seat and immediately took my hand in his when he sat down.

Julo brought us tall glasses of ice water and stayed to refill Lucas and Prescott's wineglasses with the bottle that had been resting in a nearby ice bucket.

Lucas took a sip and swallowed. "Good. I'm so glad. I'm really looking forward to seeing Peter Island later this week, especially after you told me about the Hobie Cats. Do you think you'll be up for showing me how to sail one?"

"I can show you," Worth said quickly. "Cal can sit on the beach and watch."

I squeezed his hand and chuckled. "He's talking about three days from now. I'll be fine. We'll be sailing in easy swimming depth. If I fall off, one of the island's drink servers can haul me in."

Nat and Jin joined us, followed by Mia and Jade. Once I'd answered a million versions of "Are you sure you're okay?" Julo began serving us some appetizers.

We talked about sailing and windsurfing. Jin mentioned wanting to practice paddleboarding since the water in Deadman's Bay was nice and smooth for it. Suddenly, Lucas changed the subject.

"Prescott heard from his boss today."

"Coworker," Pres corrected.

"Sorry. Coworker. She said there was an announcement today that they're laying off eighteen percent of the paralegal staff."

"Eighteen percent of the entire firm, darling," he corrected again.

"Anyway," Lucas continued, obviously fighting back frustration, "he might need to find a new job. He said JAC has a listing on their website in the legal department."

I felt Worth's hand tighten, and I sensed his entire body still in his seat. "Oh? I'm sorry to hear that, Prescott. As for JAC, I'm not up to speed on the open head count at that level."

Worth took another bacon-wrapped scallop off his small plate and popped it into his mouth. I wondered if he was using the appetizer to stall for time.

Meanwhile, Nat smiled at Prescott. "I'm so sorry, Pres. I know a law firm in the city that might be hiring. I can send you the website and put you in touch with HR."

Considering she was now co-owner of JAC with her brother, it was a strong statement about what she thought of the idea of him applying to JAC.

Worth nodded. "Good point, Nat. I could also reach out to Hank Nissing and see if their legal department needs anyone. Since they buy office space all over the world, it's a great place for commercial real estate law experience. I'm not sure JAC would be as good a fit since it's not involved in much real estate business."

I couldn't believe the gall of asking for a job the very evening his boyfriend took ownership of the company. Worth was most likely brimming with anger. I leaned over and kissed below his ear. "Steady," I breathed.

He exhaled and turned to catch my mouth with his for a soft kiss. I felt my face heat immediately. Somehow, it was different now that I knew it wasn't all for show. Or at least, I hoped it wasn't all for show anymore.

Mia clapped her hands together. "Oh my gosh! I forgot to tell you guys that I got asked to sing the national anthem at a football game next month. Well, it's really my friend Neil, but they want it to be a duet, so he picked me. Awesome, right?"

Everyone tittered over her news and congratulated her as Julo cleared the appetizer dishes and began to serve a plated dinner of jerk chicken served with beans and rice. It was close enough to a comfort meal that I wondered if he'd made it special after I'd gotten hurt. His other meals had been noticeably fancier than this simple, but delicious, fare.

At some point Jade had disappeared downstairs, and when she came back up to take her seat, she said we'd left music on in our bedroom.

"'*Who Let The Dogs Out*'—really, Worth? That must be Cal's influence," she teased.

"Shit, that's my grandfather." I glanced at Worth. "Can I... I mean, I don't want to be rude but... I never called them yesterday, and they're probably worried."

The look on his face was easy and indulgent as if he was no longer holding back quite so much around me. I didn't know if it was another part of the pretend relationship persona or if it was real, but I wasn't going to look a gift horse in the mouth. "Go ahead. Take your time."

I made my way downstairs and noticed two missed calls. As soon as I got Grandpa on the phone, I let out a big breath in a whoosh of relief.

"Hey," I said. "I'm sorry. Things are nuts down here."

"You sound good for being dead," Grandpa said. "And I appreciate that the afterlife has cell coverage because I always wondered."

Doc's voice came over the speaker. "Cut that out and give me the phone."

"I will not," Grandpa said. "Back off, Dr. Wilde. I will speak to the ghost of grandsons past."

I closed my eyes and lay back on the cool bedding while I let their familiar banter sink into me and fill me with the comforts of home. This beat chicken and rice any day of the week.

"I miss you guys," I admitted.

"Then come home," Grandpa said. "Grump went missing the other night, and we found him curled up in your bed under the covers. It's a sign."

"Oh for heaven's sake," Doc muttered. "It was the only place the air-conditioning was still working after the other unit went kaput."

"I got another job," I said. "Well, sort of. I'm... kind of hired on as a preliminary test week before the real interview. It's hard to explain. It's a yacht with a first mate who's expecting a baby soon."

The silence on the other end of the line was heavy with unspoken words, so I rushed to fill it. "You should see this ship, guys. It's a Sunseeker Ocean Club Ninety, and it's kitted out like you wouldn't believe."

"A motor yacht," Doc said. "Interesting."

"It's gorgeous," I said, as if pretty made up for the lack of sails.

"I'm sure it is, sweetheart," Grandpa said affectionately. "And if it makes you happy..."

"Major," Doc warned. "We talked about this. Stop being so understanding, dammit. Cal, we think it's time to come home. You've been hiding long enough. It's time to come up with a new plan. A new dream. And we can help you."

I knew he was right about the hiding, but I still couldn't bring myself to face Hobie now that the dream of taking over the sailing school was lying trashed in the gutter.

"I think this will be good," I said instead. "The crew is really nice, and the owner is... also really nice."

Excellent. I was doing great with the convincing.

"That's... nice," Doc said with a smile. "Really... nice."

I sighed and threw my arm over my face. "I'm not ready to come home."

"You're going to have to face Annie at some point," Grandpa said softly.

"I know. I just... if she realizes how upset I am by this, she'll get upset too. And I don't want that."

"Her family might sell for the right price," Doc said, not for the first time. "We could loan you—"

I cut off the conversation we'd already had a million times. "I don't want a loan. I want to buy the business outright. I just need to do some more work first and be patient. I'll come up with the money eventually if I play my cards right." I threw a bunch of stupid idiomatic language at them to sound more hopeful than I was. The reality was that it would take years of working and saving before I could offer to buy the camp. And by then, there was no telling what would be left of it.

Grandpa cleared his throat. "Your mother and father called."

Shit.

"They think you should come to Singapore for a visit. They have the national sailing team, and your father knows someone who—"

"No," I said through clenched teeth. "I'm not going to live with Mom and Dad and have Dad introduce me to his rich friends. I've told him that a million times. Besides, I have no interest in corporate-sponsored racing."

"Told you," Doc muttered to Grandpa. "He gets this from you, you know. The stubbornness."

"The stubbornness, as you call it, has kept me with an ornery partner for a million years. If I was quick to give up, where would we be? Huh? Tell me that."

"I love you," I inserted into the middle of their marriage quibble. "I love you both so much."

Apparently, I was feeling emotional.

Grandpa paused. "Sweetheart, are you okay? You sound... some kind of way."

I felt my chin begin to wobble. It was probably a side effect of being parented and being reminded of how much I was loved. "I'm okay. I just... I'm..." I took a breath and tried to figure out how I was feeling. They'd always been good about encouraging us to feel our feelings and communicate them. "I'm so grateful to have you, and I'm so thankful that you let me stay in Hobie when Mom and Dad moved away."

I heard Doc whisper an *Oh shit, Wes,* in the background, and Grandpa shushed him softly before coming back on. "We would do anything for you and your siblings. You know that, right? Anything at all. We love you more than we could ever tell you in this lifetime."

A tear escaped and I nodded. "Yeah. I know." I swallowed and finally admitted the real problem. "I'm scared."

"Oh, honey," Doc said. "It's okay to be scared of change. And it's okay to have to start over with a new plan. Do you think your grandpa ever imagined giving up flying helicopters to muck out stalls and raise cattle in rural Texas?"

"You mean I had a choice?" Grandpa teased. I could picture them in the farmhouse kitchen where Grandpa had most likely swatted Doc's ass.

"Things don't always turn out the way we imagine, but that doesn't mean they don't turn out amazing," Doc continued. "Come home and let us help you find your amazing."

I pictured the pink and orange sunrise glowing warmly along Worth's skin as he took his first sips of morning coffee on the deck with pillowcase creases still on his cheeks and the scent of our bodies tangled together still in my nose. Was I more enamored with the stunning Caribbean setting or with the man who made it feel like a dream?

"What if it's not in Hobie?" I whispered. "What if it's somewhere else?"

They were silent again for a few beats. "Then your grandfather will renew his pilot's license so we can fly to wherever you are," Doc said. "Do they give pilot's licenses to people born in the eighteen hundreds? We'll have to look into that. If not, I guess we could always fly commercial," he said as if the very idea was beneath him.

I laughed. "I want what you two have," I said out loud, not for the first time. And because I'd said it so many times over the years, I knew their response well enough to quote it verbatim.

"Give it time. You're still young," they said in unison.

"Pfft. Never mind, then. I'll keep sleeping around." I waited for their groans which came right on cue.

"You sound like your cousin Jack," Doc muttered. "He's having a love affair with his Grindr app, and it's unhealthy."

I threw my sister under the bus. "You know Hallie uses Tinder, right? She's on it all the time."

"Lalalalala! Don't say things like that," Grandpa said. "My heart can't take it. My precious girl."

"And don't get me started on Sassy," I said, even though it wasn't true. She was pretty low-key when it came to the dating scene.

"Now I know you're lying," Doc said. "My baby girl would never do such a thing."

"I have to go. I left a nice dinner on the table to call you back. Will you tell everyone I said hey?"

"Of course. We love you. Stay safe and tell us when you're coming home, okay?" Doc's voice was tinged with worry which was less typical of him than Grandpa.

"I will. Just... just give me some time. Um... if you see Annie, will you tell her I'm okay?"

Grandpa was the one who answered this time. "We haven't seen her in a while, but we'll tell her."

When I returned upstairs, Worth stood and pulled my chair back for me. As soon as I got close, he cupped my cheek and frowned at me. "Were you crying?" he asked softly, running a thumb under one eye. "Are you all right?"

I stepped into him for a hug and let out a breath when his arms wrapped around me automatically. I was getting way too used to this. "It's fine. Just... you know. Family."

"Is everyone okay at home?"

"Yeah. I just haven't been back in a while, you know?"

Nat's voice was laced with concern too. "Cal, is something wrong?"

I pulled back and smiled at her as I took my seat at the table. "Nope. Everything is fine. Thanks. Is anyone up for learning how to play water pong later? Worth said I could be in charge of the entertainment if I was a good boy and took my nap." I shot Worth a flirty look. "I was a good boy, wasn't I, Jon?"

His face turned bright red, but instead of sputtering a denial, he laughed. "You certainly were."

14

WORTH

WE DIDN'T END UP PLAYING A GAME, BUT WE DID MOVE OUT ONTO THE deck sofas and chairs after dinner and spent several hours talking and laughing over a few more bottles of wine. Cal curled up next to me on the love seat, and I reached an arm out to pull him even closer. As the night wore on, I realized I hadn't felt this relaxed in a long time.

"We need to make a point to do this more often," Lucas said at one point. "I didn't realize how much I needed to get away."

Mia nudged his leg with her foot. "You've been in school for a million years. Of course you needed a break."

Cal asked Lucas what he was doing now that he had his degree. "Did you get a placement at a clinic?"

He shook his head. "I'm actually spending a year in a surgery internship at a local animal charity in Chicago. We travel around doing free sterilizations and things like that. I'm considering an anesthesia specialty, but my mentor suggested this first."

Mia sat forward with a smile and a rosy glow from the sun and wine. "Tell him about the pregnant cat."

Lucas chuckled. "A woman made an appointment for her rescue cat to be spayed, but when she arrived at the clinic for the appointment, the cat was clearly pregnant. Like round enough to pass for a basketball, pregnant. Sure enough, we didn't even get her to the back of the office before she started giving birth. Ten kittens. God, they were cute."

Mia laughed. "Tell them about the goat."

Prescott's head tilted at her. "How do you know all of this?"

Mia waved her hand in a dismissive gesture. "From Friday lunches. You'd know if you ever joined us."

Pres looked at Lucas. "I thought you met Nat for lunch on Fridays."

Lucas looked confused by the question. "I do. Nat, Mia, Jade, and sometimes Jin if he can swing it. Oh, and sometimes Brady too." He turned to Cal. "That's the surgeon I work with. Great guy. Super talented."

Prescott muttered something under his breath about Dr. Perfect. I didn't mind seeing him jealous, but his peevishness made me wonder for the hundredth time what my brother saw in him.

Cal shot Pres a look that quickly turned into sticky treacle. "Prescott, why don't you meet them for lunch too? Do you work farther away?"

If looks could kill, Cal would have been a chalk drawing on the floor.

"I work through lunch," Prescott said.

Jade snapped a few pictures of the group with her phone. "I want to get some pictures tomorrow on the beach. Maybe get the three siblings together for some of them. I know Nat would love to have a photo of her with her brothers."

Nat nodded. "And the couples."

Cal shifted against me and lifted his head up to meet my eyes. He looked half-asleep already even though he hadn't had any wine. "I think I'm going to go to bed."

I leaned down and kissed his soft lips. The scrape of his whiskers teased my cheek, reminding me of the breath he'd sucked in when I scraped my own stubble on his inner thighs earlier tonight. He'd been so responsive, so fucking sexy.

I met his eyes. "I'll be down in a bit and I'll bring you some ice water. Need anything else?"

He leaned closer to my ear. "Just you." His voice was so heavy with sleep, I almost laughed. There would be no fooling around with him in this state which was fine by me. I was pretty damned happy to sleep with him even if all we were doing was actually sleeping.

I lifted his hand and kissed it before letting him go. He waved good night to everyone else and promised to be himself again in the morning.

Once he was gone, Jade was the one who gave me a knowing look. "He's the one."

"The one of what?" I asked, reaching for my wineglass.

"The one as in the *one*," she repeated.

"Your soul mate," Mia added with jazz hands.

Natalia laughed. "Stop, you're scaring him. Look at his face. He's gone pale."

"Don't be ridiculous," I said, glancing at Prescott to see his reaction. Other than flaring his nostrils, he remained still. "He's a kid."

"He's a sweetheart," Lucas offered. "And sexy as hell."

Prescott scoffed and stood up to go inside for a refill.

Lucas laughed. "You can't deny the truth. I think he's good for you too."

"I'm not in the market for a serious relationship," I reminded everyone.

"And yet..." Nat studied me. "Sometimes good opportunities come along when you're not in the market. I believe that's what my famous venture capitalist brother would say."

She was right, but that advice wasn't relevant to... soul mates.

"Anyway," I said, desperate to change the subject, "what about focusing on the other singles here. Jade, do we need to find you a soul mate this week? Mia, what about you? My sister has plenty of energy to put into this."

Jade didn't look up from her phone. "No, thanks. I'm what you call a free spirit."

Mia, meanwhile, blushed deep pink and blinked back and forth between me and Nat. "What? Me? No. What?"

Curious. I wondered if Mia had a crush on my sister.

Lucas nudged Nat's shoulder where they sat next to each other on the sofa. "Save your poor friend."

Nat laughed. "She's a big girl. And if Mia wanted a soul mate, there would be an entire arena full of men to volunteer."

Mia covered her face. "Stop. Please."

Lucas laughed. "I think this is one of those 'dish it but can't take it' things."

Mia grinned at him. "I think we should put you under the hot lamps. Why haven't you two set a date yet?"

"We're trying. But my schedule isn't very flexible right now. The only reason I was able to take this week is because Brady went to Maine to help his parents with a construction project." The breeze off the water curled a piece of his hair around his ear. "Pres keeps reminding me it's a volunteer gig and I can leave anytime. But he doesn't understand it's important in getting the recommendations I need for wherever I want to go next."

I glanced inside but couldn't see Prescott. If he was in the bathroom, I had enough time to ask my question without inadvertently starting something between Lucas and Pres. "Does he know who's behind the charity you work for?"

Jade's eyes blinked up from her phone. "Oooh, scandal alert."

Nat and Mia shushed her at the same time. Jin took another sip of wine.

Lucas narrowed his eyes at me. "No, and he's not going to."

I held my hands up in surrender. "It won't come from me. But you have to know you can get whatever time off you need when it's your foundation that runs the charity."

"Brady doesn't know that," Lucas reminded me. "And I refuse anything that requires special treatment." He looked around to make sure Pres wasn't in hearing distance. "If Pres knew, he'd make a fuss and insist on setting a date for the wedding. He's losing his patience."

"That's not fair," Mia said. "Besides, what's the rush? You already live together."

Lucas looked down at his hands, suddenly fascinated with a cuticle.

"Wait. You do live together, right?" Mia asked. "Pres mentioned the wine cellar thing."

"I mean... we pretty much live together," Lucas said. "It's just that... with everything happening with graduating and starting work, I haven't exactly been able to take time..."

His words faded out as something in my brain finally clicked, reminding me about the other night when Prescott finally got Cal alone and confronted him. Pres was nowhere to be seen inside, and he'd been gone too long for a simple bathroom break. I knew Cal could hold his own against the pushy asshole, but I also knew Cal was tired and hurt.

"Excuse me," I murmured. "I'm going to check on Cal."

As I walked inside, I heard all of them tease me about my devotion to "the kid." I grabbed a couple of bottles of water from the galley fridge and noticed Julo had already cleaned everything up and set out some things for his breakfast prep in the early morning. I could hear him and Freya talking softly from the direction of the bridge where I knew Freya would be keeping watch even though it was unnecessary while we were safely moored in the bay.

When I got to the stairs, I was relieved to see Prescott coming up. "Good night," I said as I passed him.

"Hey, Worth," Pres said, reaching out to stop me. "I wanted to thank you for earlier."

I racked my brain to figure out what he was referring to. "Earlier?"

"When you said you might be able to connect me to a job lead. That was generous of you. Thank you."

I was taken aback by his gratitude. "Oh... well, certainly. I hope you find something you enjoy."

He nodded. "I appreciate it. See you in the morning."

When I got downstairs, I shook my head. Maybe I was overreacting about him, painting him as the villain when really he was just a run-of-the-mill guy who leaned a little too much to the selfish side.

But then I saw Cal wide-awake and spitting fire when I got to our room.

"What happened?"

"That fucker needs to go," he hissed, obviously trying to keep his voice down for propriety's sake. "He... he... argh! He's such an asshole!"

I was ready to march back upstairs and throw the man off the ship, and I hadn't even heard what he did yet.

I forced myself to sit down on the edge of the bed and clasp my hands together in my lap. "What happened?"

Cal paced back and forth. "He said I was lying to everyone about who I am and he was going to tell you the truth. Then he said he saw me selling drugs in the club the night we met? Jesus. I've never even smoked pot! I promise you I wasn't—"

I leaned forward to grab ahold of his wrist and pulled him onto my lap so he was straddling me on the side of the bed. "Hey, hey. Slow down. I know you weren't selling drugs at the club."

His face was laced with concern. "I wasn't. I promise. But how can you possibly know that?"

I smiled at him and brushed his crazy hair back from where it flopped in his face. "Because when I first met you, you'd been locked in a closet buck naked. All of your worldly belongings were on the upper deck and consisted of a pair of tight shorts, a sweaty and also tight T-shirt, rubber flip-flops, and a wallet with approximately forty-two dollars in it. Oh, and your phone which is worth more than everything else put together. Not a speck of drugs or drug money in the whole pile. Either that, or selling drugs isn't nearly as lucrative as I imagined."

He seemed to calm down a little. His body relaxed into mine. "How do you know the clothes were tight if you never saw them on me?"

I couldn't keep my hands off him. I wanted to touch him everywhere. "One has to assume," I said with a sniff. "Based on the fact you were there trolling for dick."

He pinched me in the side, and I yelped. "Just think," Cal said with a cheeky grin, "if I hadn't been trolling for dick in that club, you wouldn't have an eager man on your lap grinding on your own dick right now."

He was right, and I was already hard for him after feeling his ass brush against my cock. But I wanted to know more about his conversation with Prescott.

"What else did Pres say? And why would he have made up the thing about selling drugs?"

"I think he's trying to convince me that if and when I tell you about sleeping with him, he'll be able to easily discredit me. He also said that I was crazy if I thought sucking your dick was going to result in you hiring me."

His face turned serious, and I could immediately guess what was coming. "Don't be ridiculous," I warned before he could say it.

"No. We both know he's right. I'm officially withdrawing my request for consideration for the chief mate job. I don't want to put you in that position after everything that's happened. Besides, I need to go home after this and spend some time with my family. They're right. It's time I stop sulking and put on my big-boy pants about my future."

I wrapped my arms around him and pulled him closer. "This ship and her crew would be lucky to have you, and it has nothing to do with you sucking my dick. Especially considering you haven't even done that."

"Yet."

I grinned. "Well, I hate to assume."

Cal leaned in and kissed me. It turned hot very quickly, and Cal's grip on the sides of my face was commanding. To be honest, the young man owned me in that moment whether he realized it or not. Had he asked me for the keys to the ship, I might have handed them right over. I was putty in his hands.

"Fuck me," he said against my mouth. "Want you in me so fucking badly."

My heart thundered in my chest, and my cock throbbed. "You're too tired," I said stupidly.

"Not."

"We shouldn't," I said with my hand inside the waistband of his pants. I slid my middle finger down between his cheeks to brush against his hole. I wanted to fuck him even though I was trying to be the better person and let him rest.

"We should," he corrected, reaching for the hem of my shirt to pull it over my head. "We really, really should."

I yanked his shirt off too, since he was going to have to get undressed for bed anyway. All of the skin revealed once it was gone made me salivate. I dropped a kiss on his shoulder and spread my hands across his back.

"I like that you're so small," I admitted. "Makes me want to throw you down and do naughty things to your body."

"Oh fuck yeah. Yes. Please." Cal's breaths were coming faster, and his nipples were hard. I leaned down to take one between my teeth. "Throw me down. Do naughty things," he said between noisy breaths.

I reached down to flick open his shorts before standing him up and shucking them down. Thankfully, that had the unintended side effect of presenting me with his dick at mouth level. I leaned in and sucked the tip into my mouth.

"A service top," he said, sucking in a breath. "I'll take it."

I ran my hands over the rounded cheeks of his ass. Cal's arms wrapped around my head, and his fingers dragged through my hair. He smelled like the sea, fresh lemons he'd squeezed in his water earlier, and the faintest traces of my own cologne. Smelling my scent on him made me feel savagely possessive and satisfied.

I moved up to tongue his belly button. He had the hottest happy trail of any man I'd ever seen. I dragged my stubbled chin down it to the top of his pubic hair and mouthed his dick again. Cal cursed under his breath before pulling my head back and leaning down for a kiss.

"My turn to suck you," he said. "Lie back. Get those clothes off."

He moved past me to crawl onto the bed. His pale butt flashed in the dim light of the bedroom, so I leaned over to nibble on it. He yelped and laughed, pulling away from me.

"Strip, Jon," he said. "Show me that old-man dick."

"I just lost my erection," I lied. "Try again."

"Nope. I decided as long as you keep judging me for my age, I'm going to judge you for yours. Show me those middle-aged balls."

I groaned. Fine, maybe he had a point.

"I'm not taking off my pants now," I said, crawling toward him. "Too bad since someone I know wanted a deep dicking."

His face was full of flirty mischief which turned me on more than I could express. "Who said anything about deep? I like it really shallow. Even better if you have a short penis. Do you have a short penis, Jon?"

I put my hand over his mouth and leaned in to bite his nipple again. The pink nub was taunting me, and I wanted to flick it with my tongue until he forgot the word penis.

My free hand spanned his rib cage, and I could feel his breaths heaving in and out of his lungs the more turned on he became. His groans heated the hand I held over his mouth, and when I went to remove it, he clutched it and held it there.

The nod to a little kink made my dick even harder. I moved up and rested my lips against the shell of his ear. "You want me to keep you quiet, baby? Want me to hold you down? Maybe edge you until you can't stand it anymore?"

He squeezed his eyes closed and whimpered. Twin patches of deep pink marred his cheeks as his eyelashes brushed together. He was gorgeous. The idea that I would be able to hold back long enough to edge him was ridiculous.

I dragged openmouthed kisses down the front of his throat and onto his collarbone before teasing each of his nipples again. My dick wasn't feeling middle-aged at all. In fact, my balls felt like they could probably go for several rounds of sex tonight as long as Calgary Wilde was the man in my bed.

"You drive me crazy," I said in a hoarse voice. "The things I want to do to you make me blush. And I never blush."

"Jon," he breathed against my hand.

I reached over to the bedside table drawer and pulled out a bottle of lube and a condom. "You sure, baby?"

He narrowed his eyes at me in a threat that made me laugh. "Okay, okay. I'll take the glare as a yes." I began to strip off the rest of my clothes. Cal reached for his cock and stroked it slowly. The dark nest of curls around his dick made my mouth water, and I couldn't take my eyes away from the sexy curved muscles of his thighs.

"Eyes up here, pervert," he teased.

I felt giddy and light. Free in a way I didn't remember ever feeling before during sex. "My siblings are right. You are very funny."

I leaned down and kissed the top of his foot before moving slowly up to his ankle. Part of me wanted to spend hours cataloging every inch of him while another part of me wanted to lurch up and shove my dick into him right this second.

"Stop fucking around," he warned. "Dicks as young as mine have hair triggers."

I got to the delicious curve of his inner thigh and licked it slowly.

"Oh sweet Jesus," he muttered. "Death by thigh licking. It's a thing."

I nuzzled his sac and licked his taint. His babbling continued. "Oh... oh... ohhhh."

He smelled both clean and musky in the best way, and I was tempted to rim the hell out of him, but I wasn't sure how he'd react. I moved my mouth down toward his hole to see his reaction.

Cal's fingers clamped around my wrist and held tight. "You're killing me. I want your dick. Stop the teasing."

"I was going to rim you first. Get you ready."

"I withdraw my complaint," he choked out, reaching for the backs of his knees and pulling his legs open for me. I pushed his legs back farther and began tasting him, licking and sucking and teasing until he no longer knew how to make actual words. The sounds of desperation coming out of him made me grateful our room was separated from the others by two thick walls and a hallway.

I couldn't remember the last time I'd done this to someone. Mason hadn't liked it, and before him, I hadn't been intimate enough with my partners to want to do it. The fact I went straight to it with Cal wasn't lost on me, but I didn't want to read too much into it. It was refreshing to be with someone so responsive and enthusiastic.

I moved back up to suck his dick into my mouth when he grabbed my hair and pulled my head up to his before smashing our mouths together in a hungry kiss. Cal flipped me over in some kind of ninja move and moved down to my cock, muttering about taking charge. He licked a wide stripe up my shaft and took the head into his mouth while fumbling in the sheets for the lube and condom. Within moments he had me suited and slicked and was reaching back to lube himself.

"Jesus fuck," I breathed. "I... I was going to do that, but you—"

He smiled at me indulgently. His pupils were deep and wide, his lips red and puffy, and his hair stuck up in every direction. "Next time, boo. I appreciate everything you've done, I do. But I wasn't kidding about the hair trigger, and you're seriously the sexiest man I've ever seen naked, and if you don't get your cock in my ass pretty soon, I will nut all over you just from staring at your sexy fucking face."

He punctuated the little tirade with a hard kiss before propping himself over me and putting my dick at his hole.

Then he began to slide down.

15

CAL

Maybe I wasn't being completely honest with Worth. The truth was, he was paying me more sweet attention than any man ever had before, and it was fucking with my head. His concentrated devotion to making me feel good was giving me thoughts and feelings I had no business indulging in.

So I got us right back to the physical fucking.

Except the minute he began to enter my body, he got this awed look on his face that made my heart zing around in my chest like a kid who'd eaten too much sugar at a birthday party.

"You're so damned beautiful," he said, reaching up and cupping my cheek.

Oh hell.

I closed my eyes and concentrated on the stretch and burn. When he was finally all the way in, I began to rock up and down and grind side to side.

Worth groaned and grabbed onto my hips with strong fingers, directing the movement. My cock stood out from my body like a compass point with Worth as its true north. I wanted him so much, I was leaking all over his stomach.

I propped my hands on his chest and sat up, enjoying the view as

I fucked myself on his cock. How long had it been since I'd bottomed for someone? Two years? Three? I remembered bottoming for a guy I had a crush on in college. We'd hooked up regularly for a few weeks before he'd graduated and gotten a job out of state.

"So fucking tight," Worth hissed. "Fuck. I can't... I can't..."

He flipped me onto my back and lifted my legs up before driving his cock back into me. And then he began to fuck me in earnest. Worth's thick cock made me feel so full, but his aggression was what jacked me right to the edge of orgasm. He pounded into me, grasping my ankles in a tight grip and thrusting his hips almost like he was punishing both of us.

If it was punishment, I was going to have to revisit my list of acceptable kinks to include it.

I reached back and braced myself against the padded headboard as he railed me. He continued a litany of mumbled curses as he changed the angle and lit up my entire body with a shower of sparks.

"Oh shit," I cried, feeling the edge of my release catch. My legs trembled and I reached for my cock only to find his hand there already, squeezing and stroking as he pushed me head-first into the mother of all orgasms.

By the time my muscles finished contracting, I realized I was sweaty and panting and Worth still looked like a damned movie star.

He let my legs down gently and leaned in to kiss me softly. It was sloppy and imprecise, and everything about feeling his spent body against mine was perfect.

"Holy Christ," he said after a few moments of kissing. "Maybe you were right about me being old. I feel like I just did a triathlon."

"Ready to go again?" I asked with a straight face.

The rumble of his laugh against my chest made me grin. "You're a brat," he said. "You wore me out."

He laid his head on my shoulder and blew out a breath. My heart was taking its sweet time slowing down from the gymnastics, and I felt his thumping steadily against my side as well.

"That was..." I began, unsure of what I'd meant to say.

"Yeah."

After a few minutes, he got up and fetched a wet cloth before leaning over me to clean me up like a sweet sex valet.

"Do you think there's such a thing as a sex valet?" I asked. "Like, in history. Would a king have had someone whose sole purpose was preparing him before and cleaning him up afterward?"

"That's... a very strange idea, Cal."

"It would make a good romance novel though. Admit it."

Worth sounded sleepy when he answered. "Hallmark is going to be banging down your door to get to that idea. I'm sure of it."

"Maybe a spin-off from *The Tudors*," I mused. I drew big looping shapes over the bare skin of his back after he snuggled back against my chest.

"That's unpleasant. King Henry falling for his poor jizz servant."

I chuckled. "Ooooh. I like that. Will you call me your jizz servant from now on?"

"Not in a million years. Get some sleep, Cal. My sister is going to make you pose for pictures tomorrow."

If I could have bottled this feeling of contentment, I could have made millions. "Jon?"

"Yeah?"

"If a king—"

Worth groaned, but it had a laugh behind it too. "Baby, I can't handle these difficult questions when I'm feeling fucked out. You ruined me for conversation, so it's kind of your fault."

"Fine. You sleep, old man. You probably need your rest."

He pretended to pinch me, but I grabbed his hand and kissed his fingers. After a few more minutes of quiet, I couldn't help myself.

"A douche valet. Now there's something. Just think of how helpful *that* guy would be."

Worth smothered me with the pillow and then proceeded to kiss me so thoroughly, I forgot all about douche valets.

❧

The following two days passed in a kind of fever dream including several more rounds of mind-blowing sex interspersed with long and interesting conversations, swimming, sunning, and generally indulging in my Caribbean vacation fantasies on Cooper and Salt Islands. I was walking around like a zombie. I'd barely gotten any sleep the night before after Worth had, once again, mapped my skin with his tongue and spent hours edging me before finally fucking me into a stupor. A stupor I seemed to still be in this morning.

I mentally frolicked in the clouds all through breakfast, remembering what it was like to feel the laser focus of Worth's attention on my body. Hot memories washed over me enough to make me downright stupid.

"I would say he's hungover, but he didn't drink much last night," Nat muttered into her coffee.

"He's fucked out," Jade teased. "Look at him."

Mia laughed. "Worth, what did you do to that poor guy?"

I felt Worth's fingers in my hair. "He's just not fully awake yet, that's all."

I glanced over at him and noticed endearing imperfections. There was a stubborn lock of hair on one side of his head that refused to stand down. He'd missed a spot under his jawline while shaving. And most adorably, the barest hint of a hickey peeked out from the soft neckband of his T-shirt.

I was in a heap load of trouble. Like, big-deal terrifying trouble. I blinked at Worth's handsome face and wondered if he'd ever settle down with someone and what it would be like for that person to wake up next to him for the rest of their life.

"Oh my god, he's fucking adorable," Jade muttered, pulling out her phone and snapping a picture. The sound of the camera noise jerked me to attention. She was talking about me.

I swallowed and took a sip of my coffee before acting casual. "Am not."

Worth chuckled. "Good morning, sunshine. So good of you to join us."

I looked down at my empty plate and realized I'd scarfed down breakfast at some point. "Do you think there's more? I think I'm still hungry."

Mia stage-whispered, "I think he means thirsty."

My cheeks heated. "For orange juice maybe."

"For man juice," Jade corrected.

Worth sputtered, and Nat made an *ew* sound.

I got up to find Julo in the galley. "What were those cinnamon things, and do you have any more of them?"

Julo lifted an eyebrow at me. "The cinnamon roll bites are on a very large platter in the middle of the breakfast table directly in front of your seat. Is that what you're looking for?"

I mumbled a thanks and made my way back to my chair. Worth stood and grabbed the back of my head, pulling me in for a kiss on the mouth before pulling out my chair for me. He tasted like cinnamon and coffee. "You are irresistibly adorable this morning," he murmured against my mouth. "Don't ever change."

After he let me go, I was even more dazed than before. I served myself a few more cinnamon bites and tried to clear my head by focusing on the conversation.

"You could help fund it, Worth. It might make a good addition to your portfolio," Lucas said.

"Fund what?" I asked. When I'd zoned out, they'd been talking about a family charity foundation and one of its projects supporting Special Olympics athletes. Hearing Worth speak with passion about helping disabled kids was one of the reasons I'd started daydreaming in the first place. The man was a surprise on all fronts.

Lucas's excitement was palpable. "There's a medical research group trying to partner with SpaceX to do some trials in space. They already have great results from experiments in zero-gravity test chambers, but there are some parameters that can only be replicated by testing them in space."

"It's a big risk," Worth said calmly.

"So only offer half," Lucas countered.

"That's still five hundred million dollars, Luc," Worth said before taking a sip of coffee. As if he hadn't just mentioned the GDP of a small country.

Maybe I was still dazed from the kiss. "I'm sorry, what?"

Worth turned to me. "They originally asked for a billion, but it's a nonstarter at this early stage in the process. Maybe if they already had preliminary FDA approval or some other indicator of..."

Blood began to roar in my ears. Was he... was he saying that his company had enough money to consider loaning someone a *billion* dollars? After already deciding to loan someone else a hundred and eighteen million?

They continued discussing it over coffee as if they were talking about loaning a friend a few bucks for a new video game. What kind of wealth did the Worthington family actually have? No. Not the Worthington family. Just Worth himself. This was his venture capital company they were talking about, not the family business.

I was out of my depth. Wasn't this the kind of money royal families had? Why hadn't it hit me until now?

My stomach started churning, and I immediately regretted all of the cinnamon bites I'd consumed. I needed help. I needed someone to tell me how to comport myself around people this rich.

A voice in my head reminded me I seemed to be doing fine so far. *They like you. I think?*

Still. What if I said something stupid? I was a country kid from rural Texas for god's sake. Surely I was going to put my foot in it at some point. Maybe the difference was... I cared more now about what they thought of me.

I thought about my brother-in-law Augie. He had big family money. But I knew if I asked him about it, he'd clam up like a little scared turtle pulling inside his shell.

Felix.

My cousin Felix would talk to me. He was married to an actual royal. He'd tell me what pitfalls to avoid.

"Excuse me," I murmured, standing up.

"You okay?" Worth asked with a crinkle of concern on his face.

I nodded. "Just forgot something I needed to talk to my family about. Be back in a few."

When I got back to the safety and privacy of the stateroom, I scrambled to bring up the secure app Felix and Lior used.

Cal: *You around? I need some advice.*

After only a couple of minutes, he responded.

Felix: *Yes. Thankfully, I am exempt from the sword ceremony this morning after the last time.*

Cal: *What happened the last time?*

Felix: *I accidentally cut off the top of an ornamental topiary thing with my sword. I didn't realize those suckers are actually really sharp, and I was trying to impress Lio with my sword fighting skills.*

That sounded just like my dorky cousin.

Cal: *You have sword fighting skills? Since when?*

Felix: *Since I chopped the shit out of an ornamental shrub like a boss. What's going on?*

I sighed and tried to figure out how to phrase my problem. Before I could come up with the words, the phone rang in my hand.

"Tell me," he said before I even had a chance to say hello.

"Bonjour, mon petit roi," I said. He hated it when the rest of us called him Little King, but since we'd all played a Wii game by that name when I was in middle school and Felix was in college, he was shit out of luck the minute he married an actual king.

"Ignoring you," he said. "Also, you're stalling. It's what you do."

I took a breath. "I met this guy," I began.

The squeal over the phone bore a hole through my brain. "Tell. Me. Everything."

"Stop. Be serious. It's not about that. He's not... I mean, it's not... this isn't a relationship guy. But I still need to ask you something."

Felix was quiet for a moment. "Why not a relationship guy? Is he straight? Married? Ooh, is he a closeted prince getting ready to become a king? Nah, probably not. That would never happen in real life."

"So, we're not being serious, I see," I muttered.

"Sorry. It's really good to hear your voice, Calgary," he said affectionately. "Tell me what you need. You know I'll help in any way I can."

His manner of speaking had changed slightly since moving to Europe. It was strange to notice it every once in a while. Felix was like a brother to me since we'd both spent so many years together at the ranch. I missed him, but I was thrilled he'd found such a wonderful life with Lior.

"It's kind of a long and weird story, but basically I'm on a yacht this week with a really wealthy family. I knew they were rich, right? The ship itself is a big fancy deal. But then I realized that they're like... Jay-Z rich."

"Okay?"

"And I feel like trailer trash by comparison," I admitted. "And I'm afraid I'm going to do something or say something that outs me as an imposter."

He chuckled warmly. "Ah, welcome to my life. I see why I was the lucky one to get your text, then."

"I hope you don't mind. I just figured you'd have the best advice for the situation."

"Of course I don't mind, but Cal... you're very easy to be around in every situation. I don't think I've ever seen you wrong-footed."

"No, but, like... I don't want to embarrass him. I'm bound to say something stupid." I paused, remembering the conversation about boxed wine. "But maybe if I just keep playing it off as a joke..."

"Embarrass whom?"

I flopped down on the bed. "The guy. The guy who owns the yacht. I'm kind of... his date this week. Sort of. Kind of. Pretend, you know?"

"Are you in some kind of trouble? Has someone paid you to be their plus-one? I once saw a movie like this. Richard Gere and those eyes..."

I soldiered on. "I'm not in trouble. Well, I kind of am in trouble because I'm starting to like him, and that's really bad."

"Why?"

I groaned. "Did you forget the part about Jay-Z?"

"Wait. Are you pretend dating Jay-Z?"

I sighed. "Is Lior there? Let me talk to him. Maybe he can help."

"He's at the sword thing. But listen. You already know what I'm going to say because it's what Doc and Grandpa would tell you. Be yourself. And if they don't like you, it's their loss. You know what else? Lior's friends and family find me adorably... provincial."

I scratched my head. "I don't think that's a compliment, Fee. It means unsophisticated. Like a country mouse."

"Yes, but an *adorable* one."

I laughed. Maybe he was right. After all, what did it matter if I was only on this ship for a few more days? I wasn't even sure what I was freaking out about. Maybe it was simply panic from learning how rich Worth truly was. That kind of money scared me. And I would never say this to him, but that kind of money made me feel young and incapable. Irresponsible somehow.

"I love you, Fee," I told him. "Thank you for always being there for me."

"I love you too. And if you do end up dating Jay-Z, will you ask him if you can borrow his plane to fly you over here for a visit? I promise you we have sailboats in the harbor you can use. Lio even said he'll give you a tour of the Liorland World Cup boat if it's here when you come."

I pictured the bright sails from the photos Felix had sent last year and practically salivated. "I need to find a rich boyfriend with an airplane. Hey, wait. You have a rich boyfriend with an airplane."

He chuckled. "Boyfriend, heh. I'll have to tell him you called him that."

After saying our goodbyes, I left the phone in the room and returned upstairs to the deck where everyone was still lounging over coffee. Worth stood and pulled out my chair. "Everything all right?"

I nodded. "Yeah. Yes." Maybe I needed to be more precise in my speech like Felix. "Affirmative."

Maybe not.

Worth's eyebrows twitched down for a second. "You sure?"

I sent him a pleading look that was meant to convey something like, *My thinker is offline, and I need a break from speaking.* He seemed to get the message because he turned back to the table and continued talking to Jade about something having to do with an environmental charity in Canada.

Once I settled in my seat, Worth reached for my hand without looking over at me. It was such a sweet gesture, I wanted to cry like a baby. Why now? Why did fate have to be so cruel as to open my eyes to the possibility of a relationship with the one person I could never have? He'd made it very clear he wasn't interested in an actual relationship. Mason had done a number on him, and he was understandably not looking to replace him anytime soon.

And clearly when he was ready, he'd want to find someone well educated and elegant. Someone who knew how to comport himself around big fancy money and la-ti-dah corporate people in Chicago. Beautiful, refined people like Jade and Jin. Hell, even Prescott Resnick seemed to know how to exist in this world.

That thought put me right into a funk. I shot him a glare across the table. Prescott fucking Resnick.

Pres's eyes widened in surprise when he caught me glaring at him. "Where did you go?" he challenged. And because I was stupid and immature, I couldn't help myself.

"Quick call with my cousin Felix. He lives in Monaco and has some kind of royal ceremony to go to tonight. I wanted to catch him before it got too late in the day because of the time difference and everything."

I let the words sink in while I reached for the carafe to pour a fresh coffee.

"Felix... Monaco..." Prescott's murmurs seemed to mirror the cogs turning in his head. When the pieces clicked into place, his eyes widened even more. "King Liorland's consort? That Felix? The gay royals?" His voice got higher with each question.

I took a sip of my coffee and nodded. Maybe that would help me seem more attractive to him. He needed to start flirting with me in front of Lucas if this plan was ever going to work before the week was out. "That one."

His eyes narrowed. "He's your cousin."

I nodded. "We grew up on the ranch together."

Captain Vin stepped outside and greeted us. "We're getting ready to pull up the anchor and motor over to Treasure Point on Norman Island so you can snorkel in the caves. We're going to the caves today to avoid the crowds that will be there tomorrow, but then we'll turn around and return to Peter Island for the rest of the day and night. If we need to change the plan, just let me know."

I hopped up and scrambled after him. "Can I help?"

He turned to face me when we got into the dim interior of the main room. "If you'd like. You're certainly under no obligation."

"Please. I'd really like to help. I'm sure Julo is busy, and Freya can boss me around verbally if she wants."

That caused the captain to crack a smile, and Julo looked up from where he was washing dishes in the galley. "Cheers," Julo said with a smile.

The captain clapped me on the shoulder. "Head to the bow and keep an eye on the lines, then. Thank you."

I was grateful to get away from the social situation and even more appreciative of the warm sun on my skin and the salt spray on my face as we got underway.

Out here on the bow of a ship, hauling lines and stowing rope, I was completely at home. I knew who I was and what I was supposed to do. My body moved through the tasks without overthinking, and the pod of dolphins that popped up beside us didn't give a shit about my manners or language.

Once the captain announced the dolphin sighting, everyone rushed to the bow to watch as I moved aft to check for any loose items back there. I continued moving around the deck, double-checking that everything loose was lashed down and there weren't any items that needed to be stowed.

It was Freya who finally called me on my bullshit.

"Pretty sure our top speed of twenty-six knots isn't going to dislodge the chaise pillows," she said with her arms over her chest. "It's the speed of traffic in a school zone."

I stood on the deck where I'd been methodically stacking all of the loose lounge pillows in a storage bench.

"Just making sure," I muttered, allowing two pillows to return to the giant chaise.

"Do you want to talk about it?"

I laughed. "Definitely not. What are you and Julo going to do when you have the baby?"

She lifted up her hands and sighed. "We don't know yet. Worth has offered for us to come work for him in Chicago if we want a more normal lifestyle."

I stared at her.

"Why do you look so shocked?" she asked with a laugh. "He's a good man."

"Is that what you want? To live in the city?"

"Not really." She moved to sit next to me on the chaise. "We'd love a change, don't get me wrong, but I'm not sure a big city is the place for us. Julo wants room to get a dog. We want a yard when the baby gets old enough to play outside."

"Would Julo move to the States? Or does he want to stay near his family?"

"Oh, no. He'd move. My family is in New Orleans, and he loves visiting there. He loves to cook. Give Julo a kitchen and hungry mouths to feed and he's happy just about anywhere."

Worth stepped down the stairs to the aft deck. "There you are. You missed the baby dolphins."

"I was having a moment," I admitted. "Of stupidity," I added.

His smile was easy. I could see why Nat and Lucas had wanted him to come here and relax. It seemed to be working. "I was going to go to the room and put on some clothes. Why don't you join me?"

I could tell from his expression it was a polite way of implying a booty call, and I was very on board with it.

"Is today Opposite Day?" I asked, taking his hand and pulling him back toward the main deck. "Because if what you really mean is you're going to the room to take *off* some clothes, I think I might be willing to go along with this plan."

16

WORTH

CAL WAS ACTING STRANGELY. I TRIED NOT TO ATTRIBUTE IT TO THE SEX, but it was hard not to. Had we made a mistake in crossing that line? I would have given up the sex if it meant returning to the easy banter we'd had before, because suddenly things were awkward.

"Which suit do you want me to wear?" he asked, moving over toward the closet when we entered the bedroom.

"You're asking me?"

His back was to me. When he shrugged, it lifted the hem of his T-shirt up his waist, revealing a clearer view of his sexy ass in tight shorts.

"I'm your... date. You might as well get some benefits from the arm candy."

His tone was flirty, but there was something off about it. "What's going on?"

He looked back over his shoulder at me. "What do you mean?"

Before I had a chance to elaborate, my phone pinged with a text from my assistant. There was movement on the deal I'd been waiting for.

"Sorry," I murmured to Cal. "I need to hop on a call for a few minutes. As for the bathing suit, I want you to wear the one that makes you the happiest."

I sat down at my computer and reached for my Bluetooth earbuds before dialing the office. The call was quick, but informative. The CEO had finally gotten the results of several studies he'd initiated to test the adoptability of the electronic paper tech, and he wanted to discuss it with me.

When I changed into my trunks and went back upstairs, I found Cal, Lucas, and Mia giggling over something on the giant lounger in the bow.

"You three sound like you're having fun," I said, propping my hip against the deck railing. It was another gorgeous day with the sun shining in a deep blue sky and almost no clouds in sight. Every time the boat dipped down into a swell, a light mist of seawater landed on my arms. It reminded me of the months I'd spent on the ship earlier this year. Every day after lunch, I'd come out here to doze in the sun and enjoy the combination of warm breeze and salty air. It was therapeutic.

Cal's eyes were full of laughter when he looked up at me. It was a relief to see him relaxed and happy, and I wondered if I'd been imagining the awkwardness earlier.

"Mia just convinced Lucas to tell me the Mr. Pickles story. I have to say, I'm impressed."

I groaned and shot my brother a look of betrayal. "How could you?"

He laughed and covered his eyes. "It's too good. You knew we'd have to tell him at some point, right?"

Cal reached out a hand to pull me closer. I took a seat on the edge of the chaise by his hip.

"I didn't know you had a green thumb," he teased. "Tell me more."

"It was one crop of cucumbers," I muttered. "An assignment for school, I think."

"One very special crop," Cal corrected. "So special that you became friends with your very first creation."

I sniffed and looked down my nose at him. "Until you've had the kind of relationship I had with Mr. Pickles, I wouldn't expect you to understand."

Freya came up to the bow to hook the mooring buoy, and, as expected, Cal scurried off the chaise to help her. I noticed he was wearing a pair of longer swim trunks today, and they hugged his ass as beautifully as everything else he wore. He also had on a long-sleeved rash guard which made me silently happy since I'd forced it on him for a snorkeling day like today. I would have hated to see his back sunburned from a long snorkel.

The rest of us lounged on the chaise enjoying the view. Freya teased Cal and mock-bossed him around. He impersonated a pirate's mate and had everyone laughing within minutes.

Once they had the ship secure to the mooring ball, Cal turned to me and clapped his hands. "You coming snorkeling with us?"

I pictured a morning spent lazily paddling through the crystal-blue water holding hands with Cal Wilde and searching for exotic marine wildlife. There was no other answer besides "Absolutely."

With Freya helping unload snorkeling gear from a storage locker and Nat acting as Boss of the Sunscreen, four of us were ready to jump in within minutes.

The water was the perfect temperature, and we took our time swimming over toward the caves. Vin had offered to take us closer in the tender, but there weren't many other boats there, and it was nice to get some exercise with a longer swim.

Cal was a strong swimmer like Jin, so the two of them pulled ahead fairly quickly. Nat stayed back with me at a more sedate pace, and I enjoyed keeping my mask pointed down to search for rays and barracuda. Before we reached the mouth of the caves, Nat pulled up and tapped me on the shoulder.

"You should invest in him," she said.

I thought about the call scheduled for that afternoon with the tech company. "I am. I have a call this afternoon with the management team."

"No. I mean Cal. The sailing thing he wants to do."

"Don't be ridiculous," I said. "I barely know him."

"So, do your due diligence like you would normally. Only invest if it passes your rigorous tests."

My investment portfolio was full of pharma, environmental tech, and software companies. A kids' camp was hardly an appropriate addition to my roster. "You're imagining something that isn't there, Nat. He's with us this week on the ship, that's all."

"Why can't there be more? He's a good guy. We can at least be friends and support him. So maybe you don't invest. Maybe instead you hook him up with someone else who can." She seemed to stop and think about it. "Hm... maybe I can."

"Stop," I urged. "Do you remember telling me not to hand over control of JAC to you because you were too quick to make snap decisions without thinking things through?"

She nodded enthusiastically.

"That's what you're doing now," I continued. "So I'm going to remind you that you're in lower-level management at JAC right now because you still have a lot to learn about running a business—your words, not mine—and maybe I know a bit more than you about making decisions and thinking things through since I've been at this about fifteen years longer than you have."

"I don't appreciate your patronizing superiority," she muttered. "Even if it's accurate."

"Besides," I said, trying to soften the blow, "he's not very quick to accept help, in case you haven't noticed. And he doesn't strike me as the kind of man who would appreciate a handout."

She pushed a palmful of water at my face like the little sister she was. "I wasn't suggesting a handout. I was suggesting a smart business investment. But I do see your point. We've known him less than a week."

I laughed. "Exactly. And we met him through Prescott Resnick."

"What?" Her voice had enough of a shriek to it to draw Jin and Cal's attention from up ahead. "What?" she asked again in a low hiss.

"Pres picked him up in a club the night before we arrived. Brought him on the ship and pretended the *Worthington* was his."

Nat's jaw dropped. "Wait. Wait. The ship? Pres told your boyfriend this was his ship? Didn't he—"

"No," I said, realizing I'd started the story from the middle. "He wasn't my boyfriend. *Isn't.* He isn't my boyfriend. He... I'm... we're just hoping that with Cal here, the guy Prescott picked up at a gay bar when we weren't here yet, Pres might reveal his cheating ways in front of Lucas."

"Are you guys coming?" Cal called across the water between us. He was too far away to hear our conversation, but I didn't think he'd mind me telling Nat the truth anyway. I held up a finger to ask him to wait.

"So, you're not hooking up with him?" Nat asked, shooting me a look that clearly called bullshit.

I opened my mouth and closed it again.

She rolled her eyes and shoved water at me again. "You're an idiot. Open your fucking eyes. And don't worry about Lucas. He's going to be fine."

She took off swimming toward Cal and Jin, pushing her fins up and down in the clear water with small but strong legs. I followed after her, considering her comment about Lucas.

Clearly the plan to get Prescott to act inappropriately wasn't working. Maybe I needed to stop being an interfering older brother.

When I reached the rest of them, Cal was under the water trying to get a closer look at something. He surfaced, blowing a giant spout of water out the top of his snorkel before pulling it out of his mouth and grinning at me. His teeth were bright against the darker stubble of his face. His enthusiasm was contagious. "Ready to look for buried treasure?"

"Lead on, matey."

We explored the caves for a while. Cal used a diving flashlight to point out various things to us, and it made me realize just how much I missed when I didn't dive with a local guide. He knew all the best nooks and crannies to find hidden lobsters, juvenile fish, and arrow crabs. By the time my energy started waning, Jade and Mia had joined us, and Cal started the tour all over again.

"I'm heading back to the ship," I told him.

He flashed me a smile. "No worries."

I watched him for a little while longer before swimming out of the cave and back to the boat. He truly was at home in the water, and it was always exciting to see someone living their passion. I hoped he would find a permanent opportunity on the water somewhere, pursuing his love of the water and wind.

After climbing back on board, I grabbed the handheld freshwater sprayer and rinsed off. Lucas was floating on a raft tied to one of the cleats at the edge of the deck. He had a baseball cap shading his face and seemed to be engrossed in whatever he was reading on his Kindle, so I didn't disturb him. Instead, I grabbed a towel and made my way to the large chaise in the bow to lie in the sun. Only five minutes after settling in and being lulled into a half sleep by the hot sun, I heard someone approach.

"Worth, there you are. I was hoping to get a chance to speak to you alone."

I blinked my eyes open to see Prescott blocking my sun. I bit back a sigh and sat up. "Have a seat," I said.

Prescott slid onto the chaise next to me but was very careful to keep a modest distance since we weren't friends. He had to know I didn't like him.

"How well do you know Cal?" he began hesitantly.

"Why?"

"Well, I did a little digging after he made that ridiculous claim about being related to an art thief and a royal."

I'd assumed those had been more of Cal's made-up stories, something to dangle over Prescott's head to prove he wasn't just a small-town country boy without connections. The difference between Prescott and me, however, was that whether or not Cal was related to anyone famous had no bearing on my feelings of Cal's own worth.

He was worthy with or without having big-name connections.

"All right," I prompted.

"Felix of Liorland is, indeed, from a small town in Texas called Hobie," Prescott said, "However, he is an only child who was raised by his grandparents. Alone. Every article about his past details the solitary upbringing he had. I'm fairly certain if he grew up in the same ranch house as another family of *ten* children, there would have been many, many articles about it. Besides, if he has a royal cousin, what is he doing working for peanuts as a charter captain?"

"He loves to sail. Maybe with a wealthy cousin, he doesn't need to work for money. Maybe he works as a charter captain for fun." I knew that wasn't true because I'd seen his actual fear at spending money he didn't have.

"With all due respect, Worth, the man you're... dating is a liar."

I bit back a laugh and tried to feign concern. "Really? What else has he lied about?"

He seemed to be dithering about whether or not to tell me the rest, and of course I knew why. He certainly couldn't admit to me how he'd originally met Cal. So I was surprised when he told me some of it.

"Look," Pres said. "I didn't want to tell you this because I didn't want to cause any problems... but the night before you all arrived, I saw him hooking up with a man in a bar on St. Mitz."

I blinked at him. Was he serious?

"Okay?"

Pres tilted his head. "He, ah, did more than just kiss this man. If you know what I mean."

I wanted to punch him in the fucking face, and I wanted him to never even think about touching Calgary Wilde ever again. I took a slow breath through my nose and counted to ten. "We have an open relationship," I said calmly. "He's allowed to sleep with whomever he wants. And so am I."

Prescott's eyes grew wide. "Oh."

Yes. Oh.

"Anything else?"

"I'm afraid he's using you for your money the same way Mason did."

My fingernails bit into my palms from clenching my hands to keep from decking him. "How so?"

"I overheard him talking on the phone last night. He said something about playing his cards right so he'd be able to make some kind of business acquisition."

"You were eavesdropping on his phone call?" This guy didn't even realize what an ass he was.

"No. I went downstairs to use the bathroom in my room, and the door to your stateroom was open. That's all I heard because I didn't stick around to listen to more. I only heard that tidbit as I walked down the hall."

"I see." I thought about mentioning the sailing school to Prescott, but decided it was really none of his concern. "So you think he's using me to fund some kind of corporate takeover."

"I don't know what he's doing. Listen, I'm just trying to look out for your safety and the best interests of our family," he said.

Our family.

The very idea this man and I would be family one day made my skin crawl. "I appreciate your concern," I told him. "I, too, am looking out for the best interests of my family. I promise."

I locked eyes with him until he got flustered and looked away. "Yes, well. Good. Ah… I'm going to check on Lucas and see if he needs more sunscreen."

"Good idea."

I leaned back and closed my eyes again. The conversation had left me with a bad taste in my mouth, but it had also snuck under my defenses and reminded me that, as much as I hated to admit it, Prescott was right in some ways. I didn't know Cal that well. And I had gotten mixed signals from him about financial things.

On the one hand, he could barely afford his own clothes. On the other, he'd grown up on a ranch probably worth several million dollars, minimum, and one of his grandfathers had been a doctor. On one hand, he had thousands of dollars' worth of sailing certifications. On the other, he balked at replacing his broken shower shoes.

Then there was the mystery of the wealthy family members he'd mentioned in passing conversations. The bar owner, the rare-breeds rancher, the doctor brother, the bodyguard married to a wealthy antiquities collector, and finally, the cousin who was apparently married to an actual royal family.

Even his own parents had high enough corporate careers to be expats in one of the wealthiest cities in the world.

And yet... Cal had discussed his favorite flavors of ramen noodles from the time he'd spent his food allowance in college on a keg for a party.

Maybe it was because of the inauspicious beginnings of our relationship, but I really didn't know which parts of his story were real and which were fake.

Did I think he was using me to fund the purchase of a business? Not at all. But did I think he was the kind of focused, mature partner I'd always envisioned myself with? Also not at all.

He was young and carefree, unsure of his future and seemingly not all that bothered by it. I didn't usually have much time for people without ambition, and he seemed to be floating around without purpose right now.

But Prescott was wrong about one thing. I didn't need to protect myself from Cal because I didn't have any intention of pursing anything more than what we'd already agreed to. A week in the sun and sheets.

It was all I needed right now which was good, since it was all Cal seemed capable of giving anyway.

17

CAL

I snorkeled with the ladies for over an hour before finally heading back to the ship for something cold to drink. Once we were all back on board, Freya and Vin unmoored us and pointed us in the direction of Peter Island.

It was strange not being the one in charge of the boat. I didn't prefer being a passive passenger, but I knew if I bothered them too much, the crew would soon get annoyed with me. They had jobs to do, and they didn't need someone always jumping in to do it for them.

As we got underway, I climbed up to the top deck in search of Worth. Nat and Lucas were teaching him how to play Liar's Dice, and the three of them were laughing after calling Lucas's bluff.

"Hey," Worth said, holding out his arms to me. "Come join us. You can be my competitive advantage."

I sat next to him and leaned in to press a kiss to his cheek. He smelled like coconut sunscreen and rum. "God, you smell delicious," I murmured against his warm skin.

He turned to kiss me full on the mouth, sliding his fingers into my hair to hold the back of my head so I couldn't pull away. After a deep, exploring kiss, he pulled back and met my eyes. "Missed you while you were gone."

My heart did one of those crazy-ass backflips that cheerleaders do. Fuck, fuck. I wanted him so badly, and not just for this week. And not just for sex. I wanted him to be my Lior.

This was going to end terribly.

"Oh," I said stupidly.

Nat chuckled. "C'mon. Stop the make-out sesh and join us."

I swallowed and faked a smile. "Yeah. Hell yeah. Let's do this."

We lost three games in a row because I couldn't stop feeling every single degree of heat coming off Worth's body. I couldn't stop hearing every indrawn breath and smelling the sea air on his skin. But most of all, I couldn't stop wondering *what if* and then quickly following it up with the worst kind of self-talk I'd ever experienced.

He doesn't want you that way.

His friends would laugh at him for dating someone like you.

He thinks you're a child.

He deserves better.

He lives in Chicago.

He's a workaholic.

He's never for one minute implied he'd be interested in more.

I kept my chin up through all of it and kept lying. It was one thing I was good at.

Thankfully, we ended up going straight to Deadman's Bay where we were able to rent a Hobie Cat. I wished they'd had one with a spinnaker kit so we could really have some fun, but since Lucas was new to small-boat sailing, we'd stick to the basics. When I recognized one of the guys who handled the rentals, we were able to get permission to take it farther out than the tourists could.

Worth, Lucas, and I were the first group to take it out, and I let Worth sail us slowly out of the busy bay while I explained everything to Lucas. By the time we passed the farthest mooring ball, Lucas had gotten the basics and was pretty well-versed on the "ready about" and "hard alee" warnings. All it would take was a good knock to the head with the boom to be reminded of them if he forgot.

The little lapping sounds of the water on the hull were as familiar to me as the cicadas on the ranch, and I leaned back and ran my hands through it.

"Ready to have some fun?" I asked Worth with a wink. There'd be plenty of wind once we got out from the protected area of the cove, and I wanted to show off what this little play boat could do.

Worth's eyes lit up, and he gestured for me to switch places with him so I could take the tiller and main sheet.

"Hold on to something," I warned them before finding the wind and tightening the sheet. The thwacking sound of the wind suddenly filling the tight sail lit me up inside, and I closed my eyes for a second to settle.

I was in my happy place, on a sailboat and on the water. Two gorgeous men sat beside me, and the sun was shining. There was enough wind to carry us wherever we wanted to go, and I was at the helm of one of my favorite boats. If I stayed in the present, settled into this current moment, I could forget everything else for a while.

Worth picked up my hand and pressed it to his mouth. "You are absolutely gorgeous," he said so only I could hear him. "Your passion is contagious."

I wiggled the tiller to make sure we were optimizing the angle, and I felt it when the sail found the sweet spot. The boat zinged across the water. Lucas yelped, grabbing on to the front crossbar to keep from sliding into the trampoline. Worth laughed and reached out to clap a hand on Lucas's shoulder to steady him.

"Ready about," I said, ducking and sliding to the port side as I moved the tiller and switched hands. "Hard alee." Worth made sure Lucas made the switch without getting brained by the boom, and we were off in another direction on our tack.

The sail found enough air to increase our speed until one of the hulls wanted to come up. "Hold on," I said. "We're going to heel a little so you can see what it feels like. Angle your body back to compensate for the side that comes up. Like this." I leaned back as I let the port side hull lift out of the water.

Worth let out a whoop and kept a strong hand on Lucas's elbow to keep him from tumbling forward. The three of us leaned back as the boat moved even faster across the water. After a while, I switched again with Worth so he could take control. He had just as much fun as I did before finally sailing us back toward the entrance to the bay and calmer air.

I loved watching the muscles of his arms and shoulders work as he angled the main sheet and worked the tiller. I wondered aloud if there was such a thing as sailing porn, and if so, would he consider filming some of it to make a little extra money on the side. That set Lucas off laughing so hard, he almost tipped overboard.

Once we slowed down, we moved Lucas into the driver's seat and walked him through managing the tiller and the main sheet. He loved it, and watching him take to it made Worth so happy, I wanted to bottle this day and keep it forever.

"Mia would love this!" Lucas said at one point. "We need to get her out here to try it."

"Do you want to ask the ladies to come out or maybe Mia and Prescott?" I asked, trying to be polite. "I'm not sure if Jade would be interested."

"Oh, uh, maybe. I don't think Prescott wants to sail, but Jade might. We can ask her."

I took over again and steered us toward the *Worthington*. Freya was waiting at the back of the stern deck to tie us off to the nearest cleat.

"How was it?" she asked with a big smile. "Looked like a ton of fun."

Lucas told her all of his favorite parts before leaving to find the others on the top deck. As I passed Freya, she mentioned she'd heard a phone ringing in our stateroom earlier when she was tidying up.

"Thank you," Worth said. "That might be my assistant calling back about this afternoon's conference call."

But it wasn't. It was a missed call on my phone. Worth brought it to me where I was chatting in the galley with Julo before returning downstairs to prepare for his call. The voicemail was from Grandpa, and instead of listening to it, I clicked the button to call him back.

"Cal, there you are," Grandpa's familiar voice came on the line. "Did you listen to my message?"

"No, sir. I figured I'd just call you. What's up?"

I wandered out onto the deck behind the large open living room and plopped down in a chair.

"It's Annie. She had a bad fall."

I sat up. "What? Is she okay?"

"Doc ran into Mrs. Parnell in town today and she said Annie had been washing down a boat when she slipped. They think she broke her hip. West is trying to find out more details, but I wanted to make sure you knew. She'd probably love to hear from you, even if it's just a text to let her know you're thinking of her."

I thought of the tough-as-nails woman who'd had a big hand in raising me. Her frizzled brown hair falling out of its messy bun onto her wide, freckled shoulders and the pink tip of her sunburned nose poking out beyond her faded green eyes were as familiar to me as the sound of Grump's heavy breathing while he slept next to Grandpa's feet in the family room.

"Of course," I said around a lump in my throat. "Do you think I should come home and see if she needs help? If she has surgery or something, she might—"

"No, no. Let's wait and see how bad it is. If she does have surgery, she'll probably need some help, but I think Brian and Sharon are there too. They can probably help."

Her nephew and his wife would be about as much help as a toddler would. I'd met Sharon a few times in the past and remembered her fondness for high heels and a full face of makeup. I couldn't picture her getting her hands dirty to help anyone with much of anything. Maybe this was a sign. I couldn't help her with the sailing school, but I could help her recover from surgery.

"Well," I said, trying to project more confidence in the decision than I felt, "no matter what, I'll head home on Sunday if I can find a decent flight, okay?"

Grandpa's voice was soft and steady. "That would be great, sweetheart, but only if you're ready."

I hadn't imagined I'd have to come home *and* face the couple who'd be taking over my dream all at the same time. Lord knew, I wasn't anywhere close to ready.

But it was time.

When Nat and Mia came to find me for another sail, I threw everything I had into enjoying the time I had left here. Not only would I miss most of the people on this ship, but I would also miss the peaceful, easy feeling of finding solace in the sun and the sea.

I spent the afternoon drinking in every gust of wind and spray of water that landed on my skin. As the sun shined down on me, I even forgot Worth for a little while and simply enjoyed my time in this island playground I'd fallen in love with over the past two years.

The memories would have to hold me through a north Texas winter while I tried to figure out what my life was going to be about.

18

WORTH

THE CONFERENCE CALL WENT EVEN BETTER THAN I'D EXPECTED, AND WE scheduled a meeting in San Jose for the following week to talk through specifics. I was excited to have a new project to tackle, especially anticipating being a little out of sorts after leaving Cal behind.

I'd developed some feelings for him beyond friendship and even beyond whatever part-time lover status we'd ventured into by making our relationship physical. I wasn't so short-sighted as to think those feelings would magically disappear the moment my plane took off from the St. Mitz airport.

Staying busy would be crucial, and by the time I returned to Chicago, I'd be ready to tackle my job with renewed vigor.

It was always good to have a plan. I thrived on plans.

I hopped up the staircase to the main deck, excited to share my news with whomever I found first. I looked around for Cal but couldn't find him. Jade was half-asleep on the big lounger in the bow while Prescott flipped through his phone a few feet away.

"Where's Cal?" I asked.

"Sailing," Jade murmured. "He's created a monster."

I shaded my eyes and looked out to see if I could spot the Hobie

Cat. Its rainbow sail was easy to find since it was farther out than any of the other rentals.

Mia's colorful hair clued me in to the newest sailing convert. "Oh good. Is Lucas with them too?"

"Yes, he's like a kid in a candy store on that thing."

I was happy to hear they were still having fun with the little sailboat, but I had to admit being a little disappointed neither Cal nor Lucas were around to talk to about my business excitement. I didn't care to spend more time being lectured by my sister on turning Cal into a life partner, so I avoided her and headed back inside to get a drink. I settled on the sofa on the deck behind the living room with a cold beer and my laptop. Since I was by myself for a little while, I thought I might do a little research into Calgary Wilde.

Of course, I justified the intrusion by telling myself that I was researching him as a possible investment, but that wasn't true at all. I was committed to considering investments as objectively as possible, and a twenty-three-year-old sailing instructor wasn't a proven entity yet.

I glanced up to see if I could spot the Hobie Cat from where I sat. The boat was heeling with Mia at the helm, and I had to remind myself that Cal would easily be able to right the boat if it capsized.

I went back to my browser and entered his name. Several articles about him at Texas A&M popped up. Most of them were about regattas he'd helped win on the sailing team, but two of them were about a business school presentation about the effects of community outreach on small businesses that had impressed local company owners.

There were photos of a very young Calgary Wilde winning a 4-H prize for best photo in the nature conservancy category, more recent photos of him standing next to a couple at a bar opening in Hobie, and photos of him as a teenager grinning like a goofball in front of a colorful sailboat with a bunch of other teens. He was smaller than his peers, but he had a big attitude. He wore a sailing T-shirt that said, "If you can't keep it up, don't take it out." The photo caption mentioned a fundraiser regatta at Campside Cove in Hobie, Texas, benefitting a camp scholarship program for underprivileged youth.

He was so cute, so full of life and energy. Even in an online photo, I could feel his charisma. People enjoyed being around him which must have been quite a gift to the sailing camp.

I looked up different variations of "sailing camp in Hobie" until I found the website for Campside Sailing Academy in Hobie. The site was filled with pictures of kids and adults learning to sail, colorful rigged boats, and smiling faces. Cal was in lots of them, but I also saw the woman he thought of as a second mother. Annie's face was lined with age, but she had the same easy smile Cal did, and it was clear she loved her work as much as he did.

There was a press inquiry tab on the site that led to a list of articles written about the academy and camp. While the facilities seemed due for a much-needed upgrade, the reputation of the program itself was top-notch. Graduates of the program had gone on to sail for elite college teams, and there were even two current World Cup winners from the academy.

I could see why Cal had worked so hard to be worthy of the program and why he'd been knocked so far off course after learning there was no longer a place for him there.

On the Contact page of the website, Brian and Sharon Rastall were listed as the current managers. I did a little more digging into the husband-and-wife team and discovered Brian had most recently been a youth pastor, real estate appraiser, and city council member in Denton, Texas, and Sharon had worked in the administrative offices of the Denton Independent School District. I wondered if they'd fully relocated to Hobie to run the camp or if they were staying in Denton and hiring someone else to handle the day-to-day operations. Maybe if they stayed in Denton, they could hire Cal to run the programs.

I wasn't aware of how much time had passed until Julo appeared to offer me a fresh beer and set down a tray of appetizers.

"Your man came through a few minutes ago and went to the stateroom," Julo said. "He didn't want to disturb you, but I think maybe you want to be disturbed."

He walked away without another word, and it took me about half a second to translate his words into the image of a naked Cal Wilde stepping into the shower. I grabbed my laptop and hit the ground running to the sound of Julo's chuckle.

When I entered the stateroom, I could hear the sound of the shower going and Cal singing Christopher Cross's "*Sailing*." I stripped off my own trunks and approached slowly so I could listen first.

... Just a dream and the wind to carry me...

I couldn't help but smile. He was still that happy kid, easily transported by wind and water. I wanted to learn how to let go the way he seemed to be able to do, find the joy in simple things and take each day as they came.

"Is there room for one more?" I asked carefully, trying not to startle him.

"Only if you have a penis and you're not afraid to use it," he quipped back without missing a beat.

I looked down at my hard length, already throbbing for him. "Yep. Got one of them. I found it in a bin of rarely used odds and ends."

I stepped into the marble shower behind him and slid my arms around his chest, leaning down to kiss and nibble at the back of his neck. It still tasted faintly of salt and sweat, and I chased the taste down his spine.

"How did your work go?" he asked, leaning back into me. "Your conference call."

I'd forgotten about the call in my deep dive into all things Cal Wilde and Hobie, Texas. "Oh, great. I'm flying to California to meet with them in a few days to talk next steps. They have some very promising reports about the market opportunities."

Cal reached back and grabbed my hips, pulling me closer until my dick pressed against his lower back.

"Fuck," I groaned.

"Mm, sounds like a good plan. Here or out there?" He stood on his toes and wiggled his ass back and forth until my erection slotted between his cheeks.

"Lube," I said, losing my ability to make full sentences. Cal reached out and grabbed a tube and condom from the shelf that I was completely sure hadn't been there earlier. "You're a god," I murmured against the wet skin of his shoulder.

He laughed and passed back the supplies before leaning forward to brace his hands against the shower wall. I cranked the showerhead out of the way and went to work sliding on the condom and slicking myself up. When I was ready, I slid one finger inside of him, quickly following it with another when I realized there was already lube inside of him.

"You naughty boy," I said, looking down at his ass on display for me.

"What can I say? Sailing makes me horny."

I had a ridiculous image of presenting him with his very own Hobie Cat, rainbow-sailed and wrapped up with a giant bow, but I blinked it away when I felt my finger brush over the right spot inside of him.

"Yes, fuck. Fuck. Yes," he whimpered.

When I entered his body, I almost cried out. He was so hot and tight, so perfect for me. The tanned skin of my hands against the pale white of his ass turned me on, and when I began thrusting, that pale ass jiggled enough to make me even hungrier for him than I had been.

I banded my arms around his front and fucked him hard from behind, relishing every grunt and shout he made. Cal's fingernails dug into my legs where he'd reached back to keep me from pulling out all the way, and his other hand stayed braced on the shower wall.

"You feel so fucking perfect," I told him over and over. "Never want to stop."

"Make me come. Please, Jon. Want to come," he gasped. "Close. So..."

I gripped his cock and stroked him in time with my thrusts into his body until we were both coming. Loud breaths mixed with the sound of the water spray echoed around us in the stall. I pulled out and ditched the condom before turning him around and kissing the hell out of him.

Without taking my mouth off his, I backed up until my legs hit the built-in bench and sat down, pulling him onto my lap so we could keep kissing.

My thoughts were warm and affectionate, stronger than I'd anticipated and borderline scary. He deserved the best. Hell, he deserved the whole world. And I wondered if Nat was right. Was there any way it might be possible for me to be the one to give it to him?

"We're wasting water," he eventually said in a daze.

I stood him up and washed him off, scrubbing his hair and body while he seemed to stay in a suspended state of post-orgasmic bliss. Once we were finished, I dried him off and led him to bed.

"We're napping?" he asked.

"Not really. But just lie here with me for a little while before we get dressed."

Once he settled with his head on my shoulder, his daze seemed to clear a little.

"I think I need to head home after this."

I ran my fingers through his damp hair. "Instead of staying and finding a job? What happened to change your mind?"

"You remember I told you about Annie who owns the sailing school back home?"

I murmured a yes.

"She fell. They think she might have broken her hip. I just want to be there in case she needs help. Besides..." He snuggled closer. "Maybe your seriousness is rubbing off on me. I think it's time for me to figure out what's next. And I miss my family." He shifted and angled his head to meet my eyes. "Sorry I seem to be failing on the Prescott front."

I responded without thinking. "I don't want you going anywhere near Prescott. It's done. Over. It's not worth it. I should have never let that idiot get in my head. I'll find another way to help Lucas see what an ass he is."

Cal's eyes were starting to droop, but his cheeks flushed with a sweet pink. "My, my. Someone is having strong feelings about a certain someone."

I knew he was referring to my anger toward Prescott, but as Cal drifted off to sleep, I couldn't help but think about the feelings I was actually having about a certain different someone.

There were many things I didn't know about Cal—how many crazy relatives he had or how he planned to achieve his dream of living his life on the water—but I realized I knew enough. I knew the *important* bits.

Cal was a good man. He was full of life and charisma and enthusiasm for others. He was determined to work hard and achieve good things.

For all that he was half my age, he was actually a good influence on me. He'd already taught me things and changed me for the better. I'd become too insulated and mistrustful, and that wasn't the way I wanted to live my life. He was wise and loving and generous.

But what did that mean for Cal and me? I quickly found myself playing a big round of *what if*.

What if we tried dating? I owned my own plane. We could visit each other whenever we wanted. Hell, he was between jobs. Maybe he could find something in Chicago. Maybe I could put him in touch with the Northwestern Sailing Center.

I pictured him bundled up in cold weather gear October through May when the sailing center was closed to actual sailing. It wasn't ideal, but then again, how long was the sailing season in Hobie?

What if we didn't date, but we simply met back up here a few times a year for fun in the sun and sheets?

I could do that. In fact, that would be perfect for me. The rest of the year I could focus on work and then maybe once a quarter take a break and enjoy Cal's company on the ship. Surely, that would be enough sex and fun to tide me over until the next visit.

But what if he started dating someone else?

Okay, the *what if* game was going in an unpleasant direction, but I'd humor myself. If he started dating someone, he wouldn't want to meet an old man for sex anymore. That would be disappointing. So much so, my stomach hurt even thinking of it.

But no. That would be good, actually. I wanted him to find someone. He deserved it.

I pictured him with a man closer to his own age. What if the guy didn't like sailing? Or what if he didn't support Cal's love of it? What if he tried convincing Cal to get an office job in the city?

You mean like the one you have in Chicago?

I sighed. He wouldn't be happy in a place like Chicago. I couldn't even picture him in my penthouse apartment with its windows covered in sun-blocking film and the climate controlled precisely by a home-management system.

What if I changed? What if I was the one to move for him?

I let out a soft laugh. Me, Jonathan Worthington, billionaire venture capitalist and son of the country's largest agribusiness conglomerates, chucking it all to move to Podunk, Texas—or god forbid a boat in the islands somewhere—to follow a twenty-three year-old-camp counselor.

Now who was being ridiculous?

I packed all of the thoughts away in a little box labeled *Don't Be An Idiot* and turned my focus to the funding deal I'd just greenlighted. My assistant had already reached out to the attorneys to start drawing up some contract language, but I needed to be the one to start drawing up a potential path to IPO to present at next week's meeting.

As I thought through our goals for the deal, I played with Cal's hair, lightly scratching his scalp and pulling my fingers through his spiky locks as they dried. Eventually, he woke up enough to make appreciative noises.

"We should probably get up," I suggested. "Julo was already setting out appetizers when I came down here."

"Mm, I'm hungry, but I don't want to move. You feel too good."

I leaned down and pressed a kiss to his head. "Thank you for teaching Lucas today. Maybe if he falls in love with it, I can trade this ship in for something with sails."

"I don't want you to get rid of this one though," he murmured. "I like it. Besides, it's where we first met." He opened his eyes and batted his eyelashes with a teasing look.

"Ah," I said, trying to ignore the unsteady feeling in my gut, "I see. Maybe we should dip the ship in copper and display it on my grandma's dresser like the pair of weird baby shoes she always kept there."

"Yeah, what's with that? My grandfather has those, and it's creepy."

I lifted his chin up and kissed him on the mouth, wanting to get a taste of him again before spending the next few hours around everyone else. Within seconds of fusing our mouths together, Cal crawled on top of me and began gently thrusting his hard cock into my side. I reached down to stroke it. We could fit in a quick frot before getting dressed, and it would go a long way toward calming down my wayward thoughts.

Just as I was turning to reach for the lube to help smooth the way, Cal's phone rang.

"Ignore it," he said, taking over the search for the lube in the drawer. I squeezed his ass as he fumbled for the bottle. After he pumped some into my hand, I reached down and gripped both of us together, slicking our shafts and lining us up better. Cal began sucking on my neck and chest which made me ten times harder.

"That's it," I said, unsure of whether I was talking to him or myself.

His phone rang again.

"No," he said. "Keep going. Close. Feels so good."

I jacked us as well as I could considering Cal was also thrusting into my grip and driving me crazy with his mouth. When he leaned down and took my nipple between his teeth, it was all over.

I arched up and groaned through my release, trying my hardest to keep stroking him even though my brain was short-circuiting. He came just as his phone began to ring again.

"Motherfucker," he groaned. "Whoever's calling needs to fuck off. Jesus."

I reached over for one of the discarded towels and cleaned us up before handing him the phone. "Here. I'm going to get dressed and go on up so you can talk in private." I leaned in to take another deep kiss from him before turning toward the closet. He'd already set out his clothes for the night, so I tossed them to him on the bed.

"It's Doc," he said, pulling on his boxer briefs. "No need for privacy." He dialed the phone and put it to his ear while he finished pulling his clothes on. "Hey, what's..."

He listened for a little while right as my brain began to process what three or four calls in a row would mean. Trouble at home. Big trouble.

"What?" he breathed. "What? Wait... how? Are they sure? Why didn't they..."

I turned and saw his face had gone pale. I threw on my own clothes before rushing over and squeezing in behind him, pulling him back against my chest and holding on tight. His body melted into mine as he started to cry.

"But are they sure?" he asked again. He sounded so young and afraid. I wanted to conjure up a giant bubble of protection around him and keep all the world's cruelty at bay. Whatever was happening had just devastated him.

"Doc... I... I don't know if I can get back in time. I'm on a boat and—"

I cut in softly. "I'll get you back. I'll send you wherever you need to go."

Cal turned in my arms and put his face against my chest. The warm wet tears landed on my shirt and almost crushed me.

"Will she even know I'm there?" he asked. "Will Brian let me see her?"

Fuck. It was Annie. Something had happened to her, and it was bad. I could hear the steady tones of Cal's grandfather on the other end of the line. I wanted to take the phone away from Cal and promise Doc I'd take care of everything, but it wasn't my place. I wasn't Cal's actual boyfriend. I wasn't family. I was someone who'd known him only a few days.

I reached for my phone and began typing a text to Vin with one hand.

Worth: *Need to get Cal back to Texas asap for family emergency. What's best way?*

Cal finished up his call and threw his arms around me, crying harder into the crook of my neck. I put my own phone down and held him tight. I could hear Freya's shout through the open porthole as she ran down the deck above us. The engines turned on, and Julo's voice joined the mix. They were taking care of it like the competent crew they were.

I breathed a sigh of relief and held on to Cal. "We're getting you home," I promised softly.

"She... she had a massive stroke. She's on life support. It's bad. Really bad, Jon."

"Shhh. You told me your brother and Doc are both physicians. I'm sure they'll get all the information about what's going on. Maybe they'll have a better idea of the details when you land."

Nat knocked and pushed the door open when I told her to come in. "Vin said there's an emergency? What's happening? What can I do to help?"

Lucas poked his head in behind her.

"Come in," I told them, not letting go of Cal. "Remember the woman Cal told us about who owns the sailing camp back home?" They nodded. "She's had a bad stroke. We need to get him home to see her." I tried not to use the phrase *say goodbye*, but that's what it would probably be.

Nat's face dropped, and she came to sit on the edge of the bed. Cal peered out at her but didn't take his head off my chest.

"Oh honey," she said, reaching out to rub his arm. "I'm so sorry."

"Thanks," he said with a sniff.

Nat found a box of tissues on the dresser and handed them over. "Do you want me to come with you?"

He wiped his face and shook his head. "No. I'll be okay. All of my family is there."

Nat shot me a look that had a message somewhere between "you'd better go with him" and "don't be an uncaring dick," but it was unnecessary. Of course I'd go with him.

"I'll come with you," I said, confident that he'd let me take him home since he seemed to find comfort in my company. If nothing else, I could be a friend in his time of need.

"No, thank you," he said, sitting up and moving away from me. He cleared his throat. "I'll be fine. Besides, you have your big meeting in California."

He didn't mean it. Did he?

"Meetings can be rescheduled," I said, feeling a little less steady than I'd anticipated. I was beginning to realize perhaps I wanted to go with him because of my own feelings rather than his. I wanted to take care of him, protect him, make sure he had everything he needed.

As soon as Cal met my eyes, I knew it was over. "I'd prefer to go alone. But thank you... for everything."

I stared at him in shock. Was this really the end of our time together? Of course it was. We'd known each other five days. He was only twenty-three, nowhere near ready for the kind of permanent relationship I would want if I were foolish enough to enter into a relationship again. Which I wasn't. This was simply intense emotion brought on by circumstances, that was all.

"Of course," I murmured, looking away from him to find my phone. I had travel arrangements to make. Even if I couldn't comfort him back in Hobie, I could make sure he got home as quickly and safely as possible to the people who could.

19

———————

CAL

THE TRIP HOME WAS A WHIRLWIND. MY EYES LEAKED THE WHOLE damned way, and I wasn't sure how much of it was due to the news about Annie and how much was due to walking away from Worth.

I'd wanted so badly to lean against him and let him take away all of my worries—let him accompany me back home and hold me up while I went through the impossible task of saying goodbye to Annie —but if there was one thing I knew, it was just how much harder it would be to watch Worth walk away after he'd been to the ranch and met my family.

My family was everything to me, and keeping him separate from it seemed like my only chance at protecting myself from a full breakdown. I knew if I had Worth with me in Hobie, showed him all of my special spots and places that meant something to me, I'd never be able to erase him from my hometown or from my heart.

I also knew how important his meeting in California was to him, and I didn't want my pity party to distract from the good work he was bound to do there.

As Worth's private jet touched down on the small private runway outside of Hobie, I marveled at how strange it was not to fly into Dallas. I was used to having the long drive up to Hobie to prepare for seeing my family, but today, Doc and Grandpa stood just outside of the small terminal building's double doors to wait for me.

"Precious baby," Grandpa said when I got close enough to hear him. His eyes were already red with empathetic tears as he held his arms open for me. I walked right into them and let my eyes leak some more as I clutched at the back of his shirt. He smelled like the same Old Spice he'd been wearing for decades mixed with our laundry detergent. It was one of the smells of home, and I melted into it immediately.

Doc came around behind me to rub my back. "It's so good to see you, but I wish it wasn't under these circumstances."

"Any update on her condition?" I asked, pulling out of Grandpa's hug to give Doc a hug too.

Doc's voice was calm and steady. "We went by there this morning for a visit, and they're saying there's no brain activity. I believe they're waiting for a few more tests to be sure, but it looks like they'll be making a decision to take her off life support soon. Maybe tomorrow. I'm so sorry, sweetheart."

I sniffed and pulled the handkerchief out of my pocket to wipe my tears for the millionth time. Worth had offered it to me before I'd left, and I'd made fun of the old-fashioned thing. Now I looked down at the deep blue initials JAW embroidered on it and said a silent apology. It had come in very handy, plus now I had a memento of my time with him.

"Can we head to the hospital now?"

"Of course. Let's go."

On the way there, Doc tried to warn me about Brian and Sharon. "They had a problem with your grandfather and me," he began. "Didn't want us anywhere near Annie's room."

My stomach dropped. I'd been afraid of that. Brian was a local politician where he lived and had made his religious and bigoted opinions known during some of the meetings. Annie had told me how disappointed she was to hear about it from someone else who lived there. I'd always gotten the feeling that Annie thought he'd eventually "come around" and maybe grow out of his ignorance, but apparently it hadn't happened yet, and the man was at least thirty-five.

"Will he let me in, do you think?"

Both of them nodded from the front seat of the truck. "West talked to him calmly and explained how important you are to Annie. He said you were headed back to town to see her one last time."

I scoffed. "And he gave West the time of day?"

"West passes as a dude bro," Grandpa said, surprising a laugh out of me.

"I didn't even know you knew what 'pass' meant," I admitted. "Much less the term 'dude bro.'"

"I'll have you know, your grandfather has been passing as straight for over eighty years," Doc said proudly, as if it was something to brag about. "He's masc for masc."

I laughed again. "I don't think that means what you think it means."

Grandpa chuckled. "I'm masc for Doc. How about that?"

"Better," I admitted. "Although if you were a masc dude bro, you might not have called me your precious baby. Just sayin'."

By the time we pulled into the hospital lot, I'd at least stopped crying and felt a little steadier. Doc and Grandpa pointed me in the direction of her room while they went to find West in a different part of the hospital where he was checking on a patient of his.

Sharon was just coming out of Annie's room when I arrived. "Hi," I said softly. "How's she doing?"

She shook her head. "Hi, Cal. Not good. She had a severe hemorrhagic stroke and fell which increased the severity of the brain bleed. At least, that's their best guess. She's not going to make it. The doctors told us a few minutes ago that they've done all the tests and she's gone. They're keeping her alive with machines until Brian can get our pastor here."

It was too surreal to be true. Annie wasn't even seventy years old yet. "I'm so sorry," I said, wishing I could hug her. I knew she wouldn't appreciate it though, since we didn't know each other very well and she didn't seem the hugging type.

"Me too. Poor Brian is beside himself, especially knowing she hadn't been to church in so long."

I blinked at her. "She wasn't religious. She said Sunday morning sunrises over the water were her church. She used to sit out on the edge of the dock and meditate."

Sharon sighed. "Yes, well, we're going to fix that, don't you worry. Pastor James should be here in the next hour or so, and he'll bring the comfort of the Lord's mercy."

I guessed at this point having anyone say nice things about eternal life wasn't the worst thing that could happen. The worst thing that could happen to Annie had already happened.

"Can I sit with her for a few minutes?"

"Let's wait and see when Brian comes out. He's very upset, as you can imagine."

I nodded and moved over to a nearby alcove that had a few chairs and magazines. My hands were shaking with nerves that they wouldn't let me in to see her. I remembered something my brother Hudson had told me once about how important it was to stay calm and focus on your goal when dealing with difficult people.

What will it take to get them to say yes?

I squeezed my eyes closed. *Playing the game. Acting like a contrite, meek nobody who simply wants to mourn their aunt. I can do this.*

My phone buzzed with a message, and my heart leapt with hope it was Worth. We'd ended things very awkwardly since everyone on the ship was there when I disembarked in St. Mitz.

Grandpa: *Do you want a coffee or soda from the cafeteria?*

I blew out a breath, trying not to feel disappointment surround me like a wet blanket. Even though it was nice of Grandpa to ask, I definitely didn't need coffee. If I had a stimulant right now, I might shoot off into outer space.

Cal: *Just water or juice please.*

After a few minutes, I saw my brother West approaching from the nurse's station. He was eleven years older than I was and practically radiated competence. Just seeing him there made me feel like everything would be okay.

I stood to give him a hug. "Hey," I said into the shoulder of his doctor's coat.

"Fuck, you look good," he said, pulling back to take a look at me. His blond scruff surrounded a teasing smile. "Maybe I should take Nico and the kids on a sailing trip, after all."

"I can't picture Nico on a boat," I admitted. "Especially when we tried taking him out that one time and he kept screeching every time we heeled."

My brother laughed and gestured me back to where I'd been sitting. "Kind of like the time Hudson tried getting him on a horse and he ended up arguing with Thunder during the entire trail ride."

"He's more indoorsy," I said with a soft laugh. "How is he? How are the girls?"

His face went soft and goofy. "Good. Really good. I mean... except for the fact that Pippa has entered the terrible threes and has strong opinions like someone we know."

"You?"

He laughed and leaned back in his chair. "Yeah, maybe. And then there's Reenie, who isn't even one yet and is already getting close to walking. We think Pippa's been bribing her to learn because she knows Nico and I will pull our hair out the minute Reenie's that much more mobile."

I listened to him talk about the girls for a little while longer. He probably knew that just being in his presence would help steady me for what was coming. Finally, it was time to face it.

"Are they sure she's gone?" I asked in a small voice.

He sighed. "Yeah. There are several tests they can do—EEG, cerebral angiogram, cerebral perfusion scintigraphy—to be sure there's no possibility of her recovery. They've done all of that. A head CT shows a severe hemorrhagic stroke. Even if she'd survived it, she most likely wouldn't ever be able to control critical functions again. She would have spent the rest of her life in a bed, hooked up to machines."

We watched as a man in a business suit came scurrying down the hall and into Annie's room.

"I think that's the pastor," West said. "They've been waiting for him to come up from Denton."

I bit back a groan. "She would hate that. The woman has a Buddha statue above her fireplace. She once said performative religion was like a spiritual beauty pageant."

"Well, she's not around to see it. If it brings Brian and Sharon some measure of comfort, what's the risk?"

I side-eyed him. "Since when are you so reasonable and understanding?"

He dragged a hand through his hair, leaving it even more fashionably messy than it had been before. "Since realizing that death bed prayer and ritual can be the difference between a family member handling death with grace and completely losing their shit. Honestly, it doesn't matter if religion is real. If it gives a mourner some measure of comfort in their loved one's final moments, who are we to judge?"

I opened my mouth to argue with him, but he held up a hand. "I don't mean other pain religion causes in the global sense. I simply mean, if it makes them feel better to say certain words over her body, so be it. When it's your turn to say words over her body, you can be offered the same measure of respect, right?"

"Live and let live," I muttered. "Now you sound like Neckie."

Our sister-in-law was a hippie through and through, so much so that she literally taught yoga.

West touched his thumbs to his ring fingers and mimicked a meditative chant before I punched him in the shoulder to get him to cut it out.

After a few minutes of joking around, West met my eyes. "So... Doc and Grandpa said you met someone in St. Mitz..."

Older brothers were the worst.

The image of Worth laughing in the sun popped into my head uninvited. "Not really."

West squeezed my shoulder. "Do me a favor and never play poker, m'kay?"

"He's out of my league in every imaginable way," I said.

West's eyes became stormy. "Not possible. You're in the highest league there is. There is no such thing as out of your league, do you hear me?"

Older brothers were the best.

"You have to say that. You're biased."

Doc and Grandpa walked up and handed me a bottle of apple juice and a bottle of water. Doc asked what West was biased about, but before he could answer, the door to Annie's room opened again. Brian, Sharon, and the pastor walked out, speaking in hushed tones.

I stood and clasped my hands, waiting for an opening to ask if I could have a moment alone with Annie. When Brian saw me standing there, he seemed annoyed, but he flicked his hand toward the door in invitation.

Suddenly, I began to shake. I hadn't realized until that moment how scared I was that he wouldn't let me see her. "Thank you," I whispered, moving past him and into the room.

She looked tiny in the bed, and the harsh hospital lighting made her look older than she was. Just seeing her familiar face brought back the tears as I neared the bed.

There were a couple of chairs pulled close, so I dropped into one and reached for her hand.

"I'm sorry I wasn't here," I squeaked. "I'm sorry..." I blinked the tears back and thought about what I really wanted to say to her. "Thank you for loving everyone you met. For showing me what it meant to give everyone a chance to grow and change. Thank you most especially for encouraging *me* to grow and change."

I glanced out the window, wondering how it was possible the world could continue to spin while such a force of nature was leaving us.

"You came into my life when I needed you the most," I said, voice cracking and breaking. "You gave me something of my very own to love and nurture. You gave me a future to aim for, and even if that future has changed now, I still have all of the skills and education to make a good life. Because of you."

I pulled out Worth's handkerchief and buried my face in it. Faint traces of his cologne were still there which made no sense after the way I'd abused it with my tears all evening.

Annie would hate to see me so upset. She was much more the kind of person who believed in working your feelings off rather than wallowing in them. I laughed at the memory of the time I'd come to her crying about Winnie and Hallie going off to college and how boring it was with just Sassy and me at home. She'd put me to work repairing sails all day until I figured out there were worse things than a quiet house.

"I can't even count the number of lives you changed, Annie," I said when I finally got my composure back. "Alyssa Johnson, Kev Banner, Elijah Padgitt... they wouldn't be where they are today without you. They wouldn't be happy and thriving and loved and..." I sighed. "You made a difference. And because of you, I will fight to do the same with my own life."

My eyes traced the signs of sun damage on her face from years of doing what she loved. "Thank you for every ounce of goodness you put into this world, Annie. And thank you for loving me as hard as you could. I will make you proud. I promise."

I leaned forward and kissed her hand, pressing my cheek against it until I heard the door open behind me.

"The doctors are coming in," Brian said. I could tell from his tone of voice that I was out of time.

I pressed one more kiss to her forehead and told her I loved her. Then I turned and straightened up. "Thank you for letting me say goodbye. I'm so sorry, Brian. If there's anything I can do to help, especially with—"

"We'll be fine. Thank you."

I pressed my lips together and nodded before slipping past him out the door and into the waiting arms of my family. Doc and Grandpa took me home to the ranch without a word and let me crawl into bed with Grump. My phone buzzed with a text, and I checked the screen. My heart leapt when I saw who it was from.

Worth: *Hope you got a chance to see Annie. If you need anything at all, please let me know.*

I sighed. It wasn't a declaration of love, but it was still thoughtful and sweet. I was too worn-out to do more than reply with a *thank you*.

After that, my phone buzzed on and off with texts and calls, but I ignored it. Eventually the battery must have worn out because it went blessedly silent.

I would let myself mourn for a few days. And then it was time to get a life and make a plan. Annie hadn't raised me to wallow when there was work that needed to be done.

20

WORTH

Returning to Chicago on Saturday brought a much-needed reality check. I'd had my vacation, and now it was time to dig into work. With an exciting new deal on the table, it was a good time to focus.

I might have stumbled a little after Cal left St. Mitz, but that was to be expected. He was going through something awful, and my heart went out to him.

The bed in the stateroom was strangely empty without him even though I'd enjoyed it myself plenty earlier this year when I'd been almost alone on the ship. Nat didn't stop pestering me about Cal the final night on board the ship in the St. Mitz harbor, so when we finally parted ways at the airport in Chicago, I was glad for the blessed silence.

I remembered returning home from St. Mitz after the last trip and enjoying the peace and quiet of my apartment. I'd even been grateful Mason's belongings were no longer there, and I'd been even more grateful the man himself hadn't been there.

So why was the apartment so empty today?

It felt like a crypt. The sleek, modern furnishings looked like something out of a magazine, something a grown-up would be proud of. This place represented my business success, and there had been many times I'd taken pride in the fact I'd gotten here without taking any distributions from my family's business. I'd had the benefit of the best education my father's money could pay for as well as the small inheritance from my grandparents while I was in college. I'd refused to take any money from JAC after my father had spent my entire life ranting about "good-for-nothing freeloaders" which meant I'd worked harder than ever trying to prove myself as someone who "deserved" the wealth I earned. It was a trap. I knew it was a trap, but it was still hard to dispel those words that had been hammered into my head during my formative years.

My father's views on "deserving" wealth had spilled over into his legacy. He'd deliberately left Lucas and Natalia's shares of the family business to their mother. It was a slap in the face to Lucas's hard work in veterinary school and Nat's determination to start at the bottom and work her way up at JAC. It was especially a slap in the face considering the only "work" Angela had done in twenty-seven years had been providing social lubrication for my stodgy father.

But now that JAC was completely handed over to Lucas and Nat and being managed by an incredibly capable and experienced CEO and board of directors, I could finally let go. Seven years of work finally done. Seven years of trying to manage JAC and Spinnaker Capital at the same time to keep Angela from running JAC into the ground with her negligence.

Despite having just spent the week on a yacht in the Caribbean, I was still tired. Not physically tired, maybe, but certainly emotionally tired. On Sunday morning, I decided to fight that feeling with a long run along the waterfront, something I enjoyed but hadn't been able to do on vacation.

I changed clothes and took the elevator downstairs before pushing out into the afternoon sun and turning toward the lake. My run started slowly, but by the time I hit the waterfront trails, I was flying, pushing myself harder and harder as if I could outrun the thoughts in my head. Thoughts about why I seemed to fall for every beautiful young man in front of me and why this time had seemed different. Thoughts about how Cal's body against mine and his soft breath had relaxed me in a way no Caribbean vacation could ever do. Thoughts about how, for the first time in my life, I was second-guessing my priorities.

I felt the burn in my legs and kept going. The summer heat was long gone, and the trees were just beginning to turn. A fresh breeze coming off the water helped keep me cool as I raced along the path.

When I finally stopped to take a breath, leaning forward and clutching my knees, I realized I was only a block away from Lucas's place. I headed in that direction, stopping at a nearby coffee shop to pick up some coffee and pastries.

Maybe it was time for me to accept Prescott's presence in Lucas's life. The plan to reveal him as a cheating asshole hadn't borne fruit, but maybe that was for the best. Maybe I needed to let Lucas be an adult and learn his own lessons.

Lucas needed to learn his own lesson that all the precautions in the world couldn't stop you from being sad when relationships didn't work out the way you wanted them to. And if I had to suffer through Prescott's company while Lucas figured that out himself, then so be it. I wasn't going to let the man drive a wedge between me and my brother.

Someone was coming out of the door when I approached, so I was able to get into the building without buzzing. I made my way up to the third floor and knocked on his apartment door, juggling the three coffee cups and Starbucks bag.

"Worth?" he asked when he opened the door. He was clearly still half-asleep. He had on a pair of boxers, and his hair was going every which way.

"Hey, sorry to wake you. It's after ten. I guess I assumed you guys would be up already." I moved past him into the apartment.

"Wait, wait," Lucas said. "I don't... it's not... it's not a good time right now."

I stared at him before my brain began searching for answers. "Were you in the middle of sex or something?" I wasn't sure I wanted to even think about that, but I also wasn't about to leave simply so Prescott Resnick could nut all over my brother.

"Um, no, but—"

I heard a laugh come from the direction of the bedroom. A decidedly *female* laugh.

"What's…" My brain whirred some more. "What's going on? Who's here?"

"Fuck," Lucas muttered. "Okay, but it's not—"

He didn't get a chance to finish before Mia came sauntering out in my brother's T-shirt and boxer shorts. She was busy looking at her phone and didn't see me at first.

"Babe, did you check to see if they remembered…" Her voice trailed off as she looked up and noticed me. "Creamer," she finished faintly.

I pushed past her to see who else was here, namely Prescott, but there were only two sets of luggage in the bedroom. Lucas's familiar black Tumi bags, a set we'd all gotten from our father years ago, and a giant lavender suitcase Julo had almost dropped on his foot while carrying it off the ship for Mia.

Prescott's hard-sided Samsonite was nowhere to be found.

So why wasn't I happier about this?

"Explain yourself," I grunted, feeling ancient and judgmental.

Lucas shifted from side to side, clearly uncomfortable. "Well, I—"

Mia plucked a coffee out of the tray in my hand and plopped down on the sofa. "Oh, for god's sake. Tell him, Luc."

Lucas raked his fingers through his hair. "It's just that…"

Mia sighed. "Prescott is an asshole user, and he pressured Lucas into getting engaged in the first place."

I set the drinks tray and pastry bag down and crossed my arms in front of my chest. "I'm sorry?"

Lucas paced back and forth. "I can't talk to you without clothes on," he muttered, heading to the bedroom.

Mia's expression held a warning for me. Clearly she had real feelings for my brother. "He's terrified of disappointing you," she said softly. "So you're going to listen and be empathetic, even if it kills you."

"But... why?"

"Because you love him. He's your brother."

"No. I mean why agree to the engagement?"

Lucas came back out dressed in cutoff sweats and a clean T-shirt. "Because you wouldn't have agreed to the trip otherwise. We needed a big reason to get away. Nat and I had already tried everything we could think of, and I thought if I got engaged, we could use it as an excuse to take a trip." He held up a hand. "And before you tell me how ridiculous that sounds, believe me, I know. The truth is... I didn't want to hurt his feelings. Besides. It worked. We got you out of town and onto the ship."

I gaped at him. "Don't be ridiculous. I've been to St. Mitz at least four or five times in the past two years since Mason purchased the yacht," I said. "You could have come with me any of those times without getting fucking engaged. In fact, I invited you to come a couple of those times."

"And Mason *dis*invited us as soon as your back was turned. One of the times, he asked us to stay home because he had a big proposal planned. Then the other time he told us you really wanted to be alone because of stress at work."

If I hadn't wanted to throttle Mason before for being a manipulative asshole, I definitely did now. "I'm sorry. I never knew," I said, feeling helpless and frustrated.

"And after the breakup, we asked you to come to Vail. You said you couldn't."

"I was on the yacht," I admitted. "I was licking my wounds."

Lucas smiled. "I know. Julo called me. He knew we'd be worried about you, so he wanted us to know you were okay."

I was torn between wanting to fire the man for betraying my privacy and wanting to promote him for knowing me well enough to make that executive decision.

Lucas continued. "Then we asked you to come down to St. Mitz, and you said we could go without you because you had so much work to do."

I finally relaxed enough to sit down in a nearby armchair. "That's because I'd been away so long. I couldn't leave the office again so soon." I reached for my coffee and took a sip. "But that doesn't explain you two. And where is Pres?"

Lucas looked nervous again. "He's at his own place. I told him I was on call last night and today."

"When did the two of you get together?"

Mia looked to Lucas for permission before responding. "Last night. There'd been something between us on the ship—"

Lucas cut in with a laugh. "That something has been between us for months."

Mia blushed, the pink contrasting adorably with her messy purple hair. It reminded me of the time she'd blushed at my sister on the ship, only Lucas had been sitting right next to Nat at the time. I'd completely misunderstood. "Fine, but you were dating Pres."

"Only because I'd asked you out several times before getting together with Pres, and you shot me down."

I held up a hand. "Tangent alert."

Lucas flashed me a guilty look. "I need to break it off with Pres. He doesn't know. I didn't mean to... cheat... like this."

I snorted and then started laughing for real. This was like something out of a soap opera. "I don't think you need to feel as guilty as you think."

"Why not? I've never cheated on anyone in my life. Pres deserves better."

Mia sighed but kept quiet.

"No he doesn't," I said firmly. "You know how he flew down to St. Mitz a day early because he'd gone to his cousin's graduation in Georgia?"

Lucas nodded.

"Well," I continued. "He picked up a guy at a club in St. Mitz and slept with him that night."

Lucas and Mia both blinked at me.

"How do you know?" Lucas asked.

"Because that guy was Cal."

We all stared at each other a beat before they began shooting questions at me a mile a minute. I explained as best I could, leaving out the part about trying to reveal Prescott's predilection for cheating.

"Why didn't you tell me my fiancé was cheating on me?" he cried.

Mia answered before I could. "This is good news. You don't even want to marry him. Settle down. Also, don't you remember what happened with your exes, Vic and then Zara? Hell, Worth even tried telling you when your dry cleaner was cheating you, and you didn't listen."

Lucas looked like he was truly hurt. "You seriously weren't going to stop me from marrying a cheating asshole?"

"Would you have believed me if I'd told you Pres had slept with Cal?"

Lucas opened his mouth but then closed it again.

"Exactly," I muttered.

"But wait," Lucas said, shifting in his seat next to Mia. "What about you and Cal? Cal was cheating on you? Why?"

"No, we weren't really dating. I just... I helped him out by letting him stay on the ship, and then... well, I guess we simply took advantage of being thrown together like that."

"He's a good guy, Worth," Mia said softly, hugging her coffee close.

My chest pinched, remembering the terse response to my text. *Thank you.* That was all he'd said. Not that I'd expected more. Of course not. We'd only been temporary hookups. But still, my heart hadn't seemed to have gotten that message.

"Agreed." I stood up and set my coffee down on a nearby table. "On that note, I'll get out of your hair. But first..." I locked eyes with Lucas. "I hope you know how proud I am of you. You could never, ever disappoint me. You've always been so strong, Luc. When Father wanted you to go to business school, you followed your dream instead. When your peers in vet school pressured you to take a high-profile placement, you chose to work for the charity instead. You're a man of conviction and passion. I hope you don't ever stop following your heart."

Lucas put his hand in front of his mouth and aimed watery eyes at me. "You bastard," he said.

Mia grinned. "Awww. Hug it out."

I stepped over and hugged him hard before clearing my throat of residual emotion and bolting for the door. "Later!" I called over my shoulder.

They volleyed more questions after me about my future with Cal, but I ignored them and got the hell out of there. The last thing I needed was to explain to them something I didn't fully understand myself, and I was full up enough with emotion as it was to even think about the beautiful man in Texas.

Thankfully, the following day I was headed to California on business and would have plenty of work to keep me busy while my heart tried desperately to get used to the idea it wasn't in a relationship with Calgary Wilde.

21

CAL

Sometimes my family's love was aggressive and borderline painful, like a Swedish massage. Maybe all that pushing was meant to release the toxins, but in the meantime I just had to sit there and endure the pummeling.

Nico whispered to me, too low for anyone else to hear it under the arguments going on around us in the farmhouse kitchen about *what was best for Cal*. "Hypothetically, if four of your siblings were banding together to buy—"

"Absolutely not," I snapped before facing everyone else from my spot in the corner of one of the sofas. "If any of you are thinking about trying to buy the sailing school from Brian, kindly fuck off. Even if he planned on selling—which he isn't—I don't want your damned handouts."

Everyone stopped talking and faced me, except for Grandpa, who was flipping pancakes, and Stevie, who was searching thoroughly for something deep in Chief Paige's pocket. They'd showed up with Sassy, who'd apparently sold them on the idea of free breakfast.

"Texas needs another Christian camp like a hole in the head," MJ muttered under her breath. "They'd have a better chance at distinguishing themselves if they made it a naturist resort."

I almost choked on my coffee. "Don't make me picture Brian and Sharon naked, MJ. It's too early for that sh-stuff."

"Are they even keeping the sailboats?" Saint asked peevishly. "Probably not. They probably think sailing is an abomination since there's nothing in the Bible about Jesus and sailboats."

"Wrong," Stevie interjected. "Luke mentions Jesus sailing across a lake. And I know this because my mother used to mutter, 'Even Jesus got to sail into the sunset once for fu...freak's sake.' So I looked it up." He shot a glance at my nieces, one of whom was dead asleep on Neckie's lap and the other who was too engrossed in an iPad to notice any four-letter words.

"At least they're not fighting you on your cabin," Augie said sweetly. "That was nice of Annie to make sure you got to keep a little piece of the camp for yourself."

Saint huffed. "Nice, my ass. After everything he's done for that place? One acre and a half-rotted—"

Doc shot him a warning. "Watch it."

"Augie's right," I said with a sigh. "I wasn't expecting her to leave me anything, but I sure as hell wasn't expecting her to leave me the cabin and a boat. Now I have a home base which is nice. Not sure if I'll be able to stick around during the camp season though. Seeing all the kids and not being able to interact with them..."

Doc walked over and leaned down, pressing a kiss to the top of my head. "You'll figure it out."

Otto nudged me with his foot. "We'll help you fix up the cabin. Seth's pretty good with a hammer."

"Why does that sound dirty?" Sassy muttered.

I took a breath and decided to go ahead and make my announcement. "There's no rush on fixing up the cabin. I'm going to Singapore."

All of the chatter stopped for a beat before everyone began chiming in with their opinions. I pulled the blanket over my head and tried ignoring them. My emotions were on a knife's edge, and I was one kind gesture away from losing it.

Pippa's little head appeared under the blanket. "Uncle Cow, why you hiding?"

I reached out to run my fingers through her silky hair. "Because everyone is being loud, and sometimes that's hard when you're feeling sad."

She crawled up into my lap and laid her head against my chest. I knew it wouldn't last long because she rarely stayed still, but I still enjoyed the cuddle.

After a few moments, someone pulled the blanket off us.

Doc said, "I'm proud of you for taking action. Just remember nothing has to last forever. If you change your mind, come home."

Otto was less graceful. "Fuck that. Stay here and fight. Those f— freakers aren't going to last ten seconds spending their summers outdoors with the bugs and critters."

"I'm with Otto," Saint said. "Freak 'em."

Hearing my siblings watch their mouths in front of two little girls was almost enough to jolly me out of my funk.

West looked serious. "What's your plan in Singapore?"

"Dad said the manager of one of the racing teams there wants to talk to me about joining."

"What kind of boats?"

"470s, lasers, maybe 49ers. I'm not really sure."

West frowned. "So, not the big stuff."

I shook my head. "I'm not experienced enough for that. Those guys make hundreds of thousands of dollars a year. Plus, I'm too little to be a grinder."

"Good," he said with a grunt. "That shit's dangerous."

"Not really," I said. "But it's a moot point anyway."

Hudson sat forward on the sofa opposite me. "I thought you didn't want to do that kind of racing. With corporate sponsors and stuff."

I shrugged. "I didn't. But then I realized that if I ever want to pursue my dream of running my own sailing school, I need a plan. I can live with Mom and Dad and save up money while also making great contacts and padding my sailing resume. It's a solid plan, and I'm young enough to suck it up for a few years."

The rest of my siblings volleyed questions at me one after the other until Grandpa shouted that the pancakes were defluffing before our very eyes.

MJ sat next to me at the big table once we filled our plates. "Gay sex is illegal in Singapore," she said quietly. "Lesbian sex is fine, but gay male sex is still on the books. Be careful."

Neckie leaned over and kissed my sister on the cheek. "That's MJ speak for *I love you*," she said.

I laughed. "I know. And I know it's super conservative there, but that's okay. I'm going to focus on work anyway."

Several of my brothers and sisters made a super-helpful *mpfh* sound to let me know just how much they thought of my idea. I ignored them. With eight older siblings, I'd learned long ago there was no such thing as pleasing everyone, especially when you were trying very hard to please yourself first and foremost.

After swallowing a few bites of breakfast, I turned back to MJ. "I'm hoping to write a business plan for a sailing school while I'm over there, and I'd love to get your help from a legal perspective."

Her face widened into a grin. "I'd love to help. Thank you for asking. What did you have in mind? What's your dream scenario?"

I started describing the dream I had for the school, feeling more confident now than when I'd originally come up with the concept. It wasn't easy deviating away from the way Annie had run Campside Cove, but the more I talked, the more I realized I had my own strong opinions born of the experience I'd had both in college and in the past two years of working full-time on the water. Maybe this was why Annie had insisted on me doing those things. She probably knew her own experience and way of doing things would be best supplemented by learning new ways.

It was later in the day, after almost everyone had gone home and I'd taken the dogs outside to throw the ball for them, that I overheard Doc and Grandpa talking about me.

"I just worry that he's doing the same thing Winnie did after Alex," Grandpa said over the sound of plates clinking. I'd offered to do the dishes earlier, but he'd refused. It sounded like they were sharing dish duty now.

"Maybe. But throwing yourself into work when you're only twenty-three isn't a bad thing," Doc replied.

"There's no point to work without love," Grandpa said, ever the romantic. "You can bury your head in the sand of hard work all you want, but eventually you'll come back up and look around to find yourself alone with nothing to show for it but a well-run ranch and an empty bed."

I heard the soft smacking sound of a quick kiss. "Your bed hasn't been empty in fifty years."

"It was a close thing," Grandpa muttered. "If it hadn't been for that cowhand…"

I wandered off before hearing more than I bargained for. Our family lore already sported a TMI story about Doc watching Grandpa get head in the barn. It had come out one night after Doc had drunk four too many margaritas at Taco Tuesday. There was no way I was subjecting myself to that horror again.

I walked the dogs over to Grandpa's chicken yard to check out his collection. I never remembered the names of all the varieties, but I loved looking at their black-and-white feathers and funky hairdos. There was even a peacock in the mix, but it wasn't interested in displaying its wares for me today.

I thought about Winnie. It was true she'd thrown herself into work and sworn off relationships after Alex broke her heart. She'd become bitter to the point Hallie had made it her life's goal to snap her twin out of it and at least go on one date.

Winnie refused, and I remembered her saying she disagreed with the "better to have loved and lost bullshit."

I thought back to the question MJ had asked me at breakfast.

What's your dream scenario?

I'd told her about my idea for forgetting about a big camp

program and starting with a small school first. I could work the sailing school during the season and then get another job in the off-season to help support myself and save up money to eventually offer for either the Campside Cove property or another large parcel of land to put a camp on. Only, I didn't want a camp for privileged kids with lots of money for an elite sailing experience. I wanted the camp to be specifically for underprivileged and disabled kids.

One of the jobs I'd had when I'd first moved to the Caribbean had been adaptive sailing, and I'd even talked to Annie about how we could add adaptive options to her existing programs. She'd worried about the liability issues involved, which was why I'd wanted to talk to MJ about the legal aspects.

My sister was smart as shit, and she'd immediately pointed out that there were most likely a ton of charities and grants that would help support the development of an adaptive program like the one I had in mind.

She was right. I'd thought I'd need to work hard for a few years to save up the money, but what if I didn't?

What if I could use my cabin as the school and build out a dock to house the boats? I could start small, maybe only four or five boats. I'd have all winter to apply for the grants while renovating the cabin and getting everything ready. Hell, I could even find a job in Hobie and save money by living here on the ranch. Hudson and Charlie always let me work at the pub when I was home and needed money.

I started getting excited the more I thought about it. Maybe I could build something of my very own from scratch, something to be proud of, something to work hard at and build over time.

The memory of Worth talking about his father came unbidden into my mind. One night after sex, we'd curled around each other and talked for hours. We shared the experience of being raised by parents who prioritized career ambition over family time, and he'd told me several stories about his father using "work product" as an indicator of personal value.

I'd fallen prey to the exact same thing, thinking I needed to get a career that I could use to prove myself. But what did I really want?

To help people find joy on the open water, especially people who didn't already have relatively easy access. That meant people with challenges not easily overcome.

My brain was buzzing with ideas and burgeoning excitement as I wandered past the barn and around the bunkhouse. Hudson was visible in a small grazing area past the horse ring. It looked like he was working his dog, Mama, with some of the sheep in the pasture. I wandered over to lean against the fence and watch.

After a while, Charlie came from the direction of the farmhouse to join me. We stood next to each other watching Hudson whistle Mama this way and that.

"Does this ever make you miss Ireland?" I asked.

He laughed. "The opposite. Seeing Hudson this happy is all I need. I don't care where I am as long as that man is by my side. Why would I want to be anywhere else?"

His copper hair was even redder in the early afternoon sun as a light breeze blew long strands across his face.

"That's awfully sappy, even for you," I said weakly, shoving away more stupid memories of Worth's handsome face.

"This is what it's all about. Love. Family. Being at breakfast in there with your family is a bit like plugging in the phone charger. I look at your grandfathers and see what I want—a life spent with the man I love. And now that I'm with your brother, I have it. All I have to do is hold on to it and not fuck it up."

I was sick and fucking tired of people in love. It was like everyone in here had taken tokes off the love pipe, and I wanted no part of it.

"That's nice," I said through tight teeth. "I'm going to ride into town. I need to..." I scrambled to think of something. "Loan Sassy my flute."

I walked off and left the two lovebirds to their moony-eyed bullshit. Instead of going into the kitchen where there would undoubtably be more moony-eyed bullshit, I hopped in one of the ranch trucks and took a drive.

When I ended up at the little cabin Annie have left me at the edge of Campside Cove, I shouldn't have been surprised. It was the ramshackle place I'd called home every summer since the age of sixteen, and it was furnished with various Wilde family castoffs over the years. The result of the hodgepodge furnishings was a familiar comfort I sank into as soon as the door was closed behind me.

It was chilly in the cabin, but I knew there was a thick quilt calling my name in the small bedroom. I grabbed it and brought it back out onto the porch where I plunked myself down on the single wooden rocking chair and gazed out at the water with the old quilt wrapped around me.

I pictured the rainbow colors of sails dotting the lake ahead and remembered what the cove looked like in the height of summer, full of kids getting their first taste of the water, of the wind and sails.

"They always end up in irons," Annie would mutter before inevitably calling out, "If you ever want to get moving, you're going to need to find the wind! Find a way to make it happen. Start by wiggling the tiller."

Memories fell like autumn leaves and settled over me. Her voice was loud in my head as I remembered all the great and not-so-great advice she'd given me over the years.

"Swallow your pride and go ask him," she'd said when I'd confessed to wanting to take Lew Taggart to the big bonfire my junior year in high school. "Worst that can happen is he says no."

"No," I'd said. "Worst that can happen is his brother Chuck beats the shit out of me and leaves me for dead in the school parking lot."

She'd shrugged. "Have it your way. But I'll tell you right now, if you can't find a way to face your fears, you're only shooting yourself in the foot in the long run."

"What if he says no and calls me a loser?"

"What if he says yes and kisses your face off?"

I'd blinked at her, imagining Lew kissing my face off. That had seemed pretty damned nice at the time.

She'd laughed. "Seems to me you have a choice. Chicken out and throw yourself a solo pity party or suck it up and take the chance you might actually get what you want."

An idea sparked in my mind. I knew someone who might be able to put me in touch with the right grant programs. All I had to do was suck it up and take a chance.

Take a chance...

I pulled out my phone and called Worth.

22

———————

WORTH

I was doing well... as well as could be expected anyway, considering I thought about Calgary Wilde about fifteen thousand times a day. So when I finally saw his name on my phone, I froze in shock. The voices of the legal team sitting around Spinnaker's largest conference room table faded away.

It was too good to be true.

I stepped out of the conference room into the hushed corridor, noticing the raised eyebrows of the receptionist through the glass. I shook my head to assure her I didn't need anything.

"Ah... hello?" I prepared myself to hear the shuffling noises of a butt-dial, but his sweet voice came over the line instead.

"God, it's good to hear your voice," Cal said. I could hear the smile in his voice, and it immediately grounded me.

"You took the words right out of my mouth. How are you? How is Annie?"

There was a slight pause before he said, "She was brain-dead when I got there. They took her off the machines the next day, and we've already had the funeral."

"I'm sorry, sweetheart," I said without thinking.

"I got to say goodbye to her," he said in a soft voice. "So that was good."

"Are you doing okay?"

"Yeah. Yeah, I think I am. I've been doing a lot of thinking."

My heart rate picked up, selfishly hoping his thinking had included me. Maybe he wanted to plan a meet-up. Even if he just wanted another romp in the sheets, I'd take it. I'd take anything I could get with him, even if it was temporary.

"Thinking about what?" I asked.

"What I want to do next. I have this idea... and I wondered if you might be able to help."

Yes. Please. I would help him with absolutely anything he needed.

"Of course. What kind of help do you need?"

A little voice in my head tried to warn me that this was finally going to be the part where he asked me for money, but a much, much larger voice shouted, *I don't care.*

"One of you mentioned on the ship that the family foundation did work with programs like the Special Olympics. I want to apply for some grants to help set up an adaptive sailing program for people with disabilities, and I wondered if you knew anyone who'd be a good resource for researching and applying for that type of grant."

It took me a minute to process what he *wasn't* saying. He wasn't asking me to fund anything. He wasn't even asking for our foundation to fund it. All he wanted was help learning how to do it himself.

"Of course," I said immediately. "Anything you need. Let me reach out to the foundation director and find the best person to help."

Cal let out a breath. "Great. That... that would be great. Thank you so much. I almost didn't call you because I didn't want you to think I wanted a handout. I don't. But I also really don't want to fuck this up either."

"I think that's a great idea. No reason to reinvent the wheel when someone else can show you the ropes." What was I even talking about right now? All I knew was that I wanted to keep him on the line as long as possible. "Tell me more about your idea. It sounds interesting."

He launched into an excited description of what he had in mind. While I listened, I wandered down the hallway to my office and got comfortable on the sofa.

He told me about almost moving to Singapore. My heart dropped into my stomach at the thought of him so far away. Thank god he'd changed his mind. I'd been to Singapore twice and loved it as a visitor, but I couldn't picture him being happy there as a resident. When he told me Annie's nephew's idea for getting rid of the sailing and turning the camp into a church camp, I let out a growl of annoyance. Cal laughed.

"No, it's okay. I was angry at first too, but then I realized this was good. It means I won't have any sailing competition on the lake. Kids interested in sailing won't have to choose between the two programs. You want Christian fellowship? Go to Campside Cove. You want sailing? Go to… well, I don't know what the name will be yet, but it'll be awesome," he said with a laugh.

"I know it will," I agreed. "Tell me more about what piqued your interest for adaptive sailing."

As he spoke, I could hear his passion for the subject. He told me about the first year he'd spent in the Caribbean taking as many instructor courses as he could.

"That's where I learned to teach adaptive sailing, and it was incredible. We'd had two campers over the years who'd needed adaptations, so I'd already researched it a ton before taking that instructor course. But the instructor who taught me was unbelievable. She's a double amputee and total badass."

He told me more about her and the course, and I could tell how excited he was about his idea.

"Jon, no one in this region is offering this right now. The closest adaptive sailing program is in Galveston which is a four-hour drive from Dallas and eight hours from Oklahoma City. Hell, you can't even do it yourself if you don't have the right kind of lift and transport equipment. But that's where your help comes in. If I can talk to someone who understands what all is involved in setting up a program for disabled athletes, I'll be less likely to overlook things and make newbie mistakes."

"It sounds like you have a good plan," I said. "And I'm glad you changed your mind about Singapore."

"Yeah, me too. My sister reminded me about their views on gay sex. I'm not sure I could have lived there a few years and not have been able to hook up with random guys whenever I wanted to."

I opened my mouth to tell him it was still plenty easy to find hookups in Singapore since the laws weren't really enforced, but then I closed it again. I wanted Cal to hook up with a random stranger about as much as those Rodeo Drive shop ladies wanted to help Julia Roberts pick out fancy clothes. Not at all. Aggressively not.

Just talking to him on the phone made me think of his *Pretty Woman* references.

I cleared my throat. "Right, so I'll arrange for you to meet with someone from the foundation and you can take it from there."

"That sounds great. I really appreciate the help. Thank you, Worth."

I wanted him to go back to calling me Jon. I wanted him to be the one person in the world who had special rights to call me whatever the hell he wanted.

After we got off the call, I sat back and closed my eyes.

I wanted him, full stop.

Because it was crystal clear to me now that I was in love with him.

I thought about connecting Cal with the director of the JAC Foundation. Erik Burns was tall, broad, and beautiful. And he was gay. And single.

I blew out a breath. Did I really want to help Cal learn how to apply for grants so he'd have to spend the next several months trying to convince the powers that be that he was a good bet?

No. What I really wanted to do was much, much more.

What's stopping you?

Right. What was stopping me? My stubborn pride? What was the point of pride when I didn't have the one thing I wanted most in the world?

Realizing that I wanted to make Cal happy above all else in my life was immensely freeing. Suddenly, I didn't care if he was out to take all of my money. He could have it. If my money made him happy, it was his.

Why had I never felt this way before about anyone other than my siblings? This was the difference between what I'd had with Mason, and Russ before that, and the tiniest promise of what I could have with Calgary Wilde.

I hopped up and strode out of my office to hunt down my assistant. We had work to do.

23

CAL

I couldn't remember the last time I wore a suit. If only Erik had arranged the meeting over lunch, preferably at a pizza place or diner, I could have worn normal clothes. As it was, I'd had to buy a shirt and belt in the airport shop after realizing I'd forgotten to pack them. I'd been so obsessed with not forgetting the suit itself, I'd forgotten several other essentials. My credit card was still gasping for breath from that little jaunt.

The lobby of the JAC building on West Monroe Street was crisp and cool. The windows dimmed the early autumn sun but still allowed an unfettered view of late commuters hustling by. Chicago seemed to have a very different vibe from Dallas, which wasn't surprising, and I hoped I'd have more time later today to explore a little bit.

After the security desk confirmed my identity and issued me credentials, they directed me to a bank of elevators in a recessed alcove. I hit the button for the twenty-fourth floor and tried not to hold my breath with nerves. I wasn't sure if I'd run into Worth here or not. My meeting was with the director of the JAC Foundation, but my credentials showed I was visiting Spinnaker Capital. Did Spinnaker have their offices in the same building? Was Worth even in town right now? Was he away on an important business trip? What would I do or say if I saw him?

Don't kid yourself—you'd climb him like a tree and beg for mercy.

I squeezed my eyes closed and reminded myself about professionalism and how it didn't include climbing up men's bodies. Within seconds, the elevator doors were sliding open with a muffled ding to reveal a sleek lobby decorated with colorful splashes of abstract art.

I cleared my throat and rubbed my sweaty palms together. "Um, I'm here to see..." I swallowed and tried again. "I'm Cal Wilde here to see Erik Burns, please. He should be expecting me."

As soon as I said my name, the receptionist's face softened from professional to friendly. "Welcome, Mr. Wilde. We've been expecting you." She stood up and came around her station, gesturing with one hand toward a pair of glass double doors. "Right this way to the conference room. How was your flight?"

"Oh, um, good. I wasn't expecting to fly first class. Thank you very much. You didn't need to do that. I'm pretty small, so it's not really necessary."

She opened the door to a conference room with million-dollar views of Chicago and probably the river below.

"Holy shit," I murmured under my breath. The receptionist laughed and moved around behind me.

"Yeah, kind of amazing, right? I take it for granted until someone comes in here and gasps. Would you like some coffee, tea, water, soda...?"

"Oh, uh... yeah, water please. If you don't mind." I couldn't take my eyes off the view as I moved closer to the windows.

I heard a deeper voice come from the direction of the doors. A familiar voice, one that lit up every nerve in my body and made me want to melt into a puddle right here on the immaculate carpet.

"Did I hear Cal Wilde call himself small?" Worth asked. "Because this must be an imposter. The Cal I know would never do such a thing."

I spun around to drink him in. Screw the view of the river. *This* was the view I wanted.

"Not true," I said. "I said not to ever underestimate small people."

He didn't look quite as vibrant as before. He looked paler and thinner, but maybe it was the lack of sun and surf. I wondered if he'd been overworking again.

The receptionist laid out a water bottle in front of the seat with the best view and quietly left the room, closing the door with a muffled click. As soon as the doors closed, the interior glass walls and doors turned opaque.

"Ooh, fancy," I said. "Where was that technology when I was making out in the back seat of my sister's Honda Accord with Lew Taggart and the cops showed up?"

We were separated by the giant wooden table. It would have been awkward to shuttle around it just to shake hands or hug or whatever. But I couldn't help myself.

I raced around the end of the table and slammed into him, hugging him as hard as I could and inhaling the Tom Ford scent of him.

His arms came around me just as tightly, and his entire body seemed to sag with relief.

"Hi," I said into the side of his neck.

"God, you feel good," he breathed.

We stayed pressed together like that for a long time, long enough for my soft emotions to be outvoted by my hard dick. As soon as I thought I might start humping him, I pulled back and took a deep breath to compose myself. I was here for a reason, and it wasn't to beg for his naked body on mine.

As much as I wished for that.

"Thank you for arranging this," I said briskly, moving over to take my seat. I expected Erik would be walking in at any moment, and I didn't want his first impression to be a giant Worth-boner. "I really appreciate it. You didn't have to fly me here. I could have talked to Erik over Zoom or something. Or Southwest always runs last-minute deals from Dallas to Chicago. I could have gotten one for like a hundred bucks."

I was rambling, in part so he wouldn't say goodbye yet and wander back to his own office where I was sure plenty of important work awaited him.

He moved to the seat next to me and sat down. "If you'd done it over Zoom, I wouldn't have been able to ask you to dinner."

My heart leapt. "Oh? Well. That's... true, I guess."

We stared at each other. The laugh lines next to his eyes begged me to trace them with my fingers. The tiny wayward curl of his dark hair over his ear demanded my touch. The strong, veined hands he clasped together on the table in front of him...

"... won't be coming. It's just the two of us."

I blinked up at him, aware that my perusal of his person had perhaps taken me to another mental place and away from paying attention to his words. "Huh?"

His smile was indulgent. "Erik isn't coming to the meeting. If you'd like to meet with him after I've gone over some things, then I can arrange for it, but I wanted to meet with you first."

I'd come to Chicago to meet with Erik. If I wasn't meeting with him, did that mean Worth had changed his mind about helping me? If so, why had he gone to the trouble of flying me here? "I don't understand. He was going to help me apply for the grants I need to start my program."

He reached for a thick portfolio next to him on the table and slid it closer. "You won't need those grants to start your program. Let me show you what I've done."

He opened the portfolio and slid out some documents. "The Spinnaker Foundation was created as a charitable trust. It now owns the Campside Cove property and all of the assets associated with it, including the fleet of Sunfish, Lasers, and Hobie Cats." As he pulled out more legal paperwork including deeds and surveys of the lakeside acreage that was as familiar to me as my own face, I felt all the blood leave my body.

"What?" I asked in a breathy voice. "What is this?" I thought I might hyperventilate.

"I bought the camp from Brian and Sharon and put it in trust to the foundation so you can use it for your program. According to the mission, the program can serve anyone with a unique need, whether it's financial, adaptive, or psychological." He rifled through the stack to find a colorful graph and slid it to me. "This is the preliminary budget my team drew up for the first year's expenses including necessary updates and upgrades to the facilities to make them more accessible and ADA compliant, the addition of new adaptive equipment including several new watercraft, and..."

His voice faded out behind the roaring in my ears. He'd bought the camp? The whole camp? And... what? Was he taking it over to run the program that I'd created?

"I... I don't understand. You... you bought Annie's camp?"

Worth put his hand on my arm, but I flinched and pulled away. His eyes widened in surprise. "Well, yes, but—"

My entire body started shaking as my brother's words came back to hammer my brain like a punishment.

Never trust a rich older man trying to get into your pants. They're manipulators and users.

I shoved my chair back, stood up, and shook my head. I didn't think Worth had meant to manipulate the situation, but the result was the same. He'd taken over something of mine, something I really wanted to do myself, and made it his own.

Had he thought my asking for help had been a thinly veiled attempt at getting him to fund my whole damned program? Did he think I'd come to him to ask him for money? It was like my worst nightmare. I knew, I *knew*, how much he hated people asking him for money, and now here I was doing the same. At least, that's what he must have thought.

Or did he simply think I couldn't handle it on my own and needed someone older and more experienced to take over?

I felt like I was moving through sludge. All of my dreams were going up in smoke before my very eyes, and I felt like dog shit in front of the one person outside of Annie and my family who I wanted to be proud of me.

"That's very generous of you," I managed to say around the lump in my throat. "I wish you all the luck in the world."

And then I turned around and ran out.

24

———————

WORTH

I stared at the conference room door as it closed behind him. The glass turned transparent again a moment later, and Natalia stormed in.

"What just happened?" she asked. "I was talking to Crystal at the reception desk when Cal came storming by. I tried to call out to him, but he slipped into an elevator without even turning around."

I ran my fingers through my hair and tugged. "I... I don't know. I was telling him about the new foundation and how we'd bought the camp, and he just... left."

"Wait. You... you told him about the foundation before you told him about your feelings?"

"Well... yeah. Yes. I mean... I was going to tell him about my feelings at dinner. I didn't want to..." I yanked at my hair again in frustration. "I didn't want him to think the foundation thing was based on my feelings for him."

She threw up her hands. "But it is. It *is* based on your feelings for him. Don't you see? You've never, ever done something like this for someone you're dating."

"I'm not dating him!" I said, exasperated beyond belief.

"And whose fault is that?" she shouted back. "That man wanted to make you proud. He wanted to do it himself. Don't you know him at all? He doesn't want to take your money. The last thing he wants is to look helpless and needy in front of you. He wants to learn how to help people."

"And I can *help* him help people! I don't understand. Why wouldn't he want my help when I have all of this money to invest in the program?"

She stood aside and pointed out the door. "Go. Go get him. Right now. Tell him how you feel. Make this right."

I didn't stop to wonder if she was right or not because I was too scared of missing him, of trying to catch up with him later at his hotel and discovering he'd left to fly home. Or worse, Singapore.

I raced to the elevator and used the button trick Crystal had taught me to request an express car. When the doors opened, I pressed the button for the lobby and was whisked straight there in seconds. My shoes almost slid out from under me as I ran across the lobby and out into the late-morning sun. I frantically looked both ways until I saw the spiky dirty-blond hair I knew so well.

"Cal!" I shouted as I began to run after him, weaving through pedestrians and trying to avoid the line of people queuing in front of a hot dog stand.

I continued to shout for him until I got close enough to be heard. He turned around and the first thing I noticed was tearstained cheeks. My heart shattered into a thousand pieces.

I skidded to a stop in front of him and reached for his hand, but he yanked it back.

"Please," I begged, dropping to my knees right there on the Monroe Street Bridge and clasping my hands to keep from reaching for him again. "Please let me make this right. Please. I need..." I sucked in a breath, scared I was going to say please again. "I need you to be happy. I don't... I don't care about anything else. I want you to be happy. Please tell me how to make you happy. That's all I want. That's all I need. Please tell me what it will take to give you the life you deserve, the life of your dreams."

He sucked in a sob. His eyes were wide and searching. "I... I... I don't want your money. I never did."

I dropped my chin to my chest. "I know that, baby. I know. But I would sign over every single penny to you today if it would make you happy." I looked up at him. His hands covered his mouth, and tears streamed down his face. "Cal, none of it matters if I don't have you. None of it. Please come back and tell me how to make this right. All I wanted was to make you happy. I thought I was doing that, but if we need to do something different, that's fine. I'll do whatever you want."

I remembered my sister's words about telling him how I felt.

I reached out carefully and tried to take his hands again. This time he let me. They were trembling, so I held them tightly in my grip to keep him steady. "I love you. I love you so much, and I thought it would be scary. And maybe it was, at first. But now I know that the only thing that really scares me is losing you and spending my life without your smiling face and beautiful soul. You are the love of my life, Calgary. Please let me prove it to you by helping you follow your dreams."

The world seemed to have stopped around us. Passersby held up phone cameras, and several people had clasped their hands to their mouths with soft *aww* sounds. I ignored it all and focused on the one person who had the ability to make me whole or break me for good.

He took a breath, and then the tiniest quirk of his lip came up. "You're kind of a drama queen. Who knew?"

I barked out a laugh of disbelief. "Nobody. Absolutely no one in the history of ever. Nobody's ever made me this desperate before."

I could tell from the look of affection in his eyes that we were going to be okay.

Cal pulled my hands up to his lips and pressed a soft kiss on my knuckles. "I love you too. So, so much, Jon. I don't ever want you to think—"

I didn't even let him say the words. "I don't. I never will. I don't." Okay, I was stammering. I stood up and cupped his face. "And even if all you wanted me for was my money—"

His face dropped in horror. "I don't!"

I felt light as air. "I know, but even if you did, I'd take it. I'll take whatever you want to give me, baby."

I leaned in and kissed him softly for a moment before he grabbed my shirt and pulled me closer for a much deeper kiss. Hoots and hollers surrounded us, but I didn't care. All I wanted was to revel in the moment, feel the weight of him in my arms and know that he was mine. Now and forever.

EPILOGUE
CAL - TWO YEARS LATER

"Ready to jibe!" Lottie's voice was high and clear as she called the warning and thrust the tiller with her foot and leaned down to clear the boom. "Jibe-ho!"

The warm summer wind caught the sail with a snap and thrust us into the starboard tack. Her brother Finn let out a whoop when he straightened back up on the other side of the boat and slammed the centerboard back down. "Kick ass, Lottie-bell!"

Lottie's grin was a mile wide. "Next time, I'm doing the centerboard too, okay, Coach Cal?"

I nodded. "Heck yeah. But only if your brother agrees to watch his mouth. Sailors don't actually need to curse, you know."

Lottie's eight-year-old giggle washed over me while her ten-year-old brother blushed and stammered out an apology. Hearing the sound of her laughter was like winning a regatta. She'd shown up three weeks ago with sad eyes and a defeatist attitude, insisting she wouldn't stay at camp without her brother to help her.

After sitting down with her parents and Dr. Dash, our camp psychologist, we'd agreed on a plan of action for both of them. Finn carried a heavy load of guilt over the bicycle accident that had resulted in the loss of Lottie's right arm, and Lottie had fallen into the trap of thinking she needed a literal right-hand man to accomplish anything.

The two of them were thriving at Camp Spinnaker. Finn had bonded right away with a boy in his cabin named Dex, and Lottie had quickly fallen under the spell of Sassy, who seemed to have finally found her calling as a youth activities director and DFPS liaison.

"Tomorrow you'll be on your own with me, Lottie," I said. "Finn is playing in the soccer game during our sailing time."

Even though she still gripped the main sheet in her hand, she made a fist around it and fist-pumped. "Yes! I can do it, Coach Cal. I promise."

I wasn't quite sure how I'd become "Coach Cal" to all of our campers. It had started the first winter we'd owned Campside Cove. Hobie youth soccer had needed an extra field, and we'd volunteered the use of the one at the camp. That had quickly led to me being roped into coaching a team, which I didn't mind, and then I was simply Coach Cal to any kid I met. Worth thought it was hilarious, especially when we were about to fuck and he exclaimed, "Put me in, Coach!"

He wasn't as funny as he thought.

Now that I also coached the high school sailing team, it seemed more natural to be called Coach, but it still sometimes made me feel older than I was. More capable. Worth only laughed when I started whining about being an imposter.

"You're the most capable person I know, sweetheart," he'd say patiently. "Well, besides your brother West, but he's kind of a geek that way."

Lottie dropped the sheet into the cam cleat before using her hand to raise the centerboard partway as we skimmed through a shallow spot on our way back to the dock. The motions were becoming more and more natural, and she was almost ready to experiment with a little heeling. We'd waited until her swimming proficiency increased in case she went overboard, but the swim instructor gave me the green light this morning.

This time Lottie came about and tacked slowly toward the dock until dropping the sheet and letting the boom go where it wanted as we drifted the final few feet.

"Textbook approach, Captain," I said, reaching for the edge of the dock so I could hold us still while Finn tied us up.

Lottie's camp counselor was waiting for both of them at the end of the dock, but she waited patiently until Finn and Lottie had helped with all of the tasks involved in stowing the boat for the night. After they'd headed off to clean up for dinner, I finished securing some of the other boats and latching the dockside storage bins closed. The sound of frogs and crickets ramped up as dusk approached over the lake.

I loved this time of day. It was my favorite. The gentle *ting* sounds of rigging knocking against masts as the boats bobbed in the water, the fresh, piney scent of the nearby clusters of trees, and the distant laughter of kids getting ready to head to dinner after a full day of fun and learning. I closed my eyes and breathed in. If only Worth had been here to share it with me, it would have been perfect.

He'd had to fly up to Boston for a meeting earlier this week, and I'd secretly breathed a sigh of relief for some time alone. When Worth had moved to Hobie, he'd committed to limiting travel to strictly necessary trips in order to focus on setting up the camp and spending time together in the process. He'd been terrified of treating me as secondary to his career, even going so far as to offer to sell or dismantle Spinnaker Capital. I hadn't wanted that. In fact, I'd encouraged him to set up his own Spinnaker office in Hobie so that he had a place to go to work every day and focus on what made him happy.

"Baby, *you* make me happy," he'd said a million times.

"Right, but besides me. You love helping people's businesses. You love what you do with your firm. You can do your work and I can do mine, and we can come together at night and catch each other up on it."

He'd reluctantly agreed, but it hadn't taken him long to see how beneficial it was. It didn't hurt that he'd established his office in a historical home near King's art consulting firm and West's medical practice. He was surrounded by Wildes if he ever wanted company for lunch or needed help with anything. And even when he didn't.

During the off-season, I usually hung out in his office to do camp admin work from there, and during the summer he usually stayed around the camp to help with the kids. After two years, we'd settled into a routine, and the only reason I'd been glad to see the back of him when he'd headed to the private airstrip to fly up to Boston was because I'd needed some privacy for what I'd wanted to arrange. Now that I'd finished planning his surprise though, I was selfishly ready for his return.

I made my way up the dock and past the boathouse toward the footpath that led to our cabin. One of my concessions to Worth during the combining of our two lives was allowing him to build a brand-new cabin on the property to serve as our permanent home. I had to admit to being not-so-secretly happy he'd insisted on many, many luxuries in the new house.

It was still hard getting used to the idea that I was technically a billionaire. Against my very heated protests, Worth had put my name on absolutely everything he owned, including his bank accounts, Spinnaker Capital, the *Worthington*, the plane, the house in Fire Island, the house in Hawaii I hadn't even known about, the penthouse in Chicago he kept for trips he had to take several times a year, and the ridiculously large retirement portfolio he had. My only consolation had been the look on his face when I'd insisted on signing half the Spinnaker Foundation back over to him in retaliation.

"But... but that's yours," he'd insisted.

"Not if we're partners. What's mine is yours, remember?"

I laughed remembering his sputtered argument and how I'd had to shut him up by shoving him down to his knees and pulling my cock out. He'd acquiesced gracefully after that, and the subject had been effectively dropped.

As I stepped down the path to our cabin, I noticed his sports car in the open garage behind the house. My heart jumped up, and I took off running.

"Are you home early?" I called out, slamming the front door closed behind me. "Where are you?"

"Back here," he said from the direction of the bedroom. "The afternoon meeting was canceled, so I flew home early."

I rounded the corner into our bedroom and came to a sudden stop when I noticed deep pink rose petals everywhere.

Worth was sitting on the end of our big bed with his hands clasped in his lap. He still wore suit pants and a button-down shirt, but the tie was gone and his sleeves were rolled up, showing off his hot-as-hell forearms.

"What's going on?" I asked breathlessly. Soft music was playing in the background, and I noticed a bottle of champagne along with two glasses on the dresser. "What's all this?"

"It's your birthday," he said with a smile.

"Not till tomorrow, old man. Are you getting forgetful in your old age?" I walked forward and clasped his face, leaning down to take his lips in a long, drawn-out kiss. "I missed you," I murmured against his mouth.

His hands came up to rub my back underneath my camp polo shirt before sneaking down the back of my shorts and cupping my bare ass.

"You have no idea," he said. "I was counting down the minutes like a teenager with Taylor Swift concert tickets."

I laughed and climbed into his lap until I was straddling him on the bed. "I'll give you a show, big guy," I teased, beginning to unbutton his shirt.

"Don't you want your present first?" Since his hands began lifting up my own shirt, I was pretty sure he wouldn't mind delaying the birthday stuff.

"This is my present," I said. I leaned down to kiss the base of his throat where the shirt opened. As I continued to unbutton it, I slid to my knees on the floor and kissed down his chest to his furry stomach. "God, you're sexy as fuck."

Worth's hands landed in my hair and scratched gently. "Come back up here and kiss me."

I surged back up and did as he asked, pushing him onto his back and climbing on top of him. After a while of pure, delicious make-out session, we scooted up the bed, displacing rose petals as we went.

"It smells amazing in here with all these roses," I said, moving down to unfasten his pants. "Where did you get them?"

"I love you."

His voice sounded rough with emotion. I looked up at him in surprise and saw his eyes shining with unshed tears.

"I love you too. Did something happen?"

He shook his head and reached for me, pulling me down again for more kisses. This time they were tender and sweet, heart-achingly affectionate in a way that only Worth was capable of. Sometimes his tenderness and deference toward me shocked me to my very core. It was almost like I was his kryptonite and the only person who could peel back his armor and reveal the sweet, loving soul underneath.

"Want you inside me," he said in the same broken voice. "Need to feel you."

It wasn't the first time he'd asked me to top him, but I'd definitely noticed he usually only did it when he was feeling particularly close to me. I wasn't sure what was going on in his head, but I was more than happy to take care of him. Always.

"I'm here, sweetheart," I promised, moving down to remove the rest of his clothes. "Going to make you feel so damned good. Don't move."

He watched me with that special expression of love he got sometimes that still made my stomach swoop. Once both of us were blessedly naked, I stretched out over him again and rubbed myself all over him while kissing him deeply again. I relished the feel of his big hands gripping my ass and pulling me tight against him. I loved the sounds he made as he deepened the kiss and thrust our cocks together.

I reached for the bottle of lube and began fingering him while watching his face for his reactions. When his eyes rolled back in his head, I knew he was ready for me.

"Fuck, that's good," he groaned. "Why don't I let you top me more often?"

"I've often wondered that myself," I teased. "Maybe you're ready to become a pillow princess after all."

He huffed out a laugh. "No, that tiara is reserved for you."

"Thank fuck," I muttered, pushing his knees up toward his chest. I leaned in and stole another kiss before pressing into his tight heat. The combination of both of our groans filled the room, and I took a moment to let him adjust. "Oh god, Jon. Fuck you feel good."

He pulled my face down for another kiss, but when I pulled back and thrust forward again, he lost the ability to focus on the kiss. The noises he made were unintelligible which meant I was doing an okay job of it.

I put my hand on his throat and began thrusting in earnest, watching his eyes flutter every time my dick brushed against the right spot. I loved seeing him let go like this. His whimpers and pleading noises finally turned into puppy dog eyes begging me to push him over the edge.

"I love you," I said, denying his grip on his own dick. "That's mine."

"Cal, baby. Please. I can't... I..."

I slowed down to an impossible drag in and out. His flushed face began to bead with sweat. "Killing me," he breathed. "Cal..."

"I love you," I said again. I wanted to shout it from the rooftops every day, but I especially wanted him to hear it right now, when we were the closest we could physically be. "I will love you for the rest of my life."

He blinked at me. "*Please.*"

I pulled back and slammed into him, pulling on his dick at the same time with a hand still slick with lube. He arched up and screamed, shooting his release all over his chest and my hand.

Seeing him spread out like that, knees wide open and hairy abdomen covered in cum, was enough for me even without the hot squeeze of his body around my shaft.

"Fuck," I grunted as my orgasm hit. "Oh fuck, *fuck*."

I shot deep inside him, releasing the pent-up need from several days without him. When I finally let go of his legs and collapsed on top of him, his arms came around me and held me close.

"I love you too. More than I ever thought possible," he said into the quiet room once our breathing evened out and my soft cock slipped free.

I leaned up and met his eyes. "I have something for you."

He frowned. "That's not how birthdays work."

"Really? Hm. Weird." I moved off him and made my way to our bathroom where I washed up and prepped a cloth for him.

I returned to clean him up, giving him a deferential bow as I approached. "Your jizz servant at your service, sir," I murmured politely as I assaulted him with the washcloth.

"That'll be all, Jizz Boy," he said with a sniff.

"Well, that backfired," I muttered. After tossing the washcloth back toward the bathroom, I went over to the dresser and pulled out the little wrapped box.

He looked startled and almost leery. "What's that? You... no. You shouldn't have gotten me something. I got *you* something. That's not... it's..."

I shrugged. "Okay. Then I'll open yours first. You can open this later."

He tilted his head. "Just like that?"

I nodded. "Just like that."

Worth took a moment to think about it. "How about this. How about we both take our presents out onto the private dock and exchange them there?"

The man knew how much I loved watching the summer sunset, especially from the dock in front of our cabin. I hopped up and looked around for my clothes. "Great idea! Perfect."

Worth threw on some shorts and a T-shirt while I rifled through the dresser for a clean T-shirt too. Once we were dressed, he grabbed something from his messenger bag, then bundled up the champagne and glasses into a little tote before reaching for my hand. "Let's go."

We walked hand in hand outside, across the deep wooden porch on the front of our cabin, and down to the dock where the *Wilde Man* bobbed gently on the water. Worth had given me the Hobie 16 for our first Christmas. It sported double trapezes for heeling and a gorgeous rainbow spinnaker kit. I figured it was his way of admitting he didn't need to spend much to make me happy.

When I'd pointed out that we already owned several Hobie Cats as camp assets, he'd insisted this was different. He said I needed something just for me, something that was my very own escape pod to take out whenever I wanted. Thankfully, the perfect day had come that March when the sun had shone and the winds whipped up enough to really show Worth what I could do with the little boat, and we'd had hours and hours of fun with it ever since.

Instead of sitting on the end of the dock and hanging our feet over the edge the way we usually did, Worth gestured for me to sit on the built-in bench. Maybe it would be easier to handle the champagne if we weren't sitting on the floor. Who was I to judge?

But instead of moving to open the champagne and toast to my upcoming birthday, Worth got down on one knee and reached for my hand.

My eyes must have bugged out of my head because he actually laughed. "Take a breath, sweetheart."

"But..."

"I'm known for making really good deals. The kind of deals that pay back in spades what I originally put into them." His eyes were crinkly with happiness. "I consider you to be my very best deal. When I decided to go all in with you, I knew it was a good idea, but I had no idea just how good. Cal... for the past two years you've brought a joy and lightness to my life I never even knew was missing. Every day with you is an adventure, and because of you, our lives are full of passion and meaning. Will you please marry me and let me commit myself to you forever?"

I was already a blubbering mess, but I managed to nod and say something affirmative at the same time before throwing myself at him bodily. We tumbled down onto the dock and kissed for a minute before he pulled back laughing. "I almost dropped the ring into the water."

I looked down and saw him clutching a ring box I hadn't noticed before. Inside were two bands. "Why are they different?" I asked.

"They're both for you. One is silicone for when you're racing or doing mechanical work." He shrugged. "I don't know, I just wanted you to have a safety option if you needed it. The other is the official platinum one. But we can change them out however you want."

I grabbed the box and held it to my chest. "Over my dead body!"

The sound of laughter came from the shoreline, and I turned to see my entire family standing there. Nat and Jin and Lucas and Mia stood there with everyone else and began clapping and cheering once they'd been discovered. I turned back to Worth.

"Where the hell were they when we were having sex?" I whispered, slipping the platinum band on and saying a silent prayer of thanks it fit. I slipped the box with the other one into my pocket.

"Don't think about it. You weren't supposed to come in the cabin and find me there. I'd only sat down for a minute to catch my breath before changing clothes. I was hoping to meet up with you out front and walk you down here right away."

I groaned and tucked my face into his chest. "Oh my god. They all know what we were up to."

His laugh was deep and rumbly. My favorite. "Probably. But they all do it too."

"Ew. Gross."

Nat called out, "Can we come down there and hug you now?"

Worth opened his mouth, but I clapped a hand in front of it. "Give us another minute," I shouted. Then I lowered my voice so only he could hear me. "It's time for your present. Sit."

He sat down on the bench, and I took the spot next to him before handing over the little rectangular gift. "You kind of took the wind out of my sails," I admitted. "But I still want to give you this."

He opened the gift to reveal a small wooden replica of his dream sailboat. The J-Class Rainbow by Holland.

"This is gorgeous," he said, turning it around in his hand to see all the attention to detail. "Is it a Christmas ornament?"

I nodded. "Yeah, and the steering wheel there is actually a wedding band," I said with a shrug. "Surprise. Will you marry me too?"

His jaw dropped, and I could hear enough tittering from the crew on shore to realize at least half of them, if not all, had known both of us had plans to propose to each other this week.

"Really? You were going to propose to me too?"

"Yes, you idiot. But you cheated since I didn't know you were coming home earlier."

He pulled the band out of the little boat and slipped it on. "I love it. And I love the little Rainbow ornament too."

I bit my lip and glanced around nervously. Now came the hard part. "Um... do you remember that one time you got mad when your boyfriend spent your money on a really expensive yacht?"

His forehead crinkled in confusion. "Yes?"

"Do you think it would make a difference if your fiancé did it instead?"

"Calgary... what are you saying?"

I pulled out my phone to show him the photos of the full-sized Rainbow snuggled in the St. Mitz harbor next to the *Worthington*.

"I think I'm getting better at being rich," I admitted, hands still shaking. "I mean... I only vomited the one time when I arranged for the wire transfer. But Julo was with me and said I looked very brave while I did it."

I could hear Julo's laugh from the shore. He and Freya had moved up here with us and into my original cabin after we'd fixed it up. Julo oversaw the mess hall during the season, and the three of them traveled to the islands during the off-season to take care of the *Worthington*. I was pretty sure Julo was even more excited about the new ship than I was. Their daughter, Isla, was a gem, and she fulfilled what little desire Worth and I had for our own kids without us needing to actually have any of our own.

"You bought me a ship?" he asked.

I nodded frantically. "A really expensive one." Was I hyperventilating or just dying slowly? I put my hand on my throat to see if something had constricted it. Like a snake or… or stark panic.

Worth's face widened into a huge smile. "You bought me a ship?" he asked again.

"Oh god. I might vomit again for good measure." I stood up and looked around for a bucket, but Worth caught me around the middle and spun me around. Clearly he didn't realize how close to upchucking I was.

"He bought me a ship!" he shouted. "He finally took my damned money."

I groaned and sagged against him, trying desperately to convince my brain this meant he was happy about it. "So, you're not mad?"

"Babe," he said, still grinning wildly. "If you felt comfortable spending millions of our dollars, I'm the happiest man on earth. You know why?"

"Because it means I'm just like Mason?" I grumbled, still wondering if the panic would ever fully go away.

"Not even close. Because it means you finally accept that what's mine is yours."

He waved for everyone to come join us on the dock. Julo went immediately to the champagne to open it for us while Freya produced several more bottles and plastic cups for everyone else. Someone turned on steel drum music, and the sound of happy friends and family chattering about our upcoming marriage finally served to calm me down.

"Okay, fine," I said. "But if what's yours is mine, then I own half that gorgeous wooden ship."

"Of course you do," he said, clinking his glass to mine and taking a sip.

"And you own half my boxed wine collection."

He froze midsip. "I changed my mind."

"Too late for that. You said forever," I reminded him.

He slid his arm around me and looked out over the sea of familiar faces. "Forever sounds good to me."

Check out the first book in Lucy's brand-new Aster Valley series! Right as Raine features a focused professional football player trying his very best to stay away from his adorable new personal chef. Who just so happens to be Coach's baby boy...

LETTER FROM LUCY

Be sure to follow me on Amazon to be notified of new releases, and look for me on Facebook for sneak peeks of upcoming stories.

Feel free to stop by www.LucyLennox.com or visit me on social media to stay in touch. We have a super fun reader group on Facebook that can be found here:

https://www.facebook.com/groups/lucyslair/

To see fun inspiration photos for all of my stories, including *NautiCal*, visit my Pinterest boards.

Happy reading!

Lucy

ABOUT LUCY LENNOX

Lucy Lennox is the creator of the bestselling Made Marian series, the Forever Wilde series, and co-creator of the Twist of Fate Series with Sloane Kennedy and the After Oscar series with Molly Maddox. Born and raised in the southeast, she is finally putting good use to that English Lit degree.

Lucy enjoys naps, pizza, and procrastinating. She is married to someone who is better at math than romance but who makes her laugh every single day and is the best dancer in the history of ever.

She stays up way too late each night reading M/M romance because that stuff is impossible to put down.

For more information and to stay updated about future releases, please sign up for Lucy's author newsletter on her website.

Connect with Lucy on social media:
www.LucyLennox.com
Lucy@LucyLennox.com

WANT MORE?

Join Lucy's Lair

Get Lucy's New Release Alerts

Like Lucy on Facebook

Follow Lucy on BookBub

Follow Lucy on Amazon

Follow Lucy on Instagram

Follow Lucy on Pinterest

Other books by Lucy:

Made Marian Series

Forever Wilde Series

Aster Valley Series

Twist of Fate Series with Sloane Kennedy

After Oscar Series with Molly Maddox

Licking Thicket Series with May Archer

Virgin Flyer

Say You'll Be Nine

Visit Lucy's website at www.LucyLennox.com for a comprehensive list of titles, audio samples, freebies, suggested reading order, and more!

WILDE FAMILY LIST

Grandpa (Weston) and Doc (William "Liam") Wilde (book #6)
Their children:
Bill, Gina, Brenda, and Jacqueline

Bill married Shelby. Their children are:
Hudson (book #4)
West (book #1)
MJ
Saint (book #5)
Otto (book #3)
King (book #7)
Hallie
Winnie
Cal (book #8)
Sassy

Gina married Carmen. Their children are:
Quinn

Max
Jason

Brenda married Hollis. Their children are:
Kathryn-Anne (Katie)
William-Weston (Web)
Jackson-Wyatt (Jack)

Jacqueline's child:
Felix (book #2)